DARK ANGEL

For Jim -
Thanks for the inspiration.

"Be self-controlled and alert. Your enemy the devil prowls around like a roaring lion looking for someone to devour."
—1 Peter 5:8

Dark Angel

Copyright © 2020 Steve Meddaugh

All rights reserved. No part of this book may be reproduced or transmitted in any form or by any means—electronic, mechanical, photocopy, recording, scanning, or otherwise—except for brief quotations in critical reviews or articles, without the prior written permission of the author.

This novel is a work of fiction. Names, characters, places, and incidents are either products of the author's imagination or used fictitiously. All characters are fictional, and any resemblance to actual persons, living or dead is entirely coincidental.

ISBN: 979-8-609-90203-0

DARK ANGEL

STEVE MEDDAUGH

PROLOGUE

March 23, 687 B.C.

Tomorrow Jerusalem would fall. Achior looked across the bustling army gathered before the city walls with critical eyes. An easterly wind carrying a hint of sulfur from the Salt Sea stung his nostrils as it whipped his face. Men polished their shields and sharpened their swords and spears. They moved the siege engines to the front ranks for the morning attack and tested the mechanics of the battering rams to make sure everything worked perfectly. A malfunction would be unacceptable. Achior stepped back into his pavilion, satisfied preparations were on schedule.

Inside the tent was a large table piled with food enough to feed a dozen men, but it would be eaten by none. Achior's blood pounded through his veins like 1,000 soldiers marching. Perhaps a cup of wine was in order. He had but to glance at the ceramic decanter and a servant jumped to fill his gold chalice.

Undiluted wine in hand, Achior reviewed the battle plans again. He didn't become the Rabshakeh of the Assyrian army by leaving any details to chance. He knew those plans like he knew the feel of his own sword. He had to. Being in command of such a great army, a solid plan was his most powerful weapon, but could be his greatest enemy if poorly executed.

With nothing more to glean from the plans, Achior paced the length of his tent. King Hezekiah and his people will perish. All of them. They have snubbed their noses at King Sennacherib and his most generous offer for a life of luxury and prosperity. They refuse to abandon their ways and for that, they will pay.

Achior downed the remaining wine and tossed the cup aside. He picked up the long iron sword hanging from his bedpost by a leather belt and slung it over his right shoulder so it hung horizontally at his left side, nearly touching the ground. The bronze hilt was embellished with a double lion head, intricately carved from the finest ivory. More for show than function, his sword was enclosed in a jeweled scabbard. Achior marched out of the tent, his sandaled feet kicking up clouds of dust.

As dusk settled, torches were lit and priests burned incense to appease the gods and ensure victory. Those who could speak Hebrew passed the hours shouting insults at the enemy. "Israelite dogs! You shall eat your own dung and drink your own piss! Look here at your brother whose fate shall be yours." They pointed to the lifeless form of a Hebrew soldier impaled on a spear and planted front and center for all to see. They had captured him earlier in the day then proceeded to skin him alive and pluck out his eyes while soldiers at the city's front walls were aghast, helpless to do anything but watch.

Achior stood with his first officer, relishing the skillful intimidation being played out by the soldiers. He turned to comment and noticed the man stared at something in the distance. Achior glanced at the sky and scowled. Something wasn't right.

A moment later, darkness fell over the Assyrian camp. It seemed to originate from the walls of Jerusalem and slowly spread over his army. Even the torches under the crawling blanket of pitch black no longer gave out any light, though the scent of smoke and oil told him they still burned.

As the anomaly drew nearer, screams of anguish from the men in the front ranks filled the air. A hideous creature with enormous black wings and eyes burning red led the darkness. The massive, terrifying figure floated over his army, arms outstretched.

"No. It cannot be…" It was not lost on Achior that this night was the start of the Jewish Passover, a celebration observed by the Hebrews in remembrance of the night their god, Yahweh, sent his angel of death to kill the firstborn in all of Egypt. Fables. Or so he had thought. Achior jerked his head back and forth and tried to assess the situation. He pulled at his long braids as he watched the men before him seem to burn from the inside out, while their clothes remained untouched by flames as if only their souls were on fire. He watched a dozen men near him drop to the ground, lifeless. The darkness had not even reached them yet.

His first officer turned and fled, terror etched into his face. Achior looked back at his pathetic fleeing form and spat at the ground. "Coward."

When the darkness was a spear's throw away, a chattering

sound swirled around him. He peered into the black. Something moved toward him. Achior recoiled in disgust as a swarm of rodents climbed over the dead bodies, quickly gnawing away the leather bindings on their shields and weapons, rendering them as useless as the corpses that held them.

The sounds of pain and agony rose to an unbearable level. Achior's head felt like it was being run through with a sword. Realization flooded his mind that not one of his men would survive this night. It would be a great victory for Hezekiah and his "people of Yahweh." And 185,000 Assyrian souls would be in Sheol by morning. That made it a pretty good night for Satan as well. Achior laughed at the irony.

As the great black-winged angel of death reached him, he looked it defiantly in the face. He would not die in fear. Then something he saw made him falter.

Is it… smiling?

CHAPTER 1

"Lucas! Watch out!"

Lucas Daniels jerked the wheel to the right and slammed on his brakes as a bicyclist shot out of nowhere and turned in front of him. The bike's back tire came within inches of Lucas's front bumper. His car screeched to a stop a mere whisper from the trunk of a towering Douglas-fir.

His wife, Alice, stared at him as she released her white-knuckled fingers from the dashboard. She brought her hands to her chest and blew out a sigh, then turned to their daughters in the back seat. "Are you girls all right?"

Lucas glanced at them in his rearview mirror. All three nodded their heads. Their eyes were wide, but no one seemed hurt.

"You must have an angel watching out for you, sweetheart," Alice said to Lucas as he pulled the car back onto the roadway.

"No, Mama," Abigail's tight blonde curls whipped at her face as she shook her head side to side. "An angel was watching out for that man on the bike, Mama."

"I suppose you're probably right about that, Abby." Lucas chuckled.

"I am right, Daddy. I saw the angel."

"She still thinks she sees angels?" Lucas whispered to Alice and arched an eyebrow.

"Don't be so quick to dismiss the idea, Luc. Maybe she does."

Lucas sighed. Abigail's recent obsession with angels had gone too far. She truly believed she saw them. He made a mental note to bring it up with her therapist at the next session.

Sarah looked at her twin sister, Sydney, and they both rolled their eyes. "Was the angel wearing dorky sandals?"

A smirk crossed Sydney's face. "And playing a cute little harp?" The twins giggled.

Abigail's social skills were not those of a typical 10-year-old's. Unable to read facial cues or understand the concept of sarcasm she answered, "No, Honeys, it wasn't holding a harp. It can't save people if it's holding a harp. How could the angel protect that man if it was holding a harp?"

Whenever Abigail addressed the twins together, she called them Honeys. Lucas and Alice had often called each twin "Honey," so growing up, she assumed both her older sisters were named Honey and called them that from the time she could talk. The name stuck. Sarah and Sydney acted like they hated it, but Lucas knew deep down it was a special term of affection to them both. "Girls, knock it off."

"Knock what off?" Sarah said.

"Yeah, Daddy, we just want to know about the angel, because we're, like, sooo interested." Sydney said.

Lucas bit his tongue.

"Was he wearing a pretty robe, Abby?" Sarah asked. More giggles.

"No, it wasn't wearing a robe. And it isn't even a he. Angels are not male or female. They are asexual creatures."

"Asexual creatures?" Lucas asked Alice. "Where does she get this stuff? Sometimes she talks like she's in college."

"She reads a lot at night when she can't sleep. And she likes to talk with Reverend Cooper about it. I believe he's considered a bit of an expert on the subject. He's a, what do you call it... angelologist?"

"I don't like it. I think it's all a bunch of science fiction and I don't want Reverend Cooper or anyone else filling her head with these asinine ideas. Angelologist? Are you kidding me?"

Sure, the Bible was full of stories that mentioned angels, but he believed they were just that. Stories. What reasonable, sane person would believe angels walk around among us? "Abby, there might have been angels back in biblical times, I'll give you that much, but not anymore. There are no angels left."

"That's not true, Daddy. God created a certain number of angels and they don't die, so their number never goes up or down. Of course, there are the fallen angels. That's what demons are, Daddy, angels who are servants of Satan. If the devil gets them to disobey God, they are banished from His presence forever. No second chances for the angels, Daddy."

"OK then, if demons are angels gone bad, how can you tell if you are seeing an angel or a demon?"

Abigail was quiet for so long, Lucas thought maybe she didn't hear his question. But when he looked in his rearview mirror, he saw she had her eyes closed and her face was scrunched, so he knew she was concentrating, trying to find an answer.

Finally, she said in a soft voice, "I don't know, Daddy."

CHAPTER 2

Dante opened his eyes, filling the dark room with a muted red glow. There was a battle coming. He felt it in his soul. Or would if he had a soul. Dante was created without one. What he had was a purpose. A drive. An innate need to destroy mankind. But there were rules.

It was an endless struggle. His master created him to be a killer, then unleashed him on the world with unreasonable restrictions. If he destroyed a soul that wasn't already destined for hell, Dante's own destiny would be sealed. He clenched his fists and sneered at the thought that humans, every single pathetic one of them, always had an opportunity for redemption. A fate he didn't have the luxury of considering, which made him despise humans all the more. And fed his lust to annihilate every one of them.

Dante paced the abandoned loft he liked to frequent. He had

no need for furniture. He didn't eat, didn't sleep, and certainly never had guests. He only needed a place to be alone, but he needed room. Space to roam and stretch his 14-foot wingspan. In his natural state, his form required a nine-foot overhead clearance and four feet around him with his wings tucked in. Furniture would only impede his ability to move, which he needed to do now. Dante was restless. Even in this 2,000-square-foot space he felt restricted. He needed to get out.

Dante glowered out the fourth-story window and watched people shuffle along the cracked sidewalks and drive down the wet streets, as dawn crept over the horizon. He didn't need sunlight to see them. He could spot them miles away by the glow that surrounded them, that emanated from their souls. A physical manifestation of their connection to God and the strength of their faith. Even the faintest glow meant they were off limits to him. But there it was, everywhere he looked. Taunting him. Daring him to bring his dark justice to those who deserved it, forget the rules.

Dante twisted from the window and closed his eyes to block out the mocking reminder he was surrounded by untouchables. Most of the human fools didn't have an active relationship with God. Why should he not be able to do his job and usher their souls into the eternal penalty of sin they deserved? They were sinners, every last one. Yet they were allowed to freely live their sinful lives, while grace and salvation waited for them. It was easier in the old days when sinning was enough to be fair game. But when the Son of Man came, the rules changed. It left a pathetically small population to work with.

An opportunity to unleash his power in a way he hadn't been

able to in centuries was coming, though. This is what he sensed now. The anticipation made his urge stronger. His body boiled with an internal fire only one thing could quench. He needed to take a human life, send their soul to hell. Today.

The pull was too much. Dante lashed out and smashed his fist into the nearest concrete pillar, causing the ceiling to shake. The force knocked out a chunk the size of a toaster. The piece fell among the dust and gravel of many previous bouts of agitation. Dante eyed the indentation. That one caused structural damage for sure. He should be more careful or he won't have this place to come to much longer.

He stretched his great wings. The massive black feathers ruffled in protest as if they knew they were about to be constrained again. "Time to put these away," he said as they morphed into an ankle-length, black leather trench coat, the back of which was embossed with a large, upside-down cross. His body size shrank to a mere six-foot-two-inch frame.

Dante turned back and watched his reflection in the window as the red glow of his deep inset eyes extinguished, leaving black irises around even blacker pupils. His dark gray complexion faded to a lighter, more colorless tone. His transformation complete, Dante could now pass as human. Barely.

As he headed out the door, he mumbled to himself, "Time to go see what trouble I can cause today."

But first, Dante had an important item of business to take care of.

CHAPTER 3

This was his last chance. Lucas sat on the end of his bed and laced up his Santoni Oxfords. The shoes made the man. He may not be able to afford fancy suits, but an expensive pair of handmade Italian leather shoes dressed up anything. You could tell a lot about a man by his shoes and he needed to make a good impression. A very good impression.

Today, three years of excruciating work would either be rewarded or explode in his face. Lucas would present his closing arguments and the verdict should be obvious. However, the outcome of multi-million dollar medical malpractice trials were never predictable. Over the last two weeks, Lucas had presented all the facts in a way that was difficult to dispute. His expert witnesses kept the jury at full attention, but the logic of their testimony was no guarantee. Unfortunately, in cases like this, emotion was the wild card played at the end of the game. So

Lucas needed to look sharp, give them a reason to like him, make sure he won the jury over completely.

Lucas studied himself in the full length mirrors that were his sliding closet doors. He still had the lean build of his days as a high school track star. The shoes and suit gave him the put-together look of a salesman at a Mercedes dealership.

In a way, he was a salesman. His close-cropped dark hair, prematurely speckled with gray, belied his 35 years, which worked in his favor. Juries tended to equate age with experience and ability, so the older the jury thought he was, the more likely they would trust him. But his greatest assets were his intense green eyes. He captivated people with his gaze, and made a point to make lingering eye contact with each member of the jury, reeling them in one by one. Making them believe him and trust him. This was his advantage and what made him good at his job.

Until lately.

His cases, if he could even get one, were either thrown out on technicalities beyond his control, or he found himself up against corporate legal teams he couldn't compete with. While the freedom of running his own law practice was nice, it had its disadvantages. He didn't have the resources large firms or big corporations had. Lucas only collected payment from his clients when they won their cases, and he was on a losing streak.

If he won this case, he'd be set financially for years. But if he didn't win today, he would have to look for other options. Find a job with a big law firm, maybe. Problem was, the job market in Tacoma wasn't promising and Lucas hated the idea of uprooting his family and moving.

He shook it off. No time for negative thoughts. Lucas

checked himself one last time in the mirror then strode out his bedroom door. Things were about to turn around. Today he would win. He ignored the small voice of doubt that had no place in his day and headed downstairs to the kitchen where his girls ate breakfast at the table.

"Hi, Daddy," Abigail said without looking up from her yogurt.

"Good morning, Abby. Good morning, Honeys."

"Daddy, don't call us that anymore," Sydney said. "We have names, you know."

"He calls us that 'cause he can't tell us apart," Sarah said in a conspiratorial tone then grinned at her twin.

"Of course I can tell you apart, Sarah," Lucas said.

"Daddy, I'm Sydney!" Sarah feigned offense.

This made Lucas pause, just for the slightest second, then a smile spread across his face and he waggled a finger at them. The twins both laughed.

"Almost had you, Daddy," Sarah said.

'It's easy to tell them apart," Abigail said. "You just have to look at them, Daddy." Abigail stared at her breakfast and pointed toward the twins. "Sarah has three freckles on her nose and parts her hair on the left. Sydney has four freckles on her nose and parts her hair on the right. Sarah's teeth are crowded and slightly crooked and Sydney has a slight overbite, but her teeth are straighter. They will both need dental work. Sarah has a pointier shaped head than Sydney and Sydney walks with her right foot turned in– "

"Thank you, Abby. I can tell the girls apart, but I appreciate the help."

Abigail shrugged. "You just have to look at them, Daddy."

Sydney was staring into Sarah's mouth. "Huh, you do have crowded teeth."

"Shut up, overbite. At least I don't look like a horse!"

"Girls," Alice called from the front door. "It's 7:20. Time to catch your bus."

The twins jumped up and hugged Lucas goodbye then ran to the front door where Alice stood and dangled their backpacks from her outstretched hands.

"Time for me to get to work too, I guess." Lucas went to Abigail and placed a hand on top of her head as she leaned her forehead against him for a brief second. This was her hug. Actually being held by another person was scary and uncomfortable for Abigail, but she knew physical affection was important to Alice and him so she usually allowed this much, though Lucas knew it made her bristle. "Have a great day at school, Abby."

"It's Wednesday. Wednesday is music day, Daddy. I like music day."

Lucas smiled then walked over and poured coffee into a travel mug and grabbed a bagel off the counter.

Alice waited for him at the front door with his briefcase. "Hello, handsome," she said with a smile too perky for so early in the morning. "Ready for your big day?"

"Yes." He hesitated. "I think. I mean, I don't see how we could lose this one."

"Good luck in there." Alice kissed him on the cheek as she handed him his briefcase. "I'll pray for a positive outcome today."

Lucas offered a thin smile. Big difference that would make. No, it was his job to support his family and he would win because he worked long days and nights, sacrificing time with his family to put this case together. He would win because of three years of preparation, not because his wife said a prayer. "You don't have to do that. We'll get this one. It's in the bag."

"I'll pray for you anyway."

Lucas opened his mouth to say something else, then thought better of it. He kissed Alice back, marched to his car, and headed toward the battle. He stopped at his office to review his case notes one last time. He felt confident about the way this day was going to go.

When Lucas arrived at the courthouse, he found the street lined with emergency vehicles, their lights flashing, and the entire front entrance blocked off with police tape. Lucas exhaled and felt his confidence escaping with his breath.

His day hadn't even started and it was already going to hell.

CHAPTER 4

The sky became a swirl of pulsing colors, reaching for him, as Dante passed under the glass ceiling of the Seaform Pavilion, the entrance to the Chihuly Bridge of Glass. There was something dark and sinister about the twisted forms and complex intricacies of the blown glass that appealed to him. The pedestrian overpass took him over Interstate 705, into downtown Tacoma, but sometimes Dante just paced its 500-foot span to admire the sculptures. And to watch for his next one.

The Bridge of Glass drew people from all over the world. The odds were better here for finding new souls who were ready for hell. More fresh blood passed through this landmark site than anywhere else in town. Besides, he liked it on the bridge. But now was not the time for observing. He was on a mission.

Dante marched past the Crystal Towers, twin sentinels that stood 40 feet tall and looked like giant rock candy lollipops, each made up of exactly 63 hollow crystals. Dante counted them with a glance as he crossed to the other side. The sun was rising, casting a glare off the wet pavement and causing the ice blue crystals to sparkle.

The bridge placed him on Pacific Avenue and from there it was only another block to Legal Grounds, his favorite coffee shop. Owned and operated by an ex-cop who suffered a stroke and was unable to return to duty is what he'd heard. Which explained why it was located right across the street from the courthouse. The story went, the owner opened it for the lawyers and his fellow law enforcement officers so they had someplace nearby where they could get relief from the atrocious coffee that was served at the stand in the courthouse lobby. Ironically, Legal Grounds was notorious for having the worst coffee in town. But the place was always packed.

Dante didn't like to think about anything until he'd had his first cup of coffee. He didn't need it, of course. Unlike humans, Dante had no need for food or liquids. He could eat and drink, though his body didn't require it. Caffeine had no effect on him, yet there was something about the taste he found pleasing. Coffee may not affect him physically, but it improved his mood. Slightly.

Dante walked into the coffee shop and strode up to the counter. He drew a few stares along the way and a young boy hid behind his mother's leg as he passed by. The girl behind the register had a green apron and a black ponytail that bounced like a buoy on the ocean when she moved. Her nametag said Sandra.

* * *

"Large coffee. Black."

"Would you like room for cream?" Sandra said with her best smile. Geez this guy gave her the creeps.

The man leaned over the counter, and put his face six inches from hers. His breath smelled like something died in his mouth.

"I said black." He spoke slowly through gritted teeth.

The smile fell from Sandra's face. The man's voice had dropped into a register so low she felt it as much as heard it. The sound sent shivers down her spine. She'd seen him in here a lot lately with his square-jawed scowl and leathery, grayish skin. The man looked half dead. Sandra had always been thankful he wasn't her customer to deal with, but she couldn't avoid him today. What was this guy's problem? She was supposed to ask if they wanted room. "Listen, creep… I'm just doing my job," is what she wanted to say. What came out was, "Oh, right." She struggled to stay cheerful. "Would you like anything else?"

"No."

Sandra turned to the counter behind her and poured a large coffee with no room, grateful not to have to look at his face for a few seconds. She worked on her winning smile again before she turned back around. "Here you go, that will be $2.85."

The man dropped a handful of loose change on the counter. The money seemed to flow from his hand like a fountain. The sleeve of his coat rode up his arm, revealing a tattoo of an inverted cross. Or maybe it was only upside down from her perspective. Somehow, she doubted that was the case. She looked down at the pile of coins. Was he for real? There were so many nickels. Who uses nickels anymore? She looked back up at him and continued to smile with her mouth, but no longer with her eyes. "Do I need to count this?" she said with more edge than she meant to.

He glared at her. "It's all there."

As his eyes bored into her, a wave of nausea washed over Sandra. Her chest tightened and her head felt like it might explode. It became hard to tell which way was up or down as her vision blurred, her balance in jeopardy. Was it possible he was doing this to her? How could that be? Sandra thought she might lose consciousness, but was afraid to give in to it. She fought and tried to hold on, but it was a losing battle.

When her world started to go dark, the man released her from his gaze, turned and walked away. As he did, she felt a great relief wash over her both mentally and physically. The pressure and vertigo were now gone, but she was left with an icy cold feeling everywhere except between her legs.

Candice, the barista, noticed the look on Sandra's face. "Are you OK, Sandy?"

Sandra shook her head no with tiny rapid movements.

"What is it? What happened?"

Sandra looked down at herself then slowly back up at Candice. "I just… peed myself."

* * *

Dante allowed himself a small grunt of satisfaction as he walked out of the coffee shop. He took one sip of the coffee and spat it out on the sidewalk. Disgusting. He gripped his cup tighter and watched as the coffee boiled and took on a thick, black, syrup-like consistency. Another sip. "Now that's a good cup of coffee."

Dante patrolled the downtown streets, zeroing in on the people as they rushed to work. Not many had a strong glow about them, though a few stood out. But everyone he saw had at least a faint glow. That cursed reminder they were off limits. It was a perpetual frustration. It had been months since Dante had found a human on which he could satisfy his needs without consequence. Not that time meant much to him. He had existed since the beginning of time; what was a few months? Nevertheless, when he felt his urges the rules put him in a sour mood even a scalding cup of coffee couldn't touch.

Today should have been different. Sometimes he had visions of the immediate future. Visions where he saw what was about to happen, allowing him to take action. He never had much time, though. His knowledge of the future was limited and usually only gave him seconds to react. What he felt this morning was different. It wasn't a vision, just a feeling.

Maybe a walk back across the Bridge of Glass was in order. As he headed that direction, he noticed a man half running, half walking on the other side of the street that stopped him in his tracks.

There you are.

CHAPTER 5

Dr. Craig Parker was late for work. He pushed up his glasses as he hurried down Pacific Avenue then fumbled to catch the manila folders as they slipped from under his arm. His report was due to the board of directors by the end of the week and there was still so much work to be done. His team's findings would prove to be the greatest breakthrough in cystic fibrosis research ever achieved. It would be a career changer for him. If he didn't blow it. Dr. Parker was still trying to regain control of his gravity-bound files when he plowed into the massive wall of a chest that felt more like chiseled marble than flesh and bone. The impact knocked him backward and sent his folders flying only to rain back down on him in a squall of paper.

"Pardon me, I'm sorry." Dr. Parker knelt to scoop up his fallen paperwork. "I wasn't watching—" The words caught in his throat when he looked up into a pair of dark, soulless eyes. For a second, he thought he saw something not quite human, but it was only a flash and then was gone. The man made no effort to step aside. He only stared down at him, unmoving. Not even breathing.

"S-sorry," Dr. Parker said again and quickly finished gathering his files. He stood and attempted to step past him, but the man seemed to almost surround him with his massive form. Trying to walk around him he may as well have been trying to step over the Grand Canyon. He tried to take a step back, but found himself paralyzed. Fear? Why couldn't he move? What did this man want from him? Money, probably. He didn't have time for this. He was an important scientist and he was late.

"Listen, I don't have any cash on me. I never carry cash. I don't have anything of real value to you. If you take my credit cards, I'll just cancel them before you have a chance to use them. Do you want my watch? It's not worth much, but I'll give you my watch."

When Dr. Parker tried to remove his watch, it was like his hand wasn't his. He could see it, but it seemed foreign like it wasn't a part of his body. What would cause a sudden and total loss of motor control? Possibly damage to his motor cortex. Was he having a stroke? He did not otherwise exhibit any of the usual symptoms. Probably not a stroke, but his body wouldn't do what his mind was telling it to.

People continued to walk by them in both directions. He seemed to be invisible to them. Is he actually going to be robbed in broad daylight on a busy street while having a stroke and nobody is going to do anything about it?

The stranger cocked his head ever so slightly to the left, then to the right, as if trying to decide how to attack. The man seemed to grow taller as he continued to bore into him with black, inset eyes and lips pulled tight, expressionless. Then, most disturbingly, he spoke.

"I've been looking for you." His words grated like metal being crushed on metal.

Dr. Parker felt the seed of fear in his gut bloom into full-grown terror. "Wh-who are you?"

"I am the end of you."

What?

Dr. Parker's pulse quickened. Beads of perspiration dripped down his forehead and stung his eyes. It was getting hard to breathe. The situation was worse than he thought. This can't be happening. There are too many people around. Why wasn't anyone paying attention to what was going on here?

"They can't see me," the dark stranger said as if reading his mind.

"What do you mean? How could they not see you?" As unbelievable as it sounded, it genuinely seemed to be true. Nobody even glanced in their direction. There was one way to find out. "Help! Somebody help me!"

Still, people continued to walk past them without slowing down.

"They can't hear you," he said flatly.

"They… why not?"

"This conversation is happening in your mind."

Something did seem odd about the way he was talking. He wasn't hearing his own voice like he usually did. It sounded farther away, somehow. None of this made sense.

"Time to go now," the man said.

Dr. Parker found his legs finally moving, but not of his own accord. He was being pulled along, like a reluctant dog on a leash, not wanting to go, yet compelled to move in the direction he was being led. Slowly they walked down the block. Dr. Parker tried urgently to make eye contact with someone, hoping the fear in his eyes would tell them he was in trouble. But his attempt to communicate with his eyes probably did nothing more than make him look crazy and only succeeded in causing people to look the other way. When they got to the corner of the courthouse, they turned and wound their way behind it, down to the parking lot below.

As soon as they were alone, the stranger dropped his head and shrugged his shoulders. Unexpectedly, two enormous black wings spread out behind him, the most massive set of wings Dr. Parker had ever seen. On anything. The rustling of that many large feathers was louder than he would have thought possible and the sound of it startled him.

"My God…"

The creature grunted. "Typical human. You live your life as an atheist, but when you believe it is about to end, suddenly you're crying out for God."

"It's a figure of speech."

"Not to Him." His eyes glowed red. "So you don't believe in God. What about evil?"

"Everything can be explained by science and the likelihood that there is a supreme being with a grand design that created all of this is far less than the likelihood that life could spontaneously form on this planet." His nervousness caused him to babble. "A god as a creator is simply an uneducated person's way of explaining what they don't otherwise know how to explain. I'm supposed to believe there was some omnipotent being out there before there was an 'out there'? That doesn't even make sense. The things I've seen in my medical research are proof enough that we are alone in this world. So no, I don't believe in God. But evil? You are proof to me that there is evil in this world."

"You don't know anything about evil. Though you're about to spend eternity being educated on the subject." The winged beast grabbed Dr. Parker by the shoulders and shot up into the sky, then landed violently on the roof.

Dr. Parker once again found his movements being manipulated as he was forced to walk to the front of the building until he stood on the edge in front of the great dome on top of the courthouse.

"Look!" someone shouted from below.

A crowd quickly gathered and people pointed and talked excitedly. The sound of sirens could be heard approaching.

Dr. Parker heard a whisper in his ear, "Say goodbye to this world." He closed his eyes and mentally coached himself. *You can do this Parker. Just move your foot.* Slowly he felt the control return to his body. He managed to swivel himself around, his back now to the crowd. *Good. Keep going.* He slowly squatted down. Maybe not making eye contact was the key. He forced his body to lean forward, away from the edge. A collective sigh went up from the crowd.

He was going to jump all right. He was going to jump as far away from the edge as he could and run without looking back until he could distance himself enough to call out for help or find a way into the building. Dr. Parker focused every ounce of energy he had on his legs and with a great burst of power, shot himself upward.

An icy coldness hit him like an arctic wind. Then it seemed like time stood still. Why didn't he feel himself land from his jump? He heard gasps from behind him. Confused, he opened his eyes only to discover he was plummeting backward. The roofline rapidly shrank away as the ground rushed up to meet him.

Dr. Parker did not die on impact. He lay there, his body broken and heard the voices around him.

"Did you see what happened?" someone asked. "Did he slip?"

"Naw man, the dude jumped!" another voice answered. "Did a full gainer like Greg freaking Louganis. Dang, that's a nasty way to go."

Dr. Parker heard someone throw up. With his last ounce of strength, he forced his eyelids to open. Unable to move, he was stuck gazing at the roof, where he saw the black winged monster with his eyes rolled back, his body tremoring like he was in ecstasy.

Then Dr. Parker didn't see anything ever again.

CHAPTER 6

Lucas pounded the steering wheel in frustration as he sat parked in his driveway. The day had not gone as planned. Today was supposed to be the day things turned around, but so far nothing had changed. He had been hit with one roadblock after another.

When he walked in the house, things did not get any better. The sound of Abigail's screams from the other room filled his ears. Not a good sign.

"What happened?" Lucas asked as he stepped into the kitchen.

"You don't know how glad I am you're home." Alice stood at the stove stirring something that threatened to boil over the edge of the pot, which wouldn't be the first time by the look of the stovetop. "Music class was cancelled at school today. Mrs. Schwarzbaum was sick. I had to go pick Abigail up from school early."

"She's been like this all day?"

"Yes. And she's doing that thing with her eyes again."

"OK, she's having a bad day then," Lucas said.

"She's a mess. I've hardly been able to get dinner started. Between having to deal with Abigail and the twins who are fighting over the computer, I have gotten nothing done today. I need some relief, Luc."

"I'll deal with the girls." Lucas's shoulders slumped. He wanted to deal with the girls about as much as he wanted a root canal. What he wanted to do was go put on headphones, lie down and get lost in a world of piano and strings. He turned to walk away.

"Wait, Luc… Don't you have something to tell me?"

"What?"

"About the trial. How did it go?" Her eyes were hopeful.

Lucas felt a little sting in his heart. He wanted so badly to be able to tell her they won and money was not going to be an issue for them anymore. She deserved to hear that. They had sacrificed so much over the years, Alice especially. "The jury is still in deliberation."

"Really? What could they be deliberating on? You seemed so sure about an easy verdict on this case."

"I have no idea. It makes me nervous though. And to make matters worse, I got a stern scolding from the judge in front of the entire courtroom for being late today. That can't have helped any."

"You were late for court?"

"Yeah, some idiot decided to commit suicide this morning by

jumping off the courthouse roof. The entire entrance was blocked off while the cops secured the scene."

"Oh that poor man… Well surely the judge understood the situation."

"He didn't care to hear any excuses. He was there on time, and so was everyone else. I should have gotten there earlier. Apparently I'm supposed to plan for every absurd contingency."

"Lucas, did you ever stop and think about what must have been going on in this man's life to bring him to do such a thing? You sound like you think he killed himself just to inconvenience you."

"Maybe he did," Lucas said under his breath as he stormed out of the kitchen.

Lucas slowed his pace as he entered the family room, not sure what he was going up against with Abigail. She was on the floor drawing violently, her colored pencil ripping the paper with each stroke. After the sheet was destroyed, she screamed in frustration, blinked her eyes tightly four times, then crumpled up the paper and threw it. Her wadded-up victim discarded, she flapped her hands to help calm herself, then started the process over again, crying the whole time.

Lucas knelt in front of her. "Abby."

Abigail didn't look up. She continued scribbling, tearing, screaming, blinking, crumpling, throwing, and flapping.

"Abigail."

The twins bounded down the stairs.

"Daddy, Sydney's been on the computer for, like, ever! Tell her it's my turn now."

"Not now, girls."

"I haven't even been on it for an hour. I have a report due tomorrow, tell Sarah she has to wait!"

"I said not now!" Lucas shouted. Abigail put her hands over her ears and made a low humming sound.

Sarah and Sydney both let out a loud sigh, then turned and stomped back up the stairs, as they pushed and shoved each other trying to get back to the computer first.

Lucas sat on the floor and waited for Abigail to calm herself down. When she eventually stopped humming and took her hands off her ears, Lucas said, "Bad day, huh? I had a pretty bad day myself. Things have not been going the way they were supposed to."

"Today was supposed to be music day, Daddy. But we didn't have music. Wednesday is music day, Daddy. Today is Wednesday and Wednesday is music day."

"I know how you feel," Lucas said to the ceiling. "Some days life just disappoints you. You have to accept it and move on. Tomorrow will be a new day. Maybe you'll have music tomorrow."

"Tomorrow is Thursday, Daddy. Thursday is art day!"

"Well you love art don't you? See? You have something to look forward to. Speaking of art, what is it exactly you are working on here?"

Abigail stuck out her lower lip. "I'm trying to draw an angel, Daddy. But the picture in my head is all fuzzy."

"It is? You usually see pictures in your mind like a high definition photograph."

"I know, Daddy, but not this time. It's all fuzzy and I can't get it out right."

No wonder she can't focus. Lucas hoped this didn't lead to the usual downward spiral of tantrums that would come when she couldn't clear her mind. If she went into total meltdown, it would go on late into the night until she finally fell asleep from pure exhaustion. She seemed to be quieting now, though. He had to seize this moment and keep her going in the right direction.

"I know just the thing for both of us." He got up and went over to the stereo, put in a CD of Chopin Nocturnes, then sat back down next to Abigail. "Close your eyes, Abby." As soon as she closed hers, he leaned back and closed his own.

Lucas must have dozed off for 10 minutes or so. When he opened his eyes, he saw Abigail working diligently on her picture.

"This is for you, Daddy," Abigail said without looking up.

"Thank you, sweetheart. I can't wait to see it when you're finished." He pushed himself up to a squatting position. "In the meantime, I guess I'd better go deal with your sisters." He rose and took a single step away.

"Daddy?"

Lucas turned back toward Abigail. She set down her pencil, stood and placed her forehead gently into his abdomen. He barely reached up his hand to lightly touch the top of her head when she dropped back down and returned to her drawing.

Lucas looked up to see Alice across the room, leaning against the wall with her arms folded, smiling at him.

"My hero. Where were you when I needed you five hours ago?" she said with a smirk. "You are such a good Daddy."

But Lucas didn't feel like a very good father. Not until he could come home and say he won his case. Not until he could say they didn't have to worry any more about how they were going to pay their mortgage, or cover Abigail's therapy and medications. When he could provide for his family the way a man should, then he would feel like a good father.

He smiled sadly at Alice. She looked tired, exhausted as usual. There would be no intimacy in the bedroom tonight. She'd be fast asleep by the time he put the girls to bed. Not that he was in the mood. Lucas turned and headed upstairs.

Tomorrow would be a new day.

CHAPTER 7

The call didn't come until late Friday afternoon. Lucas was to appear back at court. Two and a half days the jury deliberated and long deliberations never worked in Lucas's favor. After he arrived in the courtroom, the judge had the jurors file back in and take their seats.

"Will the foreman please rise?" Judge Erikson said. A middle-aged gentleman in a too-tight brown polyester suit stood and faced the judge. "Has the jury been able to come to an agreement on this matter?"

The jury foreman said, "No, your honor. We have reached an impasse."

"Do you feel if you were given more time, anyone's minds could be changed?"

"No, your honor."

"Very well," Judge Erikson said, not masking his annoyance.

"In that case, I declare a mistrial." He banged his gavel. "Ladies and gentlemen of the jury, I thank you for your service. You are now excused. You do have the option to wait and speak with the attorneys if you wish." Then he got up and walked out of the courtroom.

Lucas dropped into his chair. A hung jury. Unbelievable. Did that really happen? It felt like someone was taking a Hoover to his lungs. Lucas closed his eyes and tried to remember how to breathe again.

"You OK, counselor?" The defense attorney stared down at him.

No, he wasn't. "Uh, yeah. I just…" he let the words trail off, not knowing how to respond.

"Yeah, tough break, kid. What do you say we go over and see exactly what that jury was thinking?"

Lucas forced himself to rise and, with the other attorney, approached the jurors. "Before you all leave, would you mind answering a few questions?" The jurors all looked at each other as if not sure how much they should say, then slowly nodded their heads.

"Good." Lucas forced a smile even though he wanted to give them all a collective smack to the head. "First, what was the vote? Where were you guys at?"

The jury foreman spoke for the group. "We were 11 in favor of your client. One against."

One person hung this jury? His life was crumbling apart because of one person? Lucas could not believe this. If they had been split 50/50, he could accept it. But one person ruining this case for him? Almost inconceivable. "Was there anything in particular that was preventing this one juror from agreeing with the rest of you?"

"Yes, sir. One of us did not believe the testimony of your primary expert witness."

"Didn't belie… all witnesses were under oath." Lucas was incredulous.

"Interesting," the defense attorney said.

An elderly man in the back piped in, "He lied through his teeth! I know he did. I could see it in his beady little eyes. Never trust a man with beady eyes."

Lucas dug his fists into his eye sockets and shook his head. He had to be better about the jury selection. No sense arguing with him, the trial was over. There was absolutely nothing he could do about it now.

The defense attorney said, "Thank you all for your time. We appreciate it."

The jurors slowly parted ways. Some exchanged handshakes and business cards before they walked out the door. Lucas gathered up his things. What was he going to do now? This case was his last hope for keeping his own law practice going. There was no way he could afford to retry it. He didn't look forward to the conversation he would have to have with Alice.

As he slogged down the hallway, Lucas took his cell phone out of his pocket then stopped and stared at it for a moment. No, this was a conversation to be had in person. He slipped the phone back in his pocket and continued toward the lobby doors with a sense of dread when it rang.

He answered the call. "Dad?"

"Hello, son."

"Dad, what's wrong? Is Mom OK?"

"We're both fine. Your mother is making one of her casseroles for dinner. Can't a father just call his son to check in?"

He can, but why does he seem to have this superpower where he calls only at the worst possible times? In the background he could hear his mother's voice. "Is that Lucas on the phone? Hi, honey. Kisses!"

"Your mother sends her love."

"I got that Dad, thanks. Listen, I'm fine, but I really need to—"

"You don't sound fine."

Lucas wanted nothing more than to end this conversation as quickly as possible. Probably best to lay it all out there and be done with it.

"I just lost a big case today. I'm not much in the mood to talk right now."

"It seems like you haven't won any cases in quite some time."

"No." But thanks for the salt laced with cayenne pepper for my open wound, Dad. Lucas regretted answering the call more with each passing second. Why didn't just let it go to voice mail?

"Maybe this wasn't the right career for you, Lucas. Have you thought about doing something else? You need to be providing for your family, it's what a man does."

"Dad…"

"You always were too much of a dreamer, holding on to fantasies of being able to do whatever you want, instead of what you need to do. Remember when you thought you wanted to play guitar for a living? Maybe it's time to let go of this one too."

Lucas wondered if his dad could feel the heat coming off his face right now. "Anything else?"

"No need to be defensive, son. I just want to make sure my grandchildren and your lovely wife are being taken care of."

"Got it. Time to man-up." Lucas paused. "Give my love to Mom." Without waiting for a response, he hung up.

When he stepped outside, the rain poured down in sheets, like a giant faucet in the sky had been turned on full. Of course he hadn't brought an umbrella. "A perfect ending to a perfect day," Lucas muttered. He pulled his coat up over his head and ran to his car, which was parked behind the courthouse. It was dark in the parking lot and before he knew it, Lucas stood ankle deep in a giant puddle that had formed next to his car door, his $600 Santonis ruined.

"Aw…"

CHAPTER 8

Dante entered the coffee shop on Pacific Avenue, dripping from the rain. As he stepped inside, he noticed the recognition and fear in the eyes of the girl behind the counter. Sandra, was it? When he reached the counter, she pushed a full cup of black coffee across the counter with trembling hands.

"Here you go, sir. It… it's on the house." Sandra stepped back and looked at him with anticipation. She probably wondered whether he would be pleased with her offering, or enraged by it.

Dante looked at her a moment then grunted and gave her a nod. He picked up his cup and boiled it to a thick tar as he walked back outside. The rain came down harder now. He quickly cloaked himself from view and released his wings, which snapped like a sail that just caught wind. He rose up with a single flap and floated over the courthouse building. He set down on the back side of the roof where he had a view of the shipyards.

It was barely dusk, but the rain clouds made the sky black as midnight. Dante arched his wings up over his head to form a massive hood. Better than any umbrella. He sat and stared down at the marina while he inhaled the aroma of his burnt coffee. Somewhere, from the darkness of the parking lot beneath him, he heard a man cursing wildly.

Hmm. Colorful.

Dante reflected on the life he had taken the other day, on how good it felt. Not like the days of old when there were millions of unenlightened souls for the picking, when he could take hundreds, sometimes thousands of lives at once. Those days were long gone, but at least it scratched the itch. For now.

Dante sipped his coffee. He thought about the look on that man's face right before he died, the way the pathetic fool looked up at him. His face didn't register a realization he had been wrong about God, only confusion and fear showed in his eyes. The corner of Dante's permanent scowl twitched ever so slightly, the closest he came to a smile. He felt whole in that moment. He had done what he was created to do and it made him feel complete, but the feeling wouldn't last long.

A car door slammed and Dante heard the engine sputter to life. Tires spun on the wet pavement as the car squealed away. Silence now, except for the rain. The background score of profanity that had accompanied Dante's thoughts for the last few minutes was gone.

Why couldn't he have been created for some purpose other than to send faithless souls to hell? Why did he have to suffer this constant feeling of emptiness and anxious anticipation? The power and anger built up inside him like pressure that needed a release. But that release had to be controlled carefully or he would pay a price he wasn't sure he wanted to pay. Would he ever find peace? He drained the last of his coffee and incinerated the paper cup in his hand with a look. The ashes left behind nearly matched the color of his skin.

Sometimes Dante loathed his creator for forcing him to live out all time surrounded by mankind, a population who, in his opinion, had no redemptive value whatsoever. He was forced to protect them until their souls became so utterly lost, their journey to hell was guaranteed. But he didn't want to protect them. If it were up to him, he'd simply destroy them all. He had his directive though and the consequences for going against the wishes of his master were too grim to consider. Dante tried not to think about it. He would continue to wander this earth and look for every opportunity to satisfy his need, no matter how small.

Dante stood and stretched his wings. Maybe it was time for him to move on, to hunt for lost souls in another part of the world. Maybe he could find a less educated population who had no knowledge of God. But no, something was going to happen here and soon. Something worth waiting for, he could still feel it. He would wait a while longer. Whatever was going to happen, would things actually change for him? Frustrated, Dante flew up into the dark and rainy night.

Send the faithless to hell? His existence *was* hell.

CHAPTER 9

Lucas arrived home soaking wet. He had taken his shoes off at the door, but still left a puddle in the entryway. His briefcase and coat had been dumped right there on the floor, next to his ruined oxfords.

Alice heard him come in and came to greet him. When she saw him slosh up the stairs leaving a trail of water behind she said, "Lucas? What—"

"Not... now," was Lucas's only reply as he continued to climb the stairs.

Abigail came and saw the puddles all over the floor. "Did Daddy do that? Is he in trouble? Because if *I* did that, *I* would be in trouble."

The twins came to see what all the fuss was about. "What the heck happened?" Sydney asked.

"Daddy's in trouble." Abigail said.

"He's not in trouble," Alice said.

"What's going on?" Sarah asked.

"I don't know yet. I'm sure your father will fill us all in when he's ready."

Abigail's cat wandered in and started to lick up the water. He was a solid black cat Abigail had picked out from a no-kill cat shelter up in Arlington, that she named Scratches for his tendency to scratch everyone but her. It was as if the two of them had made some sort of pact that sealed the adoption deal.

"Why don't you girls go get washed up for dinner. Abigail, take Scratches out of here before he tracks water all over the house."

Abigail picked up her cat and when the girls were gone, Alice debated following Lucas up the stairs to find out what happened, then thought better of it. He needed space right now. Instead, she went to get towels to mop up the mess. He'd talk when he was ready.

* * *

Over dinner, Lucas filled everyone in on how the trial turned out and why he had come home drenched.

"I'm afraid this is it," Lucas said. "My law practice is done. I can't afford to do it anymore. I'm going to have to find something more stable, more secure." What that something would be, he had no idea. Lucas had put feelers out there for the last few months and there were no openings anywhere. But he didn't need to tell his family that. Not yet.

"What about your office space?" Alice asked.

"My lease is up at the end of the month. Obviously I won't renew the contract. I have a couple weeks to clear my stuff out. Until then, I'll use it as a home base to job hunt." Lucas looked his family over and tried to assess how they were all taking the news. Abigail hadn't looked up from her plate since dinner started, which wasn't unusual. "Abby, do you have any questions?"

"Um... can I have more milk?"

"Sweetheart, you have a full glass right in front of you."

"Oh. Then no, Daddy."

Lucas wondered if she was even listening. He looked at the twins, who seemed a little on edge. They looked at each other, then at Alice, then at him, then back at each other. Finally, it was too much and they alternately fired their questions off in rapid succession.

"Does that mean we don't get our allowance anymore?"

"Does it mean we can't go to horse camp this summer?"

"Does Mom have to get a job?"

"Are you still going to buy us things?"

"Do we have to like, start shopping at Value Village?"

"Are we poor?"

"Do we have to move?"

"Are we going to lose the house?"

At this, Abigail looked up. "Lose the house? How can you lose a house? It's big and it doesn't move. You can't lose a house." The emotional state of everyone else at the table had Abigail a little concerned and she started to blink her eyes.

"Everybody relax." Lucas tried to sound more reassuring than he felt. "None of those things are going to happen. Monday I will start to look for a new job and if I find one within the next month or so, you won't notice a thing."

"What if you don't, Daddy? What if you don't find a new job, Daddy?" Abigail asked. She was flapping her hands now.

"Girls, your father will find another job. If not right away, then we'll simply have to make some small adjustments. We'll be OK."

The twins looked at Alice, uncertain whether to believe her or not. Abigail looked at her big sisters and waited to see how she should react.

"Listen," Lucas said. "Don't worry yourselves with grownup things. All you need to know is my job is going to change and until then, things might be a little tighter than usual. Now, why don't you go on and play."

The girls got up and cleared their dishes from the table. Lucas and Alice sat in silence.

CHAPTER 10

Lucas came down after he tucked the girls in to bed. He found Alice at the kitchen table with the laptop.

Alice looked up. "The girls go down OK?"

"I think they're fine. They probably aren't sure what to make of the situation."

"Neither am I," Alice said.

Lucas plopped down in a chair. "Yeah…"

Alice eyed him. "You aren't so sure yourself, are you? We'll get by somehow."

"How do you know?"

"You have to have faith, Luc." She rested a hand on his forearm. "I believe God will provide for us."

"Yeah that's working out great so far." He paused. "So what are you doing there?"

Alice lifted her hand off Lucas's arm and looked away, then

fidgeted with her blouse. "Oh, I'm just posting a few things on Craigslist."

"Craigslist? What happened to God providing for us?"

"God helps those who help themselves, Lucas."

He wasn't sure that was true, but something in her tone said he shouldn't question her right now. Alice seemed a little stressed. "What are you selling?"

"The living room sofa. It's too big and we don't use it. Besides, I never liked it. Also, our china."

"That was a wedding present!"

"Lucas, we've been married for 13 years. How many times have we used the china?"

Lucas thought about this. "Three or four times?" he guessed.

"Never. We have never used that china. It's just sitting there collecting dust."

"Fine, anything else?"

Alice dropped her head. "My mother's wedding ring."

"What? No. No way. You are not selling your mother's ring!"

"That's not your call, Lucas."

"It's a bad idea. I don't like it."

"Well I'm doing it. I've already posted it."

"Why, Alice? Why are you doing this?"

"Because somebody has to bring in some money around here!" Alice's eyes went wide and her hands flew to her mouth as if she could stop the words that already left her lips.

Lucas felt like he'd been hit in the chest with a sledgehammer. He shot up so fast, he knocked the chair over onto its back.

"Luc, I didn't mea—"

"Stop." Lucas said with a finger pointed at her. "Just... stop." Tears of anger and hurt formed at the corners of his eyes. He needed some air. He needed to get out. Now. Lucas left the chair where it lay on the floor and stormed out of the house.

Not wanting to be seen by anyone, Lucas decided to cool off in their detached garage. It was a good place for a man to be alone with his thoughts. He went inside and closed the door, leaving the lights off. The rain had stopped and a bright moon shone through the side window, illuminating everything with a silvery glow.

Lucas sat on a stool at his workbench and stared at nothing in particular. He thought about all the events of the day. Not one thing had gone right. He was a failure. He was failing in his career, he was failing as a family provider and he was failing in his marriage. When was the last time he was intimate with his wife? He couldn't even remember.

Why was his life such a wreck? Lucas thought he did all the right things. He worked hard, went to church on Sunday, lived honestly, was kind to others, and what for? For nothing, apparently.

Lucas looked around the garage. A gleam from the moonlight caught on something on a shelf. It was one of the buckles on his guitar case. His guitar! Lucas got up and took the case down, opened it and removed a beat-up old acoustic. It wasn't anything special, but Lucas had worked hard mowing lawns around the neighborhood and doing extra chores around the house all summer when he was 13 and bought it himself. He used to practice for hours. By the time he was 18, he had gotten quite good.

He sat back on the stool and casually strummed a chord, but it didn't sound like any chord he'd ever heard before, or would want to again. The thing was colossally out of tune. Lucas spent a few minutes tuning it back up and then tried the chord again. Better. He continued to play some scales and noodle around for the next half hour. Lucas could feel the strain of nearly two decades of not playing. His fingers ached, the pads of which had gone soft and the lack of calluses made it difficult, if not painful, to work the frets. Still, there was a sense of peace it brought him.

He ran his hand over the familiar curves of the wood. It had been too long. Lucas remembered the last time he played it, he was getting ready to go off to college and had been packing up his things. He had taken a break to play around on his guitar when his father walked in.

"You aren't taking that to school, are you?"

"Why not, Dad?"

"It's a distraction. It was fine you played it while you were a kid, but you are becoming a man now. Time to give up childish pursuits and get serious about your life. You need to start being realistic." The hurt must have been evident on Lucas's face. His father sat and put his arm around him. "Look, son… a real man provides a financially stable environment for his family. If you end up marrying Alice, or anyone else someday, you need to be able to support them. You can't waste your life with foolish pursuits. It's time to be smart. You're leaving for college now and you need to be focused on the task at hand so you can be successful. Do you understand what I'm saying?"

Lucas nodded.

"Good. Good." He patted Lucas on the back.

Lucas wanted to be successful. He wanted to have a family someday and be able to support them. He wanted to make his father proud. Maybe Dad was right. It was time to set aside any distractions that would prevent him from being a success in life.

Sadly, Lucas packed his guitar away in its case and there it had stayed, until now. He continued to run his hand over the body then up onto the rosewood neck, which he grabbed with both hands as he stood and raised the guitar over his head. Anger and frustration overtook him. He brought the guitar crashing down onto the garage floor.

"Be a man, Lucas. Be a real man!" Over and over he smashed his instrument on the ground, splinters flying. A piece flew up and embedded itself in his cheek, but in his state he didn't notice. The body was in broken shambles and hung awkwardly from the strings still attached to the neck. He continued to slam and smash until the body finally detached itself completely, leaving no further damage to be done.

Emotionally and physically exhausted, Lucas dropped what was left of the neck and covered his face with his hands as he slumped to the ground. There he stayed deep into the night, and wept.

CHAPTER 11

The devil was in his lair. His face was distorted and shifting rapidly, moving in and out of reality, but there was no mistaking who it was. The lair was a dark cavern, but more like a cave turned inside out, wrapped around the world which was nothing more than a dim ball of light in an abysmal pocket. Someone, or something, else was with him. It lurked in the shadows or may have been the very shadows themselves. It was impossible to tell.

"Foolish humans. If only they knew what hell was really like. Of course, they are incapable of even conceiving of the pain and suffering they would endure here. If they could, they would all be devout worshipers of our enemy. But they depict this place as a cartoonish underworld of fire and brimstone."

The hidden creature laughed as it came forward and took shape from the darkness. Like the devil, it was hard to make out what it looked like exactly as its form kept shifting, but it had a vaguely human physique and was shrouded in something like a robe or a cape. Perhaps even giant wings. "Yes, your highness. For all their creativity, you'd think they could do better."

"I admit I have had a bit of a hand in encouraging their thinking."

"Credit where credit is due, sir."

"Humans are so easily influenced. It is rather pathetic, really. They imagine a place where there is weeping and gnashing of teeth. Can they not see how absurd that idea is, Vetis? They know perfectly well their bodies do not go into the afterlife when they die, that their flesh is eaten by maggots until they decompose into nothing more than fodder for the earth."

"Mmmm." Vetis bowed his head. "Ashes to ashes, dust to dust."

"And yet, they believe hell is a place where they will feel physical pain. There are no eyes to weep or teeth to gnash. No, in hell they will experience a whole new level of pain and suffering, unlike anything they have ever experienced. Their souls will be separated from God forever. There is no underworld where all the unrighteous people are gathered up to torture each other. No, they will be very much alone."

"They will feel like a young child in a large crowd, separated from their parents, lost and panicked."

"Well said, Vetis. Except the fear and anxiety will feel a hundredfold what they have experienced in their earthly lives. But they do not understand that. Instead, they have conceived of a place that is nothing more than a hot cavern where they are to be chained and forced into everlasting manual labor, or until they can be rescued. That is not so scary, right?"

"Indeed," Vetis said.

The devil smiled to himself. Humans made his job so simple. "But there will be no rescue. Their condition will be permanent and irreversible. They will be mine to torment for all eternity."

"Yes, master."

"So, Vetis, tell me more about this human."

"He is nobody of importance, sir."

"Nobody of importance?" The devil did not hide his exasperation. "Fool!" The boom of his voice shook the lair, causing what appeared to be rock and dirt to rise as if falling upward until it dissipated into a cloud of dust that floated into the ceiling of eternal blackness. "Have you learned nothing after all this time? It does not matter if they were a king or a beggar during their life on earth. A soul is a soul. All are equal in God's eyes and so are they in mine. Every soul I can take is one less my enemy gets and that brings me no end of satisfaction. Every soul is a great victory."

Vetis tried feebly to apologize. "Sir, I didn't mean…"

The devil sighed. "It is no matter, Vetis. The truth is it is getting harder and harder these days to win souls. I do not seem to have the appeal I used to. And with the advances in human technology, the word about God and his insipid son has fast spread to the far corners of the earth, making my job more difficult."

"Understood, sir. But I think this one will be quite easy. His name is Lucas Daniels. Married, father of three daughters."

"Hmm, people with families always prove to be more difficult."

"This one is in a bad place right now. We must take

advantage of this opportunity."

"Yes, to be sure, Vetis. Where does this Lucas live?"

"North America. Tacoma, Washington."

"The Pacific Northwest. I believe the one who goes by Dante is in that area. He has proven useful for me in the past." The devil pondered this for a moment. "Yes. Yes, this will work out nicely. Vetis, I want you to use him. I want this Lucas to belong to me and Dante is just the one to assure I get what I want."

"I will take care of it, Sir."

"Let me be clear, Vetis. I do not want to lose this one. If anything were to happen to him before his soul belongs completely to me, all will be lost. So until that time, protecting his life is of the utmost importance. Understood?"

"I understand." Vetis bowed deeply before his master, then vanished back into the shadows.

The devil's form grew, filling the seemingly unfillable space around him with light. "Lucas Daniels, your soul will be mine. My demon is coming for you. It is time... It is time… It is time…" The words repeated, getting louder each time, like a feedback loop, until they echoed and shook the lair like an earthquake.

"It is time..."

"Abigail! It is time to get up!"

Abigail woke to find her Mama shaking her and instinctively screamed and pushed her away.

"I'm sorry, Abigail, I know you don't like to be touched, but I was calling and calling for you to wake up. I even turned on your light and you just wouldn't wake. It's time to get ready for school."

Abigail sat up. Wet curls clung to her face. "Mama, he's coming for Daddy."

"Who is?" Then, "Honey, you are drenched in sweat. Did you have a bad dream?"

"Not a dream, Mama. The devil is after Daddy's soul. Daddy's in trouble, Mama. He's in trouble. Daddy's in trouble!" She flapped her hands and blinked.

"Abigail… calm down, it was just a dream, I promise you. Your father is going to be just fine."

Abigail stopped flapping and blinking. She wanted to believe her mama, but she wasn't so sure she could. It didn't feel like a dream. It felt like pure evil.

CHAPTER 12

Dante stewed over his cup of coffee. A direct order from his master is not what he wanted. He had gotten used to the freedom of doing what he desired, but now he'd been tasked with an assignment. Lucas Daniels. Who was he and why was he so special? Was this some sort of punishment? Dante knew he toed the line a bit and pushed his luck with the rules. This time it was obvious he was not to bend the rules. Not even a little bit.

To make things worse, Lucas was a man of faith. The chances of him completely denouncing that faith were pretty slim. So why all the attention? Dante would much rather spend his time in search of people he could immediately claim for his own dark purposes. People who had no faith. It seemed such a waste of time to hover over someone who, in all likelihood, would never completely give up his beliefs. Faith had a funny way of hanging out, even in the darkest places of the heart, never completely willing to let go. Once planted, it was always there, somewhere, to pull from. It's normal for humans to question and doubt. But when it really came down to it, all the questioning, all the doubting and uncertainty, it all boiled down to that seed of faith. If it was there, they would turn to it eventually. A fact Dante knew all too well. It was the thing that made it so difficult to find victims to satisfy his urges.

Then there was the other thing. Dante was told there would be "another." That other forces were attending to Lucas's soul. Dante would have his work cut out for him. Was this the event he sensed was coming? Dante wasn't entirely sure what was going on, but it was made very clear he'd better not screw this up. He wasn't usually in the business of actually protecting humans from harm, but as long as this Lucas still had faith left in him, that was his job.

Dante's coffee had grown cold. His situation had put him in such a bad mood, he'd lost all interest in it. Lucas lived not too far away, but he worked right here in the downtown district. Dante got up from his corner table at Legal Grounds and left his cold cup of black sludge.

It was time to find Lucas Daniels and get to work.

CHAPTER 13

Lucas walked down Pacific Avenue, headed back to his office located a few blocks up from the courthouse. He couldn't have asked for a more convenient location and was going to miss it. His lease was up at the end of the week and it was time to pack up his things. May as well, the job hunting had only lead to one dead end after another.

Having been in his own practice for so long, none of the big law firms were going to take him. He wouldn't fit their culture. The big firms like to groom their lawyers right out of law school and conform them to their ways. Can't teach an old dog new tricks was their way of thinking. Like it or not, Lucas was an old dog. Then there were the in-house jobs with corporate legal departments, but in this economy, there was nothing available out there. There were smaller firms around, and though Lucas had a small caseload of 30 or so active cases he could bring with him, it wasn't enough to make him an appealing prospect. These firms ran as lean as possible and kept as busy as they needed to. Adding another lawyer would only add more cost than the revenue they would likely bring in. If he could consistently pull his own weight, he wouldn't be looking for a job in the first place, right?

Lucas decided packing up his office would get his mind off things for a while. As he walked by the courthouse, he heard the most amazing guitar playing coming from down the block. He saw a man on the corner with an acoustic guitar playing his heart out, lost in his music. Lucas walked up to him and stood there and listened. The man's fingers flew over the fret board in ways Lucas didn't know fingers could move. This guy was incredible. When the man finished playing, Lucas pulled a $10 bill out of his pocket and looked at it for a second. He wasn't in the habit of handing out money to homeless people on the street, but something moved him and he dropped it into the open guitar case on the ground.

"Thank you, brother." The man had an Irish accent.

"You're very good," Lucas said. "You should have a recording contract, not living on the streets playing for change."

"Well thank you very much. But I'll let you in on a little secret, brother. I'm not homeless; I choose to make my living this way."

Lucas glanced at his $10 sitting in the case. "You make a living playing on street corners?"

"Oh yeah, you'd be surprised. It's not a great living, but I'm doing what I love." The guitar player brushed his shoulder length hair out of his face and tucked it behind his ear, only to have it fall back in his face. "I used to have a regular job, made good money, but I wasn't happy. Playing the guitar is all I've wanted to do me whole life, so here I am."

Lucas got it and had a fleeting desire to follow in this man's footsteps, then heard his father's voice in his head, "fantasies."

"I noticed the way you were watching me, do you play?"

"I used to, a little." Lucas subconsciously reached up and touched the small scar on his cheek left by the guitar splinter. "So what did you do before this?"

"Lawyer. Good one too. But it wasn't enough for me soul. Of course I didn't have a family to take care of. You look like a family man, am I right?"

"I am. I'm a lawyer too. Looking for work at the moment."

"Are you now?" The man had a gleam in his eye. "I may not practice anymore, but I still have connections. What's your name, brother?"

Lucas offered his hand. "Lucas Daniels."

"Seamus." He took Lucas's hand and gave it a hearty shake. "Seamus Robert White's the name. Mighty fine to meet you, Lucas Daniels. This be your lucky day." Seamus reached into his pocket and a produced a small stack of business cards. He flipped through them then handed one to Lucas. "These guys are new in town. I think you might be a good fit for them."

Lucas read the card. "Hawkins, Wall and Associates? Never heard of 'em."

"Like I said, they're new in town. Relocated here from California."

Lucas was highly suspicious. He'd been scoping out the job market for months and there wasn't anything out there. If this firm truly existed, they weren't likely hiring or interested in him. He didn't want to be rude though, so he made a show of carefully putting the card in his wallet and said, "Thank you, Seamus."

"Ah, I can see you have doubts. Understandable, but try to ignore my appearance, I really do have high connections here. Give me until tomorrow to work some magic. Call them first thing in the morning. I'll have everything taken care of."

Was this guy for real? Could he actually arrange a job interview? "Why would you do this for me? You don't even know me."

"I know you, brother." He looked intently at Lucas. "I have a sort of… gift I guess you'd call it, for looking someone in the eye and seeing who they are."

Seamus's gaze made Lucas feel violated.

Then Seamus relaxed and gave him a warm smile. "It's why I was a good lawyer. Trust me, you are right for this. I will get you this job."

Lucas highly doubted that. But he would at least call, he decided. "Thank you, Seamus. I don't know what to say."

"Say you'll call. Tomorrow. First thing."

"I will. Um… good luck with the music."

"You take care, brother." Seamus thrust his chin in an upward nod.

With a nod in return, Lucas started to walk back to his office. Was it really his lucky day? If this at least led to a job interview, it would be a lot more than he'd accomplished himself in the last couple weeks. He tried not to get his hopes up, but he was beginning to have a good feeling about this. Maybe he was just desperate, latching on to any hope he could. What if this panned out? He would want to be able to give Seamus a proper thank you. Maybe there was a way he could get in contact with him. Lucas decided to find out, but when he turned around Seamus was gone.

Had he imagined the whole thing? Man, he was losing it. He pulled out his wallet to check for the business card. It was still there. Obviously he hadn't imagined it. That was something at least. He walked back to the spot where he had seen Seamus play his guitar and looked around.

Seamus was nowhere to be found. And there on the ground, was Lucas's $10 bill.

CHAPTER 14

Dante stepped out of the coffee shop into the mid-morning sun. He knew Lucas should be somewhere nearby. Dante stared across the street at the courthouse where he had probably seen Lucas come in and out many times. Time to go into stealth mode.

Dante ducked into the alleyway behind the coffee shop. After he glanced around to make sure nobody was watching, he allowed his body to take on its true form. As his body grew to its full size his trench coat split down the back and unfolded into giant black feathered wings. The front of his black leather coat morphed into gray leathery skin. He felt a dull burning behind his eyes as he floated upward. None of this was visible to most humans. In his natural state, he was like a shadow. Had anyone witnessed the transformation, it would have appeared as if he simply vanished into a puff of dark vapor.

Nothing felt more comfortable to him than his true form,

which was human-like, but different. Aside from the wings and larger size, Dante's natural state lacked the hard edges of a physical body. Even when he chose to reveal himself to a human in this form, their eyes are unable to completely focus on him. His extremities would appear to them like they dissipated into wisps of vapor, like a dark spirit floating around. In this form he can seamlessly pass between the physical world and the spiritual realm. In fact, he exists in both at the same time, allowing him to move about, denying the laws of human physics.

Dante remained cloaked so he could observe unnoticed and move more quickly and freely as he searched for his target. With a lurch, he rose on flapping wings until he had an overhead view of the downtown area. His eyes worked like high-powered binoculars that could zero in on any object for miles around. He had been given a vision of Lucas, like a movie of the man's entire life up to this point, downloaded instantly into his consciousness. He knew Lucas's heart; he had seen his soul. Dante would be able to spot him in an instant the way a mother can pick her own child out of a crowd. Finding him would be like instinct now.

Within seconds Dante spotted him. He was close. Dante floated over and positioned himself across the street from where Lucas stood watching a man play guitar. As he observed the interaction between Lucas and the guitar player, he noticed the man with the guitar kept glancing up in his direction.

Does he see me?

It wasn't unheard of to be seen. Even though he had made himself invisible to the normal human eye, there were some whose brains were simply wired differently. They saw the world around them in a completely different way than most people. These people could sometimes see his kind. They didn't always understand what it was they saw, but they definitely recognized a presence, which the man with the guitar seemed to be doing now. Then the man looked directly at him. Looked him right in the eye.

Oh yes, he sees me.

There was something about the look on the street musician's face that Dante couldn't put his finger on. Something seemed off, a blip on his warning radar. He'd been spotted before, but this felt different somehow. Maybe it was time to move on. Perhaps it was time to go meet Lucas's family. As Dante turned and headed for the Daniels's residence it finally occurred to him what was wrong about the way that man looked at him.

The man had seen him, really seen him… and he wasn't afraid.

CHAPTER 15

"Mr. Wall will see you now," the receptionist said to Lucas. The name placard on her counter said, Louise Tully. "If you'll just follow me…"

Lucas got up and followed her down the hallway to a small conference room. She was a plump, middle-aged woman who wore cat eye glasses and walked too fast. This whole thing felt surreal. He hadn't been able to find any decent jobs in weeks, even months of searching. Yet somehow he found himself here with an interview. Where did this firm come from? Why didn't he come across it before? Seamus actually came through for him. Lucas called this morning, half expecting a disconnected number. But when the receptionist answered and he gave her his name, she said he had an appointment already set up for this very afternoon. Lucas had shown up a half hour ago with his resume and sat and waited while the partners reviewed it.

"In here, Mr. Daniels." Louise held the conference room door open for him. "Mr. Wall will be right in."

Lucas sat at the small table, not sure what to do with his hands. A few minutes later a large man with white hair entered the room. He wore an expensive suit and a chubby frown.

"Mr. Daniels." His voice was higher pitched than one would expect from a man of his stature.

Lucas started to get up, but the man shook his head, his jowls flapping side to side, and motioned with his hand for Lucas to sit.

"I'm Marcus Wall," he said as he sat across from Lucas. "I regret my partner, Adam Hawkins, could not join us. He had to be in court." Wall busied himself flipping through Lucas's resume.

Lucas felt like he should say something. "I—"

"I've looked over your resume," Wall cut him off, "and reviewed your current case load. Let me put you at ease so we can get down to business. You've got the job."

What?! Lucas was beside himself. He hadn't dared to think he would even get a real interview today. He figured at best he was being humored as a favor, but here he was being offered a job. He didn't even know what the job was yet.

"I'm going to be up front with you. I'm not happy about this, but I had no choice in the matter. This came from higher up. Some debts were collected on and I was told to hire you."

Lucas started to sweat. He didn't understand what was happening. It was all so fast, so unexpected. Unbelievable, really. Once again, he was nearly speechless. "Uh, thank you… sir."

"Here's the deal. We are from out of state and new to this area. Our bar certifications are all updated and we are endorsed in Washington now, but Washington law is still new to us. We are looking to take on a new partner, one who is experienced in this state. All of our associates came with us from California, so none of them are eligible for the partnership. You will start as an associate and be on a six month probation. That's all I had to promise. If it doesn't work out, you're out of here. But if you can prove yourself to be an asset to us, you will be made a partner. Any questions?"

Questions? There were too many questions. Lucas didn't know where to begin. "Sir, I… this is incredible. I don't—"

He held up a hand to silence Lucas. "I know what you are thinking. You're wondering about salary. You will start off with a flat salary of $140,000 a year, paid weekly. Does that sound reasonable to you?"

Lucas's jaw dropped. Reasonable? A steady income half that would be reasonable compared to the income he was used to. But a hundred forty grand? Pull yourself together Lucas, don't seem too eager. "I don't know anything about your firm yet. Can I think about it?"

"Mr. Daniels, this offer is on the table right now, but once you walk out of here it's gone and my obligations will have been met. This is your one chance, and with the job market being what it is out there, I suggest you take it."

He was right, of course. This was a once in a lifetime opportunity. Lucas couldn't afford to let it slip away. Even though he didn't know all the details at this point, it didn't matter. At least it was a salary. "I understand. In that case, I'll take it." Lucas stood and offered his hand. "Thank you, Mr. Wall."

Marcus Wall stood, gathered up his papers and completely ignored Lucas's outstretched hand. "You will start first thing in the morning. Be here at 7:00 am sharp. See Louise at the front counter on your way out. She'll give you an advance check on your first month's salary. Get yourself a nice suit."

He started to leave, then turned back to Lucas and added, "And a decent pair of shoes."

CHAPTER 16

It was 2:00 am and something wasn't right. Everyone in the house was asleep, including Scratches, who was curled up in his usual spot under the covers at her feet. Abigail crept out of bed and tip-toed to her doorway. She had heard something. Not the usual night creaks of the house or groans of the pipes she was all too familiar with. This was a new kind of sound.

Abigail was what Mama and Daddy called a night owl. Her mind didn't shut off like a normal kid's. Part of her winding down routine was to flip through mental images of everything she had seen since she woke, like a high speed slideshow of her day, and carefully store each memory for perfect recall. Abigail could not relax until she had analyzed and processed every last detail. So, by the time everyone else had gone to sleep, her mind was still busy going over everything. It wasn't usually until late into the night she could mentally start to shut down. Her parents gave her medicine at bed time to help speed up the shutting down process, but even so, she probably only slept four or five hours a night.

Nobody else should be up at this hour. Abigail knew the noises of the house at night and something was different tonight. When she peeked down the hallway, what she saw made her gasp. The sound of her quick intake of breath did not go unnoticed. The creature in the hall spun around and looked right at her.

Abigail stared back. It was an angel. Abigail had seen them many times, but never one so close. It was much larger than she thought it would be. The angel was so big it seemed it shouldn't be able to fit in the hallway, but somehow it did. It was as if the space around it conformed to accommodate its presence. Almost like it was there and it wasn't. Abigail's mind felt fuzzy.

The angel drifted toward her. Abigail should have been frightened, but instead she felt warm and calm as it drew near. It was an intimidating creature whose imposing form now towered before her. Its wings were so incredibly beautiful. Abigail wanted to reach out and touch the downy feathers, but she didn't dare. She looked up and asked, "Why are you here?"

"Your father needs looking after." The angel's voice seemed to come from inside her head.

"He's in trouble, isn't he?"

The angel looked at her for a long moment. "He is a lost sheep and there are wolves on his scent."

Abigail looked around nervously and contemplated whether wolves could actually get in the house. "Oh," was all she could think to say.

"This is not your concern, child. Return to bed."

Not her concern? There were wolves after her daddy; of course she was concerned. She started to protest, but the angel vanished and she was left staring into an empty hallway. Abigail felt cold, like she had just stepped out of a warm car into a chilly winter night's air. She thought about waking her daddy, but the rule was not to wake her parents up unless it was an emergency. Abigail wasn't sure if this was an emergency. On the one hand, wolves in the house would definitely be an emergency. But on the other hand, she wasn't sure the angel was really talking about wolves. After all, her daddy wasn't really a sheep. She decided against waking anyone up for the time being.

Just to be safe, Abigail kept watch from her bedroom doorway. In case any wolves happened to come.

CHAPTER 17

Lucas crept down the hall, careful not to wake anyone. He didn't want to be late the first day at his new job so he got up extra early. When he told his family over dinner the previous evening that he'd gotten the job, he felt like a hero again. There was money left over from his advance after he bought himself a new wardrobe, so he surprised everyone and took them out to The Old Spaghetti Factory for dinner to break the good news. Not a very fancy place, but for them, going out to eat at all was a real treat. And this was one of the few public places Abigail would even eat. She was familiar with the restaurant and always ordered the same thing— macaroni and cheese with ketchup. Things were finally turning around and Lucas was beginning to feel like a man again. He hadn't felt this way in a long time.

As he passed Abigail's room, he noticed her asleep on the floor. She was lying in her doorway, her right arm sprawled into the hallway. Had he walked down the other side of the hall, Lucas would have stepped on it.

That's new.

Abigail was known to fall asleep in some pretty interesting positions and locations within her room depending on what she was doing when her mind eventually shut down, but never right in the doorway.

What was she doing?

Lucas knew if he tried to move her now, she'd wake up and Abigail needed what precious sleep she could get. He decided to leave her where she lay, but only after he carefully lifted her stray arm out of the hallway and set it gently where it wouldn't be stepped on. As Lucas padded down the stairs, he heard a tiny voice from behind him.

"Daddy?"

He turned around and saw Abigail standing at her door. Dang. He'd woken her after all. He walked quietly back and knelt to whisper to her. "Abby. You should be in bed, asleep. Why were you sleeping in your doorway?"

"I was watching for wolves, Daddy."

"Wolves?"

"Yes, Daddy. There was an angel here last night and it told me you were a sheep and there were wolves coming after you."

"Oh, I see. And why was there an angel here?" Lucas didn't have time to get into a discussion about this so he went along with it.

"It was checking on you. Because of the wolves, I think."

"We'll talk about this later, OK? Do you think you could go back to sleep? It's still very early."

Surprisingly, Abigail walked to her bed and lay down. Maybe she wasn't really awake and was just talking in her sleep. Their conversation would make more sense if that were the case. Lucas watched her for another second. Satisfied she would stay in bed, he headed downstairs for a quick breakfast before he went to work.

When he walked into the kitchen, he could already smell the aroma of freshly brewed coffee. Alice must have set the timer last night for him. Stuck to the coffee machine was a yellow sticky note:

Knock 'em dead today, counselor.
I'm so proud of you.

Love you,
Alice

Lucas smiled to himself. Things were definitely looking up.

CHAPTER 18

Lucas arrived at Hawkins, Wall and Associates at 6:45 a.m. Nice and early. When he entered the front doors there was no one in sight. Maybe he came a little too early. Should he wait here in the reception area?

A well dressed, late middle-aged man with slicked back silver hair walked by and noticed Lucas standing there. "You must be Lucas." He smiled and strode confidently over to Lucas with his outstretched hand. "Adam Hawkins."

Lucas shook his hand with a firm grip. "Lucas Daniels. Nice to meet you, Sir."

"Bah! Adam, please. You're early. I think you're going to fit in nicely around here. Follow me."

Lucas felt a little smug, proud he made a good first impression on the boss. That is until Adam led him into the back offices which, to his shock, were already teeming with activity.

He wasn't so early after all. It appeared he was, in fact, a bit late. Lucas would have to get used to getting up earlier if he was going to get anywhere in this place.

"This will be your office, Lucas." Adam led him into a small office with windows that looked out over the port of Tacoma. A 30-inch monitor sat atop a large mahogany desk. The walls were lined with cherry file cabinets and bookshelves stuffed with legal reference books. Behind the desk was a plush, red leather executive chair.

Are you kidding me? Lucas couldn't believe his luck.

"Did you bring your existing case files?" Adam asked.

"Yes, I have all my file boxes in the car."

"Good. Good. Why don't you start by bringing those in and then get yourself settled. I will be pairing you up with one of our newest associates who will work those cases with you. I want you to mentor her. Hayley is a really sharp gal. You'll like her." Adam winked. "Once you get organized in here, I want you to start familiarizing yourself with these cases." He pointed to a tall stack of folders that towered precariously at the edge of Lucas's new desk. "You will be working on these as well. I'll go over them with you after you've had a chance to read through them."

"Sounds good." Lucas's feeling of luck was being replaced by a sense of uneasiness. This job, the nice office, it all came with a price. He was going to have to work hard to earn it.

"It's nice to have you here, Lucas." Adam turned to leave then stopped and gave the doorjamb a couple taps with his hand. "Louise at the reception desk will be in at 8:00. If you need anything at all, she can take care of you. We'll do introductions around the office later. You good for now?"

Lucas nodded. After Adam left he stared out the window of his new office for a few moments and took it all in. This was incredible. He was going to make sure this job worked out. He'd been given an amazing opportunity and wasn't going to blow it. He'd probably have to make more sacrifices with his family time. More than before, but he was finally going to provide for them the way he should.

By mid-morning Lucas had brought in all his current case files and organized his office. He decided to call Alice and tell her all about his day so far.

"That's great, sweetheart. I can't wait to see your office, but listen I need to get going. I'm volunteering at the church for a few hours." Alice paused. "I have Abigail with me."

"Abby? Why isn't she at school?"

"She was really upset this morning when she woke up in her bed and you were gone. She kept repeating something about wolves. Abigail is really worried about you. Do you know what this is all about?"

"I guess she didn't remember talking to me this morning. She wasn't completely awake. I found her asleep in her doorway."

"Her doorway?"

"Yeah, something about seeing an angel in the house last night who told her there were wolves after me, so she was keeping watch. I think we might need to talk to the doc about switching her meds."

"That's so strange. She was so worried wolves were going to get you that I couldn't get her to calm down. I couldn't send her to school like that. She's doing better, but she's still really agitated. I told her she could come with me to church and that maybe she could talk to Reverend Cooper. The idea seemed to get her to settle down."

"I don't know if that's such a great idea. He's probably going to fill her head with more crazy ideas about angels."

"Or maybe he can calm her down and help explain what it is she thinks she saw. Besides, I really don't have any other choice but to bring her along."

"You're right. Do what you need to do. I'll see you tonight. Tell Abby I'm fine and that there are no wolves here, so she doesn't need to worry."

Lucas hung up and glanced over at the towering stack of cases he was supposed to look through. Time to get busy.

He proceeded to rearrange his desk, peruse the collection of law books on his shelves, and change the desktop background on his computer. Anything to avoid getting started on the overwhelming pile of work that stared down at him. When he ran out of excuses and distractions, Lucas forced himself to settle in and get started. He was just reaching up to grab the first case file when he was saved by a knock on his open door. Adam was poking his head in.

"Hi, Lucas. This a good time?"

Couldn't be a better time. "Sure, come on in."

Adam smiled and waltzed in. Behind him followed the most stunning young woman Lucas had ever seen.

CHAPTER 19

Abigail sat in Reverend Dr. Mark Cooper's office on a small couch under a window that looked out over the church's 10-acre property. It was a comfy room with a big desk, lots of books and even a fireplace. Reverend Cooper said she could talk to him while her Mama made phone calls. She liked talking to him. He had a son, Caleb, with Asperger's Syndrome, like her, so he understood her better than most people. And he knew everything about angels. He always listened to her and believed her when she said she saw them. Even her own parents didn't really believe she saw angels. Abigail didn't know who else she could turn to about this. Luckily, this was the day her mama usually came to the church. He could explain things to her about what she saw.

Reverend Cooper sat right next to her. "Abigail." He smiled gently. "I hear you had a very upsetting dream last night."

"Not a dream, Reverend Cooper. I saw an angel and I was awake. It was not a dream."

"Interesting… Tell me what you saw."

"It was big. Real big. But fuzzy. I couldn't see it right." She rocked slightly as she talked and focused on a spot on the carpet.

"I'm not surprised, Abigail. Angels don't have physical bodies. When they appear to us, they give themselves a very human-like form so we won't be so afraid. In their natural state, I can imagine it would be hard to perceive their shape at all. We humans don't usually see them unless they want us to. How is it you can see them like this?"

Abigail shrugged. "I just do. I see everything different than most people."

Reverend Cooper nodded. "Indeed you do, Abigail. Indeed you do. So what was so upsetting about this encounter you had? I know you have seen angels before."

"It said Daddy is a lost sheep and there were wolves on his scent. I don't understand what that means, but I don't want wolves to chase my Daddy. My Daddy isn't even a sheep. Why would wolves be chasing my Daddy?"

Reverend Cooper pressed his fingertips together and looked up at the ceiling. "Jesus said, 'I am the good shepherd; I know my sheep and my sheep know me' John 10:14. The angel didn't mean your father was literally a sheep." He gave her a kind smile. "He meant your father is a child of God who has lost his way."

Abigail looked up at Reverend Cooper's smiling mouth, then back at the spot on the floor. "He's not lost; he's at work. Mama just talked to him!"

"No child, not lost in this world, lost in his relationship with God. It means he is struggling with his faith. You see, we all go through peaks and troughs in our relationship with God. Sometimes we feel very close to Him, but other times He pulls away and we feel distant."

"Why does He do that?"

"He does it to test our faith. This is probably what your father is going through right now."

"Oh." Abigail stared thoughtfully at the wall opposite her for a moment. "But what about the wolves? What does wolves mean?" She looked at Reverend Cooper again without making direct eye contact.

Reverend Cooper's face turned very serious. "It means the angel fears the devil will take advantage of this trough period in your father's life and seize the opportunity to attack with his demons while your father's faith is weak. That's usually the way he works." Reverend Cooper relaxed his face and smiled again. "But God always has his angels watching over us, as you have seen. Your father is a good man. I'm sure he's going to be just fine, so don't you worry."

Abigail couldn't help but worry, though. Demons. That sounded even more scary than wolves.

CHAPTER 20

The young woman who entered Lucas's office had the most fire-red hair he had ever seen. Her pale, freckled skin indicated she was probably a natural red-head, though the color was anything but. Lucas was absolutely mesmerized. When he finally tore his eyes away from her hair, he noticed her slim but very well proportioned figure, dimpled smile, and an ever so slightly upturned nose which gave her an almost pixie-like look. Lucas felt an odd warm sensation in his chest, like someone placed a hot water bottle underneath his sternum that pleasantly warmed his lungs while uncomfortably crushing them.

"Lucas, I'd like you to meet Hayley Simons. Hayley is fresh out of law school and I'd like you two to work together. You'll be her mentor. She's ready to help out on some cases so she will assist you with yours for now."

"Hi, Lucas, nice to meet you." Hayley stepped toward him,

her hand outstretched.

Lucas stood and reached across his desk to shake her hand and knocked over the stack of case files in the process. The files crashed to the ground and spread all over the floor. Papers slid out everywhere. Lucas's cheeks grew hot. "Aw Geez... Sorry. Lucas, I'm Hayley. I mean Hayley, I'm Lucas... Daniels... is my name." Why was he so flustered?

Hayley stifled a giggle. "Nice to meet you Lucas Daniels is my name."

"Well I see you've got everything under control here Lucas." Adam grinned. "Why don't you two get acquainted, then Hayley will show you around and introduce you to everybody."

"Don't leave me," Lucas wanted to say. But Adam was already gone.

"Here, let me help you get these files back in order," Hayley said as she squatted down to scoop up some of the folders.

Her skirt rose up well past her knees and Lucas tried not to look, but his eyes didn't seem to want to focus anywhere else. He cleared his throat and said, "I'll get this later. Sit down, let's chat."

"OK, sure." Hayley stood and placed the small stack of folders she had gathered back on the edge of Lucas's desk. She sat in one of the chairs that faced him and crossed her legs.

Lucas sat back down and after a short awkward silence asked, "So, are you from California too? Where did you go to law school?"

"No, I'm from here. Went to law school at the UW. I don't know how I got this job, I would have thought they'd want a more experienced Washington lawyer."

I think I know how you got this job. No, that's not fair. Adam said she was smart. He needed to give her a chance. Get to know her before he made any assumptions.

"But I guess that's why they hired you," Hayley continued.

"Actually, I've been wondering how I got this job as well."

"Guess we're both lucky," she said.

They talked a while longer and shared their histories, then Hayley took him around to meet everyone else. Lucas was surprised by the intelligence and professionalism of the other Associates. Many of them were a lot more experienced than he was, and yet he was supposed to beat them all out for the partner position simply because he was an experienced Washington attorney? He would have to work hard to keep up around here. They were all pleasant enough to him, but it was clear he'd have to earn their respect. It would be sink or swim. Adam Hawkins seemed like a nice guy who was willing to give him a chance, but Marcus Wall, the other partner, seemed like he'd just as soon see Lucas drown.

Lucas spent his lunch hour cleaning up the mess of case files on his office floor and got things sorted back in order. Hayley joined him in the afternoon to walk him through the cases. She had worked on some of them personally, but was at least familiar with all of them. She really was sharp. Lucas was impressed with her knowledge and thoroughness for someone so young. They had gone through about half of the cases when Adam asked to see him in his office.

"Lucas, I just wanted to touch base with you before the end of the day. So, what do you think? You up for this?"

"Absolutely."

"Sorry to throw Hayley at you like that, but she needs a mentor and you need someone who has the time to help get you up to speed quickly on our caseload and the way we do things around here. It just made sense."

"Makes sense to me." On paper it made sense, but Lucas wasn't sure about reality. To work with such a beautiful, intelligent, young woman was a bit distracting. More than once while he reviewed cases with Hayley earlier, he found his mind would wander. He'd contemplate her fiery hair and wonder how soft it was, or watch her perfect lips move, fascinated by them without hearing a word she said. And when he did listen, he was taken with how articulate and smart she was. Did he actually have a crush? Nah, he was a married man with three children and she was practically a kid herself. Even if by some crazy chance she were interested in him, he would never act on it. He could keep this very professional.

"Lucas?"

The sound of Adam's voice brought Lucas back from his wandering thoughts. Even when he wasn't with Hayley, she distracted him. This was bad. "Sorry, what?"

"I asked if you could take Hayley to the courthouse tomorrow to file a motion on the Jenkins case. I want her to spend some time in a courtroom. Will you be ready?"

"Absolutely." What else could he say? He had his work cut out for him tonight. As he walked back to his office, he tried to remember which one the Jenkins case was. When he came up blank, he stopped at Hayley's desk to ask her.

"Adam wants us to file a motion on that one tomorrow," he said.

"Great! We'd better dive into it then. I could order Chinese delivered here for dinner. How does that sound?" Hayley seemed almost excited at the prospect of working late.

Lucas was about to answer when his cell phone rang. He slipped it out of his pocket and looked at the screen. Alice. Lucas held up a finger as he stepped away to take the call.

"Hey Luc. Sorry to bother you at work. I just needed to know if you were going to make it home on time for dinner?"

"Umm…"

CHAPTER 21

Lucas walked in the house right as Alice was about to serve dinner. He'd spent the last couple hours of the day reviewing the Jenkins case with Hayley. Lucas decided he needed to spend time alone to look through everything. He thanked her for the offer to work through dinner, but told her she should go home and he was going to do the same. The motion hearing wasn't until tomorrow afternoon so they would have all morning to regroup and go over the case again when he was more familiar with it.

"Luc, You're just in time!" Alice pecked him on the cheek, then glanced down at the large stack of files under his arm. "Busy first day?"

"There's the understatement of the year." Lucas dropped his things and followed Alice into the kitchen.

"We want to hear all about it during dinner. Help me set the plates out?"

She handed Lucas two plates loaded with ham covered in a hollandaise sauce, mashed potatoes, and broiled asparagus dusted with red pepper flakes. Dinner looked and smelled amazing. She was amazing. After he set the plates on the table, Lucas came back and she handed him two more plates like the first set, only with smaller portions.

"For the twins," she said.

As Lucas carried them to the table, Alice called the girls down to dinner.

Lucas had just reached the table with Abigail's plate, which had only mashed potatoes and peas in two simple piles, when the girls came in.

"Daddy!" the twins shouted in unison and ran to him.

Lucas turned to embrace them as he set Abigail's plate down, causing the peas to roll all over the plate. Abigail sauntered in and looked at him with a curious expression, then pressed her head against him while he gently rested his hand on top of her head. Then without a word, she sat in her seat at the table.

Abigail looked down at her plate then turned back to Lucas and said to his left shoulder. "I can't eat this, Daddy."

"Why not?"

"The peas are touching the mashed potatoes."

Lucas realized what he did. "Can't you just push the peas away, back into a little pile?" He asked the question, but knew the answer.

"They already touched. You can't make them untouched, Daddy. I can't eat this."

"You'll have to dish her up fresh servings on a new plate,"

Alice said. "You know that."

He did. Sometimes being home could feel more exhausting than being at work. Lucas dished up a new plate for Abigail and they all sat to eat.

Alice said grace, then Lucas asked, "So, why no meat tonight, Abby?" He started mixing his peas in with his mashed potatoes, unsure if he was silently protesting Abigail's aversion to letting her own food touch or if it was because it was one of those things he had always liked to do and never outgrew.

Abigail gave no indication she even noticed. "Mama has never made ham this way before. Mama doesn't have enough experience with the recipe yet."

Lucas waited for a smart aleck comment from the twins, but they knew better than to say anything. Abigail never tried anything the first time Alice made it. He took a bite of the ham and let the lemony, buttery flavors of the hollandaise roll around in his mouth. There was a little bite to it, but not hot spicy. Paprika maybe?

"Well, Abby, I think your mom has all the experience she needs with this one." He looked at Alice. "This is really delicious, hon."

Taken as a cue, the twins dug in, but their faces went sour after the first bite. They looked at each other, silently scheming, then continued to shove bites into their mouths as they taunted Abigail.

"You haff got to try thish, Abby," Sarah said with her mouth full.

"Yeah, Abbs, this is the best dinner ever!" Sydney shoved another forkful in her mouth. "Mmm-mmm!"

Oblivious to her sisters' actual distaste for the meal, Abigail replied, "No, I'm good. I'll let Mama have one more practice making it."

Lucas didn't say anything because even though the twins were being brats, Abigail had no idea. And they were actually eating their dinner, which was a small miracle. Besides, though it was lost on the kids, it really was delicious and Lucas just wanted to enjoy his meal.

Midway through dinner, Lucas noticed Abigail had hardly taken her eyes off him. He wondered if she had noticed his pea and mashed potato mixture after all. "Abby, is there something you want to talk about?"

"Do you believe in God, Daddy?"

The question caught him off guard. "Of course I do. Why would you ask that?"

"You're a lost sheep. The angel said so."

The twins rolled their eyes and scoffed. Lucas glanced at Alice, who simply shrugged.

"I'm worried about your soul, Daddy. An angel was here for you."

Lucas shifted in his chair. "Yes, I believe in God. You don't have to worry about my soul, Abby."

"Do you really, though?"

The question made Lucas pause. Why was his 10-year-old daughter challenging him like this? He wasn't so sure about his answer, if he was being completely honest. Although his life was, without a doubt, turning around. So maybe someone was looking out for him. It sure felt like it. Lucas wasn't comfortable with this conversation though. Then he felt uncomfortable for not being comfortable with it.

Alice saved him and changed the subject. "So tell us about your first day."

Grateful for the diversion, Lucas answered, "Incredible. My office is more than I dreamed of. I've got a good thing going with this job. It will be very intense for a while, though. I'm going to have to work hard to keep up. They've got me mentoring a recent law school graduate named Hayley."

"Is she pretty?" Alice kept a straight face.

Another unexpected question. He couldn't tell if she was kidding or not. "Um, she's young is what she is, sweetheart." Why did he avoid the question? Because the truth was, she's gorgeous, that's why. Lucas now felt more uncomfortable than he was before, if that was possible. Hayley was just a young co-worker. Sure, she was cute, so what? Why not admit it? He now wished he was still discussing his faith with Abigail.

"Well, I'm sure you'll be a great mentor," Alice said, moving on.

Lucas proceeded to fill everyone in on his day, and tried to prepare them for the fact he may not be around as much while he worked to secure his position as a partner. The next six months would be critical and he needed the family to understand that.

Later, after the girls had gone to bed, Lucas approached Alice, who had been unusually quiet since dinner. "Alice, what's wrong?"

"Nothing, it's just... I'm not sure how I feel about the idea of you working so much. I need you here. Do you appreciate how much work it is with the twins and Abigail? I can't do it on my own, Luc."

"What good is it if I'm here helping you out if we have no money?" Lucas didn't want to get in a fight. If anything, he wanted to celebrate. Things were going his way for once. "Please," he tried to be understanding. "I know I'm asking a lot of you, but we need this. It's the best thing for the family." He pleaded with his eyes for agreement.

Alice asked, "What happens when you get the partnership? Will the hours back off then?"

Lucas had no idea. He suspected not, but right now he needed Alice's full support. "Yes, definitely. I need to make partner, then things can go back to normal. OK?" He gave Alice his best smile. He was doing it again. Why wasn't he being honest with her? It was for the greater good, he convinced himself.

Alice let out a sigh. Her shoulders dropped and her face visibly relaxed. "Six months?"

"Six months. Just give it six months." He knew in his heart it was a lie. And he suspected it was the first of many.

CHAPTER 22

When he found out Hayley had never even been in the courthouse yet, Lucas thought it would be a good idea to go early so he could show her around before the hearing. "Why don't we go grab a cup of coffee and finish going over this file, then I'll give you a tour of the courthouse. There's a place right across the street from there that serves a terrible cup of joe." Lucas smiled at his own wittiness.

"No," Hayley said seriously.

Lucas felt his heart drop to his stomach. Did he say something wrong? Was he being too forward? Too flirtatious?

Hayley's face brightened. "I'll have tea." She grabbed her purse and coat, then spun on her heels and headed for the door. Without slowing down, she called out, "Come on, old man. You're buying."

Old man? He probably did seem like an old man to her, but

he was hardly old yet. Although, the way she said it made it sound almost sexy. As he frantically tried to scoop up the case files and catch up to her he thought, *who was flirting with whom?*

They found a table at Legal Grounds, Lucas with a non-fat hazelnut latte and Hayley with a chai tea, and reviewed the case one last time. They discussed how the hearing would go and what Hayley's role would be, but the more they talked, the more Lucas found his mind drifting. He would focus on the way her hair cascaded over her shoulders, or the way her eyes danced with expression when she talked. Lucas wondered what she thought of him. If he were single, would he have a chance with her? Or would she think he was too old? Clearly, she was aware of their age difference, but he figured she couldn't be more than 10 years younger. Not so big an age difference at this stage in life. As he stared into her gleamy blue eyes, time seemed to slow down. What would they be like together?

Lucas snapped out of it and time resumed its normal pace. What was he doing? Why was he having these thoughts? This wasn't normal. What was going on with him? Then he noticed Hayley had stopped talking and was staring somewhere behind him with a look on her face like she ate something sour. "Hayley, what's—"

"Don't look," she stopped him. "There is a majorly disturbing man sitting against the wall behind you and he's just staring at the back of your head. Like, really intensely staring."

Lucas started to turn, but Hayley reached over and placed a hand on his arm.

"Lucas, don't turn around. He's looking right at you!"

"Well, what does he look like?" Lucas was unnerved.

"Big. Scary. He has the blackest black hair and his skin is this… off color. Almost like it doesn't have color. He does not look happy." She dropped her voice to a whisper. "Like he's trying to decide whether to come over and kick the you-know-what out of you. Someone you screwed over in court maybe?"

It was killing Lucas not to turn around. Now he needed to get a look at this guy. He tried to turn just enough to get a glimpse of him in a reflection somewhere, but he saw nothing.

"Wait, he's getting up now," Hayley said.

This is it. I'm going to be pummeled right here in front of a beautiful girl. Lucas decided he may as well face his attacker like a man. But when he turned around, all he saw was a very large man in a long black coat with an inverted cross on the back walk out the door of the coffee shop.

* * *

Dante sat in the coffee shop and watched Lucas and his female companion. This was an interesting development. Dante knew it was not Lucas's wife. He sat there, a boiling cup of black coffee cupped between his giant hands, and tried to influence Lucas's thoughts. Tried to give him a little push in the right direction, but something fought him. Dante didn't know what it was or where it came from, but something else powerful was at work in Lucas's mind.

He finally felt himself break through into Lucas's thoughts, but had focused so hard he didn't notice at first the woman was staring at him. Then Lucas twisted his head like he was trying to look behind him without turning around.

I've been spotted. Time to move on.

Dante had done all he could do here anyway. He needed to find out what was working against him, but it wasn't going to happen here. Not now. So he got up and briskly strode out the door before Lucas could get a good look at him.

He needed to find a different angle.

CHAPTER 23

Davis Jackson couldn't stop sweating. He fingered the cold steel in his pocket, seeking some comfort, but it brought none. It wasn't his gun. He didn't own one. He'd never even shot one before. Guns were nothing but trouble. They were the thing that took his mama away. His big brother too. Both gone in an instant while he watched helplessly, too young to understand what was happening at the time. Davis had done a lot of bad things in his life, made many mistakes, but he always drew the line with guns. Until now.

He stood in front of the courthouse, unsure whether to follow through. A demon had visited him in the middle of the night. A dark form in the shadows that whispered to his soul. The demon knew everything Davis had ever done, good and bad. Unfortunately for Davis, it was mostly bad. He was certain the demon had come to usher him directly to hell. Instead, he made him an offer.

Davis only had to do this one simple thing. One tiny favor and he would live like a king on earth. His soul was doomed anyway, he may as well be able to enjoy himself while he's here. The demon promised him all his dreams would come true if he did this. It seemed like a simple enough request. Davis wasn't sure it was as cut and dried as it sounded, but what choice did he have? He could go to hell now, or… make the devil happy and maybe have some time to live it up in style.

When he woke this morning, the whole encounter felt like a nightmare. The events of the night before were already drifting from his memory like little clouds of unwanted knowledge. Maybe it had all been nothing more than a dream. Then he looked over at his nightstand and saw the dull black metal. A 9mm Glock sat there like the devil himself, staring him in the eye. The horror of last night consumed Davis all over again. His whole body was seized by small tremors. He wished it were a heart attack, but knew it was only fear and realization of what he had gotten himself into. *This is happening.* Davis rushed to the bathroom and in the process, knocked over a lamp which made a loud popping sound as the bulb crashed to the floor. Mistaking the sound for the gun going off, Davis instinctively dropped to his hands and knees and frantically crawled the rest of the way, then hurled in the toilet.

After he pulled himself together, Davis was able to clean himself up and get to the courthouse. As he watched people empty their pockets and proceed through metal detectors, he became even more unsure about the whole assignment. The demon assured him he'd be able to pass right through security screening. All he had to do was enter the courthouse building with the gun hidden somewhere on his person and wait. Wait for what? Was he supposed to give it to someone? Rob someone? This was insane. He should turn around and go home. But to what? Another visit from the demon? No, whatever this was, it was bound to be better than that.

Davis ran his coat sleeve across his forehead to wipe away the beads of perspiration. He didn't want to appear too nervous. After he took a deep breath, he pulled open the front doors and entered the courthouse.

Inside, he faced a row of three metal detectors and paused, not sure what to do next. The officer on the line marked "General Screening" was waving him through, making impatient circles with his arm. Davis sucked in a quick breath and walked quickly, but slowed as he passed through the arch. To his grave dismay, the detector beeped at him like a cacophony of devils shouting, "He's got a gun!" Davis was sure this was the end for him. That all hell was about to break loose. He froze.

The officer stepped up to him, his skin blotchy, green uniform crisply pressed but untucked by his protruding belly, every hair on his head perfectly in place. All two of them.

"Sir, do you have any metal plates or limbs?" The officer made it sound more like a statement than a question.

No, he did not. "Yes, sir, I have a metal rod in my leg. Car accident." Where did that come from? Why did he say that? He had no metal rod in his leg. He wasn't in any car accident.

The officer ran the wand over his leg and it made a high pitched *weeeee-eeew*. To Davis's amazement, the wand didn't make a sound as the officer moved it over the rest of his body.

What the?

"Thank you, sir. Have a nice day." The officer waved him off and was already on to the next person.

Davis couldn't believe it. The demon told the truth. All he had to do was come in with the weapon, and the rest was taken care of. But now what? He looked around the huge lobby. The courthouse used to be the main Tacoma railroad station. It had an impressive entrance with giant glass sculptures hung from the great domed ceiling and on the walls and along the windows. The glass art was done by some local dude who was famous. Chilulu… Pichuley… something like that. Davis took it all in, and momentarily forgot why he was there.

Without warning, his hand shot to the pocket that held the pistol and, unable to control his movement, he drew the gun out. He looked down at the gun in his hand, his mouth wide open. He looked up to see if anyone was staring at him, but nobody had noticed. Yet. Slowly he felt his body turn. What the heck? When he stopped, he faced a well-dressed man in a suit. Probably a lawyer. He was about 20 feet away and Davis watched in bewilderment as his arm raised itself until the gun pointed directly at the man.

"Yo, man! Get out the way!" Davis swung his free arm wildly in an attempt to get the man to move out of his line of fire, while the hand with the gun held like a rock. Steady and true. "Move, dude! I ain't got control of this mutha!" But his finger was already slowly squeezing the trigger.

Someone yelled, "Gun!" and the room filled with screams of hysteria. Davis gritted his teeth and clenched every muscle as he tried to stop himself, but it was no use. He dropped his head and closed his eyes, hoping if he couldn't see a target maybe it would all stop. When the gun went off, Davis was tackled from behind. He never saw what happened. There was a small army of officers holding him down and yelling at him.

"Yo, I didn't do nothin'!" he pleaded lamely. "This wasn't my fault, I don't know how it happened!" Davis tried to raise his head up to get a look at whether he hit that man or not, but one of the officers slammed his face back into the tiled floor. He felt a shock of pain that ran all the way to the back of his head. A wet, sticky substance oozed down to his lips and he tasted copper. Blood. His nose was broken for sure. He cried out as the handcuffs were cinched too tight behind his back.

As he was roughly yanked to his feet and dragged away, Davis caught a glimpse of the man in the suit, lying on the ground. But his wasn't the only body.

There were two.

CHAPTER 24

Lucas grabbed Hayley's arm and pulled her in a wide arc around the man who stood in front of the courthouse. Homeless, by the looks of him.

"Lucas, wha…"

"Sorry, did you see that guy? Something is wrong with him." Lucas released his grip on Hayley's arm, then placed it behind her left shoulder and gently guided her toward the bank of doors. "I didn't want you to get too close. They shouldn't let people like that loiter in front of this building." As he pulled a door open for Hayley, he turned back to look at the man. The nut-job was sweating profusely and seemed lost in his own world. *Probably going through withdrawals.*

"I see chivalry isn't dead after all." Hayley smiled at him as she walked into the building.

Inside they were allowed to bypass the general security

screening with their IDs. The officer who checked them through was unfamiliar. Lucas tended to see the same guys working security here day in and day out. This guy looked like a new recruit. Actually, he looked like he belonged on a surf board in California. Not here in dark, drizzly Tacoma. The officer checked Hayley's identification and smiled, revealing perfect, white teeth. His ice-blue eyes sparkled like diamonds. "Thank you. Have a nice afternoon, ma'am."

Lucas noticed Hayley blush slightly. He held up his ID and noted the nametag above the officer's right breast pocket read "K. Stiev." With his blond hair and strong bone structure, he was an extremely handsome young man, Lucas gave him that much. He found himself staring when Officer Stiev looked up and made eye contact.

"Thank you, Mr. Daniels. Have a nice day."

Lucas stammered, "How did you know my—"

"Your name is right there on your ID, sir. The one you are still holding up. You can put it away now, you're good." He gave Lucas a friendly smile.

Now Lucas was the one blushing. Officer Stiev stepped back so they could walk past and into the lobby.

"Wow, this place is amazing," Hayley said, as she looked all around, taking in every detail.

"I'm surprised you haven't been in here yet. We have time still, go ahead and look around at the glass art if you want."

"Really? I won't take but a minute, I promise!"

Lucas smiled as he watched her saunter across the lobby, inspecting every detail. He pulled his phone out and checked his email and appointments. Lost in thought, he didn't hear the shouting at first. He looked to see a gun pointed right at him. His phone dropped from his unresponsive hand and shattered the screen in a spider web of a hundred tiny cracks.

"Move, dude! I ain't got control of this mutha!" It was the man he had seen out front, who was now waving like a maniac, yet that gun didn't move an inch. It was trained right on Lucas even when the man closed his crazed eyes.

The whole lobby was in chaos. People ran every which way, screaming and shoving, fighting their way out of the room. But Lucas couldn't move. He was paralyzed with fear and could do nothing but stand there and gawk at the business end of a pistol. Shouldn't he at least duck? Is this how it was going to end? Just when his life was getting back on track, it's over because all he can manage to do under pressure is stand there like a statue.

Lucas heard the gun go off, echoing in the large space like dynamite. He saw a wall of green, then felt the impact as he was knocked backward. When his body hit the ground, his head whipped back and struck the hard floor. There was a flash of white light behind his eyes.

Then everything went dark.

CHAPTER 25

Dante watched Lucas enter the courthouse. Invisible to human eyes, he floated among the glass sculptures and waited for the right opportunity to get to Lucas. He had not been very successful in the coffee shop, but he would have his way with him here.

He watched as the man with the gun walked in. Lucas had his head down, sucked into an electronic world, oblivious to the real one around him. Dante almost felt bad for Lucas as he watched the terror rake across his face when he realized a gun was pointed at him. Almost.

Time to end this.

Dante was in the head of the man with the gun. But he soon realized he wasn't alone. There was that presence again. The same powerful one he sensed in Lucas's mind earlier. Dante struggled to overtake it and gain full control, but perhaps he underestimated what he was up against. He watched as his mental battle played out physically in the man's wild movements.

The gun went off. Dante left the man's head immediately and watched the scene play out. A security officer was there out of the blue. He jumped in front of Lucas and took the round square in the chest. The force knocked him backward off his feet and into Lucas. The two of them tumbled to the ground, but the force of the officer's extra weight was too much for Lucas, whose head was thrown back on impact and hit the tiled floor hard.

People continued to scream and flee the courthouse. There were shouts from the officers who tackled the man with the gun as they restrained him swiftly and without mercy.

"Yo, dudes," the man shouted. "The devil made me do it!"

The man was right, of course. Too bad nobody would believe him. Dante watched the officers roughly drag him off as he kicked and screamed like a madman.

The officer who took the bullet for Lucas slowly sat up, coughed, then grimaced at the obvious pain it caused. He tried to adjust the Kevlar vest under his uniform shirt then looked up at the sound of a screaming woman who ran toward him.

"Lucas! Lucas, oh no, no, no, no... Lucas, please be OK!"

It was the redhead from the coffee shop. She rushed up and knelt next to him. The officer looked down at him too, then back up at the redhead. Their eyes locked and they looked at each other with what appeared to be great concern. Why, because Lucas wasn't moving? He probably passed out from overexcitement. Dante floated over for a closer look. Then he saw it.

A pool of blood rapidly formed around Lucas's head.

CHAPTER 26

Abigail gripped the strings of her drawstring bag tightly as she followed her mama around the seventh floor of the St. Joseph Medical Center. She brought everything she thought she would need for a visit to the hospital; Kindle, headphones, notebook and colored pencils, her favorite Garfield comic book, hand sanitizer, tissues, binoculars, emergency utensils, and a now-empty snack bag of Goldfish crackers she nervously ate on the car ride over. Her mama kept wiping her eyes as she tried to read the room numbers through her tears. Her sisters trailed behind, silent for once.

"Room 709, Mama. He's in room 709."

"I know, sweetheart. Maybe it's in the next quad."

St. Joe's was an odd four-leaf-clover shaped tower. Her mama said the design was meant to give more rooms views of the port and downtown Tacoma, but in the hallways it was just confusing. When they reached room 709 they all froze. The door was open, revealing her daddy lying in a bed, his eyes closed and his head wrapped in gauze.

"Is he dead?" Abigail stared at his body and jerked down on the drawstrings repeatedly as if it might help produce the answer she wanted to hear. She gave up on that and flapped her hands and blinked her eyes.

"He's not dead, you ignoramus." Sydney said. "They don't leave dead people lying in their rooms." A pause. "They don't, do they?"

Sarah punched Sydney in the arm. "Who's the ignoramus?"

"Ow! Hey!"

A quick word from Mama shut them both up. She turned to Abigail and squatted down to her level, trying to make eye contact. "He's going to be OK, sweetheart. Abigail, look at me."

But Abigail couldn't look at her. She couldn't look at anything when her eyes were blinking so rapidly. She tried to squeeze them shut, but they only flew open wide then began to blink again. She was losing control.

This was a bad place. Abigail didn't like it here. Not at all. There was a funny smell in the air, like pine, alcohol, and urine. The smells, the beeping and whirring sounds, the patterned wallpaper that didn't match up at the seams, it was all too much sensory input. Her skin felt like hundreds of ants crawling all over her. She started spinning. Around and around. Better. Abigail could feel the ants fly off one by one.

"Oh my gosh, that is sooo embarrassing," Sarah said.

"Yeah, can't you make her stop doing that, Mom?" Sydney added.

"You know I can't, girls. To restrain her right now is the worst thing I can do. Just let her calm herself. She'll stop when she's ready."

Her family thought she was not all there sometimes. That her mind went away and she couldn't hear every word they said. It wasn't true, though. Abigail was perfectly aware of everything going on around her. What they didn't understand was her mind worked fine. Differently, yes, but worked all the same. She was simply trapped in a body that did things she couldn't control. Abigail felt her mama gently guide her toward the room as she continued to spin.

When they stepped in the room, something caught Abigail's eye that made her stop spinning. She looked out the window and saw it. Then Abigail felt a great release wash over her. Her arms dropped to her sides, motionless, and her eyes stopped their uncontrollable blinking. It felt like she was a marionette and all the strings controlling her had just been cut. Abigail glanced over at her sisters. "Honeys, don't you see the…" then dropped the thought. The twins looked at each other and shrugged. She looked to see if her mother possibly saw it, but Mama was looking only at Daddy. Abigail calmly walked over to the window and stood there, staring out with a smile on her face.

Mama quietly said, "Lucas, are you awake?"

"Mmmm…" He stirred.

"Luc?"

"Wh- Alice? Girls?" He smacked his lips and made a loud gulp.

"Daddy!" the twins squealed in unison.

"Could you bring me my water please? I have a cup here

somewhere," he said.

"Of course," Mama said. Then, "Here you go. Sorry it took so long for us to get here. By the time I pulled the girls out of school and got to the ER, they had already moved you up here to neurology. The police explained everything that happened. I just can't believe it. You must have been so scared. Were you scared? Are you OK? Thank the Lord that officer was there. You are OK, aren't you? Listen to me, I'm babbling now." Then Mama started sobbing.

"I'll be fine, hon. But I owe my life to the security officer." he paused. "Where's Abby?"

"She's over there, at the window."

"Abby? What are you doing over there? I didn't even see you in the room. I'm so glad you're here."

"I told you Daddy," Abigail said, still smiling at the window.

"Told me what?"

"An angel is watching out for you."

CHAPTER 27

Lucas was showing his girls the stiches in the back of his head when a portly, older man with white, slicked-back hair, a bushy white beard, small round glasses and a white lab coat walked into the room reading a clipboard. If his coat had been red, he could have passed for Santa Claus.

The man looked up and smiled at everyone, then looked at Lucas. "I see the whole family is here. How are we doing today, Mr. Daniels?"

"I've had better days."

The man laughed a full belly laugh. "I'll bet you have. Well, I'm Dr. Scott and I'm going to check you over real quick." He slipped a pen out of his breast pocket and clicked it three times. "Can you tell me your name?"

"Susan."

Dr. Scott looked at Lucas over the top of his glasses.

Lucas grinned. "I'm just messing with you Doc. It's Lucas."

"A sense of humor! Always a good sign. Do you know where you are?"

"St. Joe's... I'm not sure which floor."

Dr. Scott smiled. "Good. No, that's fine. I'm not sure what floor I'm on half the time. They all look the same around here!" He pulled a pen light from one of his lab coat pockets then shined it briefly in each of Lucas's eyes. "And what time of day do you suppose it is?"

"I have no idea, I've lost track today."

"Well, roughly. Morning? Evening? Midday?"

"Late afternoon, at least."

"Excellent. Well, you seem oriented and alert. Do you remember what happened right before you hit your head?"

"It's all sort of a blur. I remember I was in the courthouse lobby, and there was this man with a..." Lucas glanced at his daughters unsure of how much detail he should give in front of them.

Dr. Scott let him off the hook. "That's good enough. No memory loss, which is a good sign." He checked Lucas's blood pressure and temperature, then held out his hands. "I want you to take my hands and give them a squeeze." Lucas squeezed as hard as he could. "Whoa, easy there, Iron Man! Are you always such an overachiever?" Lucas smiled sheepishly. "Well the good news is, your vitals are fine and I've looked over your MRI and the results are unremarkable."

"Unremarkable? Doc, are you insulting my intelligence?"

More belly laughs. "In this case unremarkable is a good thing. It means I don't see anything of concern."

"So what's the bad news?" Alice blurted a little louder than necessary.

Dr. Scott looked at Alice and the girls. "The bad news is, Dad here has suffered a mild concussion and we need to keep him overnight for observation. Standard procedure for this type of injury. That's bad for you because you don't get to take him home with you tonight. And it's bad for him because we're going to come in here and do neuro checks on him every couple hours making sure he gets a lousy night's sleep." He threw a wide smile then looked back at Lucas. "Have you experienced any nausea or vomiting? Dizziness? Blurred vision? Sluggishness? Sensitivity to Light or noise?"

Lucas answered "no" to each.

"Good. I think you should be able to go home tomorrow morning then. Your head might throb for a day or two. If it does, just take ibuprofen. I'll write you a prescription for the good stuff. Otherwise, you'll be good as new and can go back to your normal routines." Dr. Scott stayed until everyone's questions were answered. As he was leaving, he stopped in the doorway and turned back to Lucas. "You're a very lucky man, Lucas. You escaped both a bullet and a serious head injury. I'd say someone is watching out for you."

Lucas nodded slowly. But why didn't he feel so lucky?

CHAPTER 28

Lucas's head throbbed, and the twins' relentless questions weren't helping. He needed more painkillers. Abigail wouldn't stop moving. Something was making her restless. Lucas pressed the call button on his bed.

"It's almost 5:30." Abigail blurted out. "5:30 is dinner time. Nobody has started dinner yet. We're not even home. How are we going to eat dinner on time? It's almost 5:30 and 5:30 is dinner time."

A nurse had stepped in the room and overheard Abigail. "There's a cafeteria down on the main floor, hon. They have all sorts of good stuff. I know people who come here to the hospital just to eat." She smiled.

Alice said, "I can't bear to leave Lucas right now. Can you girls please wait a little while?"

"It's almost 5:30, Mama."

The nurse said, "Tell you what, why don't you sit here and have a little time with your hubby. I can take the girls down to the cafeteria."

"They might not have the right food for me." Abigail said.

"Do they have pudding?" Alice asked the nurse.

"Sweetie, it's a hospital. We have pudding galore."

Alice looked at the girls and they all shook their heads vigorously. "Thank you." She reached into her purse, pulled out a twenty and handed it to Sydney.

"Sweet!" Sydney said as she snatched it away.

"I want change, young lady."

"Whatever, Mom."

The girls followed the nurse without so much as a glance back. Abigail was already pulling one of her sealed disposable utensil packets from her bag.

As much as Lucas liked having his girls with him, he was grateful for time alone with Alice. But it was not to be. The girls hadn't been gone 30 seconds when there was a knock on the doorframe.

"Mr. Daniels?"

It took Lucas a second to realize who it was. He wasn't in uniform, but the good looks and flashing smile were unmistakable. "Officer, um… Stive is it?"

"It's pronounced Steeve, actually. Stiev is a German name, so you say the second vowel. But please, call me Kevin."

"Only if you call me Lucas. I think we're past formalities at this point."

"Deal."

Alice gave Lucas a questioning look.

"Alice, this is Officer—I mean… Kevin. He's the one who took that bullet for me. He saved my life today." He looked back to Kevin and waved him in. "Come meet my wife, Alice."

Kevin stepped into the room, and offered Alice his hand, which she ignored as she wrapped her arms around his neck and planted a kiss on his cheek. "Thank you, thank you. Thank God for you, Kevin." Tears welled up in her eyes.

"Just doing my job, Ma'am."

"Now you drop the formalities with me too, young man. It's Alice."

"Yes, Ma'am." Kevin smiled, but looked a little uncomfortable.

Alice jumped back. "Oh my gosh, I'm so sorry! You must be terribly sore and here I am squeezing away. I wasn't thinking…"

"No, it's fine. Really. It was only a 9mm round. My Kevlar vest distributed the force of the impact well. It left a good bruise, but I'm OK."

Lucas was shocked. "You got nothing but a bruise? I would have been dead!"

"They just finished checking me out. Physically I'm fine so they've sent me home. I'll be on mandatory paid leave until I meet with a psychiatrist to make sure I'm mentally fine as well. I wanted to stop by and check on you before I go. To make sure you were doing OK." He looked down at his feet. "And to apologize for knocking you down. I feel responsible for your injury."

Lucas was incredulous. "Kevin, I can't believe you are apologizing to me. I'm trying to figure out how I'll ever be able to repay you for what you did."

Kevin put up a hand. "No, sir. Don't mention it. I just needed to make sure you were alright. You had me worried, there was so much blood."

"Yeah, I guess a lot of blood is normal with head injuries. A lot of capillaries near the scalp, or something like that."

"Well, I'm glad you're alright. I have no idea how that guy got through screening with a gun, but this is all my fault. It was my job to protect you, not take you out."

Lucas thought he was making a joke, but Kevin truly looked unnerved. "So, who was that guy anyway? The shooter?"

"We don't know yet. As far as we can tell it was just a random shooting and you were in the wrong place at the wrong time. But I'll tell you this… that guy's life is over."

Something caught Kevin's attention and he looked to the window. His face darkened. Lucas caught a flash of something behind his eyes. Anger? Then it was gone as quickly as it came.

Kevin smiled broadly. "Well, I better let you folks have your time. I didn't mean to intrude." He backed out the door.

Alice threw herself at him and stopped him with another big hug. "Thank you, Kevin." She stepped back, took his hands in hers and looked deeply into his blue eyes. "Thank you."

Kevin smiled at her then looked to Lucas. "I'm sorry I wasn't a better protector." He looked out the window again and the dark look crossed his face once more. Then he spun on his heels and was gone.

Lucas turned to the window to see what had agitated Kevin and triggered his sudden departure.

But there was nothing there.

CHAPTER 29

The angel was outside the hospital, searching. He had just checked on Lucas. Today was too close a call, he almost slipped up. When your lord and master tells you to protect someone, you make sure you do. He was already on thin enough ice with God these days and needed to get back into His good graces. When he looked at Lucas in the hospital room, he could see Lucas's brain better than any MRI or CAT scan. The doctors wanted to keep Lucas overnight to make sure there weren't any unseen complications, but the angel could see all. Lucas was fine. Physically, anyway.

Then it showed up again. The fallen angel who chose the master of darkness over the master of light. Now a demon of blackest intent, that dark shadow of a being pursued Lucas with a boldness and passion that surprised him. Why? What was it about this human that has stirred up so much interest?

The demon emerged from the shadows and approached the angel without fear, without hesitation.

"You," he said.

"You," the angel replied. "What name do you go by?"

"I go by many names. The name is not important. What is important is your interest in Lucas Daniels. You are not usually in the business of babysitting humans. So now you are the great protector?"

"What is your interest in him?"

The demon shrugged nonchalantly. "He's an opportunity."

"Not on my watch."

"Oh, we'll see about that. I doubt you are all that committed to this one. I know you. You'd rather be doing, hmmm... shall we say, other things?"

"I do what my master tells me."

"Yes... what He tells you." The demon began to smolder, charcoal vapor rose from his body and evaporated into the air.

"Don't be so smug. You answer to a master too."

"Sure, there are still rules I must follow. Believe me, I struggle with them every day. But it's nothing like the strict and watchful eye of God. I do get away with satisfying my own internal urges... to a point. Things you deny yourself out of fear. Do not be so afraid of the consequences. You should join me. Together we could roam the earth and wreak havoc until the end of time."

Could what he was saying be true? There must be something the demon isn't letting on. He couldn't imagine going against God the eternal father. It's a trick, of course. That miserable fiend of darkness wants to pull me off Lucas because he's afraid.

He's afraid he might fail with me around. Now things are getting interesting. "Liar. You will not deceive me. And you will not win Lucas Daniels's soul."

The demon let out a howl, spread his wings and propelled himself into the angel, lifting him high into the air. The angel spread his own wings as a buffer to slow his ascent. When he gained control of their momentum, he turned it around and slammed the demon back into the ground. Unfazed, the demon returned to the sky for a superior position and dove at the angel again and again. Each time the angel met him with fierce resistance, but the demon was just as powerful. Neither seemed to be gaining an advantage over the other.

Back and forth they fought outside the hospital, tearing at each other like savage beasts driven by nothing more than a primal urge to kill. The sky crackled and sparked with lightning under a single black cloud that appeared where the angels battled, but they were otherwise unseen and unheard by the oblivious humans around them.

"Surrender to your urges," the demon shouted. "You know you want to be free like me."

"You are an agent of the prince of darkness. Your intent is born of deception. Be gone!"

The angel spun and collided with the demon at an angle that caused their wings to lock. The two beings struggled to free themselves as they made a rapid descent earthward. The angel cried out in desperation as they neared the ground and gave a final, desperate pull as he twisted and yanked himself free with a crack and a tear just as they hit the ground. The angel and demon rolled away in opposite directions. They may be eternal creatures, but they aren't impervious to affliction or injury.

The angel had had enough. He wasn't sure what the extent of the injury he just sustained was, but he knew he couldn't keep fighting in this condition. Hopefully the demon took the greater damage. He rose seven stories into the air and let his body vibrate, giving out a low hum and creating waves that disrupted the space around him. He was getting ready to slip into the heavenly realm. The demon saw what he was about to do and with a final scream of fury flew at him, but too late. As he reached the angel's glowing form he was met with a burst of blinding light that tore his physical form into shreds of smoke.

* * *

Abigail returned to room 709 with her sisters. Mama sat on the edge of the bed talking quietly to Daddy. Then she noticed something outside the window that made her stop in her tracks, causing her sisters to slam into her.

"Hey! Watch it, dork!" Sydney said.

"You almost made us spill all our food, you goober!" Sarah said. "Hello? Earth to Abigail."

But Abigail ignored them. She was focused on what she saw outside the window. A great flash of light, then tendrils of black smoke that dissipated into nothing. Only the smoke didn't stay nothing. It reappeared and swarmed together taking on a physical mass. A terrifying creature formed before her eyes, floating on large wings. It stared right at her.

Abigail let her chocolate pudding drop to the floor. It splattered everywhere, staining her white sneakers. She could feel everyone's eyes on her now.

"Abby, what—" her daddy started to say.

Then Abigail screamed.

CHAPTER 30

Should he be here? Dante sat at the end of the same pew as Lucas and his family and glared at him. It was a risk. On the one hand, church was the perfect place to try to influence him, but it could also backfire. Churches were a tricky thing.

While some could be spiritually uplifting, others could suck the life right out of its members. They were flawed, exclusive, self-serving institutes. Full of politics and grand ambitions, many churches grew to become a church of self, rather than a church of God. They become so focused on how big they can grow, or how much good they can do in the community and around the world, they forget about the spiritual health of the congregation.

Churches are full of hypocrites, who come one day a week in order to ease their own consciences. They come and go like zombies to read words and sing songs without an ounce of spiritual connection to what they are doing. Many churches know how to tap into one's emotions and create the illusion of a spiritual experience, that only fades by the time they get home and leaves a need to return the following week.

Most of the humans who sat here were in a state of confusion, whether they realized it or not. They were more susceptible to influence in church than anywhere else. A church is one of the devil's favorite hangouts. But it is also God's house. Dante wasn't sure he could accomplish anything here with Lucas. He had to try something though. So here he sat.

He knew he wasn't the only one after Lucas's soul. At the very least, he could keep a close eye on him here. Especially here.

* * *

Alice leaned over and whispered to Lucas, "Don't look now, but there is a… an unusual man sitting at the end of the pew. I think he keeps looking at us."

Lucas felt a sickening sense of déjà vu. Was he being followed? He tried to look down the pew out of the corner of his eye, but there were too many people. It was all a blur. He leaned forward and pretended to adjust the hymnal in front of him then glanced casually toward the end of the row as he sat back. Nothing. He looked at Alice, who looked back at him expectantly. "I don't see anyone strange."

Alice bit her bottom lip. "OK, it was probably nothing."

Lucas couldn't shake the uneasy feeling he had for the rest of the service. As they walked out of the sanctuary, Alice frantically tapped his shoulder.

"Lucas, isn't that Kevin over there?"

As if he heard her, Kevin turned and caught Lucas's eye. He smiled and waved as he navigated the throng of people toward them, like a salmon swimming upstream.

Alice greeted him with a hug. "Kevin, it's so nice to see you!" Kevin winced and she noticed. "Oh, I'm so sorry, Kevin. Did I hurt you?"

"Nah, I pulled something in my back working out at the gym. It's fine. Not your fault."

Lucas offered his hand. "What are you doing here, Kevin?"

Alice threw him a sharp look, followed by an even sharper slap to his outstretched hand. "Forgive my husband's manners, Kevin. What he means is, we've never seen you here before. Do you go to this church?"

"Naw, it's alright. I've never been here before. After everything that happened last week, you know... I started questioning some things. Thought I might give church a try. I had no idea you guys went here."

"Well, we're happy to see you, Kevin. You picked a great Sunday to come! I thought the service was especially powerful today. I feel so recharged and uplifted! Don't you? And oh... the music today! I couldn't stop myself from standing up and throwing my hands in the air."

Kevin looked down sheepishly. "Well... I kind of have a theory about that."

"Oh? You have a theory about me throwing my hands up in praise?"

Kevin laughed. "No. Well, yeah in a way. About the way you felt in general. No offense, but none of that felt real to me."

Finally. Someone else who thought the way he did, just when he thought he was the only one. Lucas never understood how people became so spiritually possessed during a service. It seemed more like an act. Were they honestly that caught up in the moment? Or were they trying to draw attention to themselves to show what a spiritual experience they were having. *Look at me, everyone! I'm dancing with God!*

"What do you mean?" Alice asked.

"Well, it's the music. Music stirs an emotional response in people. Have you ever watched a suspenseful scene in a movie with the music turned off? It's not so suspenseful. Or a touching scene that without music is nothing more than dialog, but throw in the soundtrack and bam, you have tears in your eyes. You don't even notice the music most of the time, if it's done right, but take it away and you notice a huge emotional hole in the drama. Churches understand this. That's why they spend so much money and effort on their music programs. They know the music controls emotions and evokes that feeling of spirituality they want people to think they have."

"I agree with you 100 percent that music triggers emotional responses."

All three of them turned around. Reverend Cooper stood there, smiling. It was apparent he overheard the conversation.

"But the reason it does this is music is a gift from God. It has that effect by design. We use it to create a feeling of spiritual connectedness because that is what God intended. It's why He gave us music. I will have to respectfully disagree with you that the feelings it invokes are fake. It is His gift to us. A channel through which He can touch us in our very souls." He smiled and held out his hand to Kevin. "Mark Cooper, I don't believe I've seen you here before."

"Kevin Stiev."

"Nice to meet you, Kevin. Are you a friend of the Danielses?"

"Kevin is the officer who saved my life the other day," Lucas said.

"Well! Then it is very nice to meet you! What a blessing you are, my son. Kevin, I hope you will consider what I've said and, more than that, I hope to see you here next Sunday." He smiled broadly and shook Kevin's hand again, then Reverend Cooper glided off and shook more hands like a campaigning politician.

Alice looked at her watch. "Omigosh! I'd better go get Abigail. If I don't pick her up from her classroom on time, the rest of the day will be ruined. Why don't you boys catch up? I'll get the girls."

Kevin arched his eyebrows at Lucas when Alice hurried off.

"It's a long story," Lucas said. "Let's just say my youngest daughter doesn't handle even the smallest variations in routine very well."

"Speaking of routine, when do you think you'll go back to work? How's your head?"
"Aw, I'm fine. I'm back to work tomorrow. I was going to go back Friday, but my boss insisted I rest at least through the weekend. Honestly, in my household, being at work is far more relaxing. What about you?"

"I have my psych evaluation later this week. After that, as long as the doc signs off that I'm mentally OK, I can go back on duty immediately."

"That's great. Then I'll see you at the courthouse as soon as this week?"

"As long as I can convince the psychologist I'm mentally stable." Kevin grinned and crossed his eyes.

"Good luck with that!"

Lucas chatted with him a few more minutes, then decided he'd better catch up with Alice and the girls. As he walked, he thought about the things Kevin had said regarding the whole church experience and feeling manipulated emotionally. It was nice to meet someone who shared similar viewpoints. The things Kevin said, it's like he could read his mind. He felt the exact same way. But he had to admit, Reverend Cooper made some good points. This was the problem with church. Always more questions than answers.

* * *

Lucas strode down the hallway. He did not notice the figure that stood in the shadows. Dante stepped out and watched him walk away. Was it enough? He couldn't tell how much he got to Lucas today. At least Lucas was questioning and not blindly believing the lies he was being fed. Yes, coming here today was a good thing.

But it was only the beginning.

CHAPTER 31

"Are you sure you're ready for this?" Adam Hawkins looked at Lucas with what appeared to be genuine concern. "It's been one week to the day since the, uh… incident at the courthouse. You don't need to go back so soon. One of the other associates can go with Hayley."

Lucas shook his head. "No, I have to do this. I can't avoid the courthouse forever. I'm fine, really." He was anything except fine. He was a wreck. The Jenkins case was his now, though. The court granted him an extension on his motion due to the shooting, but he wasn't about to ask for another. He had to face his demons eventually.

Adam blew out a sigh. "OK. Well then, you and Hayley better get ready."

Lucas turned to leave, but Adam said, "Wait."

Lucas looked back, expectantly.

"It's gonna be fine."

Lucas paused, then nodded and headed back to his office to prepare. Sure, it was going to be fine. It was ridiculous to think something would happen today. These things almost never happen to begin with. What are the chances he would be involved in another random shooting? At the same courthouse. And after what happened last week, security must have been ramped up a notch. No, this particular court was probably the safest place for him to be right now.

On the way there, Hayley didn't say a word to him. She must be as nervous about this as he was. Neither of them had been back since the shooting. As they approached the front doors of the courthouse, Hayley put her hand on his arm and stopped him.

"Listen, Lucas. I've been thinking about this and I need to get something off my mind, OK?"

Lucas could tell by her fidgeting and lack of eye contact she was struggling with something. "Sure, Hayley. What is it?"

"I just... I'm partially responsible for what happened to you."

Lucas stiffened. Could she have been involved somehow? It's not possible she would have had anything to do with that scumbag. He narrowed his eyes. "Hayley, what are you talking about?"

"Well, if I hadn't been looking at the building and artwork and left you standing there... if we would have just filed the briefs, you wouldn't have been in the lobby and wouldn't have gotten hurt." Hayley's eyes welled up, but she didn't let a single tear fall. "I wasn't professional and you paid the price."

Lucas softened. "Hey, hey..." He wanted so badly to comfort her, but he didn't know what to do. What was appropriate in this situation? Then Hayley leaned into him and his arms automatically went around her. "It's OK. I don't blame you. At all. What happened was nobody's fault but that lunatic with the gun."

Hayley looked up at him. "Really? Are you sure you aren't harboring some resentment?"

Lucas moved his hands to her shoulders and gently pressed her away, just enough to make eye contact. "Not even a little bit. Now what do you say we go face this place?"

Hayley straightened and said, "OK, then." She smiled and gave a nod. Together, they entered the courthouse.

But what they saw inside, Lucas was not prepared for.

CHAPTER 32

Lucas looked at the courthouse entry in disbelief. It looked like the security checkpoint at an airport. A long line of people snaked around roped-off lanes waiting their turn. Something had slowed the process way down. Lucas scanned the room and noticed security officers armed with rifles stood sentry around the lobby. The place suddenly felt more like a prison than a courthouse.

After he watched people file through the security process for a while, Lucas saw what was slowing things down. Some were being selected for a full pat down. Lucas had learned the man who took a shot at him had gained entrance with a gun due to a faulty scanning wand. The physical pat downs made sense as a backup precaution, but yet it all seemed a bit crazy. Where was the lawyer entrance? Lucas looked around for an indication of where to go.

"Lucas." Hayley tapped his shoulder. "Over there."

Lucas followed her gaze until his eye caught someone waving him over. Kevin.

As they sauntered over, Hayley asked, "He's back to work already?"

Kevin greeted them with his usual charming smile. "Mr. Daniels, it's good to see you here. First time back?"

"Yes. And seriously, would you drop the formality already?"

"Sorry, Lucas, habit of the job." Kevin grinned as he shrugged his shoulders and raised his hands, palms up. The perfect picture of innocence.

"I'm surprised to see *you* back so soon."

"I was able to get in to the department psychologist right away and he signed me off with a clean bill of mental health. And departmental investigations verified I followed all procedures correctly. My mental state was solid, there was no reason I couldn't return to work."

"But you were shot. How can your mental state be solid?"

"Believe me, I've been in scarier situations. The kind of things that would haunt most normal men with nightmares that rob you of sleep until you lose your mind."

"So… you're not normal?"

Kevin laughed. "Let's just say I live for this stuff."

Lucas bobbed his head a few times as he looked around again. "I was expecting more security, but this seems extreme."

Kevin snorted. "It's all a show. What happened with you was an embarrassment to the court and to the city. The extra presence is a sort of knee-jerk reaction in an attempt to assure the public they are safe to come here. Gradually things will go back to the way they were before. The shock of the event will wear off and people will forget about it." He glanced at Hayley. "And how are you, Miss Simons? That must have been a pretty traumatic experience for you too."

"I'm just glad everyone's OK. Not something I want to go through again though." Her cell phone chirped. Hayley looked at the screen. "It's my brother. I should take this. Lucas, meet you in there?"

Lucas waived a hand and he and Kevin watched her walk off with her phone to her ear.

Kevin whistled. "Man, how do you do it?"

"Do what?"

"You're a married man. How do you work with that hot little piece of action and not be tempted?"

Lucas harrumphed. "Even if I weren't married, she wouldn't be interested in a guy like me. It's simply not an issue."

"You really don't see it, do you?"

"See what?"

"The way she looks at you. She's got that whole puppy crush thing going on, in a big way. The entire time we stood here, she hardly took her eyes off you. You don't see that?"

"Um… no, you must be mistaken." *Could it be possible?* Lucas's mind was spinning. Sure, he was a happily married man. Or at least a satisfactorily married man. But the thought of a beautiful young woman being interested in him stirred an excitement in his soul he hadn't felt since… well, since he and Alice first started dating. Lucas felt his ego boosted. The idea someone might find him attractive, desire him even, inflated his confidence. Lucas stood a little taller. Then reality settled back in and Lucas slumped. He shook it off. "No. No way. Nice thought though."

Kevin gave him a knowing look. "Open your eyes. She's after you. You need to be careful she doesn't destroy your perfect family."

Kevin's warning rang a little too true. Lucas's attraction to Hayley was one thing, but the possibility of mutual interest smelled like danger. He tried to put it out of his mind but a seed that didn't exist before had been planted and Lucas now felt completely uncomfortable. "I should get going." As he walked away, Kevin's words echoed in his mind.

Open your eyes. She's after you.

CHAPTER 33

She was supposed to get ready for school. But Abigail had to investigate the tapping sound coming from the front of the house. She wandered toward the sound until she discovered its source. A small bird was perched on the tiny ledge outside the front window. It flew up a foot and tapped the glass with his beak, then landed back on its perch. The bird flew up again, higher this time, gave the window a single peck then landed. It was almost as if he was testing the window for a way to get in.

Abigail squealed with delight. He was beautiful. Abigail was an animal lover. She loved animals of all kinds, and generally preferred them to people. Animals didn't judge you or make fun of you because you were different. They didn't say confusing things that contradicted the look on their face or the tone of their voice. They didn't tell jokes that made her wonder if the laughter was at her expense, or if there was actually something funny in what was said. Animals were honest and straightforward about their needs. They didn't say things like, "Gee, Abby, make yourself at home, why don't you?" when what they meant was, "Get out of our room, Abby."

Animals were so much easier to understand than people. But what did this bird want? Why did he repeatedly tap at the window? It's not like he was trying to fly through it. Maybe if she knew what kind of bird it was. Abigail ran to get her *Northwest Backyard Bird* guide. When she came back with the pamphlet, she walked very slowly back to the window, hoping not to spook the bird away. It cocked its head and looked at her with an unblinking eye. Abigail studied its features for a moment. It was a sparrow-sized bird with a coal black head, skin-colored beak, and a brown body with a white abdomen. She opened her guide and tried to find a bird that matched its shape and features. The bird, having apparently determined her not to be a threat, gave a few hops then resumed its short bursts of flight to tap at the window.

When it flew up, she could see white along the sides of its tail. Abigail frowned, not seeing a picture that looked like the bird at the window. She turned the guide over and found it immediately. A dark-eyed junco.

"Mama! Honeys! Come see it! There's a dark-eyed junco tapping at the window!" She didn't even try to contain the excitement in her voice as she let herself ramble. "I don't know why he's tapping at the window. Maybe he wants to come inside. Maybe he sees something he wants. I found him in my bird guide. Come see the dark-eyed junco!"

The twins trotted up to see what all the excitement was about.

They watched the bird for half a minute, then Sydney turned and yelled, "Mom, Abby's not even dressed yet!"

Her mama stormed in. Her brow was furrowed and her face looked tight. "Oh, Abigail, honestly. You should be ready for school by now. You need to hurry!"

Abigail would not be sidetracked, though. "Mama, look. I found him! He's a dark-eyed junco. He's right here on my bird guide." She pointed to the picture. "See the black head and gray-brown body with a white belly? It's a junco. A dark-eyed junco! That's him, Mama."

"That's great, dear. You are an excellent bird watcher. But right now I'm much more interested in seeing you get ready for school." She took Abigail by the arm and led her away from the window.

Abigail turned and waved. "Bye, birdie! Don't hurt yourself."

CHAPTER 34

It was the end of the day. The tradition at Hawkins, Wall and Associates was to close shop a little early and go out for drinks on the last Friday of every month. This was that day. No wonder everyone seemed in lighter spirits today. The associates insisted Lucas come and would not take no for an answer. It was on the company's dime anyway. Who was he to argue?

Lucas pulled out his brand new iPhone as they all headed out together and called Alice. "Honey, looks like I'm not going to make it home for dinner tonight."

"What? You never work late on Friday nights!"

Lucas could hear more than a hint of annoyance in her voice. "We have a work function. It's uh… mandatory."

"Don't forget to call and get permission from your mommy too, Lucas," someone called out, which prompted a great deal of laughter.

Lucas stuck the index finger of his free hand in his other ear to block out the noise. "I'm sorry, honey, what did you say?"

"I said, when do I get a mandatory work function that doesn't involve the kids? I need some time for me, Luc. I've had a rough day, you know." She paused for a few seconds. "You owe me big time, Mr." Then she clicked off.

Lucas pulled the phone away from his ear and stared at the screen for a second. He was not looking forward to going home tonight. He would have to postpone it as long as possible. Maybe Alice would cool off.

Hayley slipped up next to him and hooked her arm in his, then hooked her other arm with a guy named Elliot. She looked at each of them in turn with a big smile on her face and said, "Let's go, boys."

The group walked a couple blocks down the street to an Irish pub called Paddy Coyne's. Marcus Wall opened the front door and held it open for his employees. "Go on in, I've got our usual area reserved."

Inside, the place was alive with singing and shouting of some old Irish folk tune. There was a man on a makeshift stage in the front corner who played a guitar and led the crowd. Lucas made eye contact with him immediately. Seamus White? A nod from the performer verified it. Lucas hadn't seen him since that day on the street when they'd met. Seamus wasn't singing then, but he sure was now. The man had a golden voice. He was baffled why this guy wasn't famous.

Lucas looked back as the last of the group filed in to see where everyone headed to sit. As Wall brought up the rear he looked toward the singer and went white as a sheet. He recovered quickly, but Lucas was sure of what he saw. What was that all about? Seamus got him this job, what kind of hold did he have on Wall? Lucas saw Adam Hawkins and decided to ask him about it.

Adam frowned. After a brief pause, he shrugged. "You probably misread that. Wall nearly has a coronary every time we do this. As soon as we walk in, he starts to worry about how much the night is going to cost him. This group is known to tip a few back." Adam smiled broadly. "So let's get started shall we?"

They headed to a back section where a bunch of tables had been shoved together to accommodate them all. The tables were already filled with plates of chicken strips, sliders, fries, and lamb skewers. "How were you able to reserve such a large section on a Friday night? This place is already packed."

Adam cocked his head. "We give them a lot of good business." He gave Lucas a quick smirk. "So what'll you have?"

Lucas got the feeling he was in for a wilder night than he anticipated. "What's good?"

"I know just the thing for you." Adam headed to the bar and returned a few minutes later miraculously carrying eight opened bottles of beer. He passed them out and saved the last two for himself and Lucas.

"Cheers, Lucas." They clinked bottles, then Adam was off to mingle.

"Sit and stay a while."

Lucas turned toward the sound of the voice. Hayley sat at the table, patting an empty chair next to her with one hand and holding an already half empty glass of beer in the other. Yes, he was definitely going to stay a while.

Lucas felt good. After some delicious food and well-crafted beer, the stress of his job, his family, his life, all washed away. He was there in the moment without a care in the world. Lucas even found himself joining in with the crowd and singing along to an Irish tune or two. It didn't hurt he was sitting with a beautiful young woman either.

"Lucas Daniels! How's it goin', brother?" Seamus pulled up a seat across from Lucas and Hayley.

Lucas hadn't noticed the music stopped. "Seamus, it's good to see you. You sound great up there!"

"Thanks, bud! And who is this vision of beauty with you?" He gave Hayley a big smile and extended his hand.

"This is my co-worker Hayley Simons. Hayley, meet Seamus White, the man responsible for getting me this job."

"Don't be so modest, Lucas. I only got you an interview. You got yourself the job." He turned to Hayley still holding her hand. "You, my dear, possess a beauty only the Irish can claim. You do have Irish blood in you, yes?"

Hayley giggled. "Possibly. My grandparents came here from the Netherlands. My family is Dutch."

"Are they now? Well you certainly have some Irish in you. I mean look at you!" They both laughed.

Lucas had had enough of Seamus flirting with his… co-worker. She's just a co-worker. What was he thinking? He's a married man. So what if another guy is putting moves on Hayley?

"So what are we drinking?" Seamus now looked at Lucas.

Lucas shook himself from his thoughts and glanced at his bottle. "I've never had this before. Smith-wicks? I guess it's an authentic Irish beer." Lucas got a puzzled look from Seamus so he turned the bottle to show him the label.

Seamus burst out laughing. "You Yanks... yes, it's an Irish beer, but it's pronounced 'Smiddicks'. I'm surprised the barkeep even served it to you for pronouncing it wrong."

Lucas felt his cheeks flush. "My boss has been bringing them over."

"It's all right, brother! I'm just having you on. Let's have a toast. But for this, we need the good stuff." Seamus turned and caught the bartender's eye and held up three fingers. The bartender nodded and a minute later, each of them held a fresh pint of Guinness.

Seamus stood and raised his glass. "An Irish blessing!" The crowd around them went quiet. "For my good friend, Lucas. May the cat eat you and the devil eat the cat." Then he proceeded to down the entire pint.

There was utter silence for a brief moment, then Hayley burst out laughing. She pitched forward into Lucas and slapped her hand down on his arm, leaving it there as she tried to regain control. How much had she had to drink? Was it really that funny? The crowd had turned their attention back to what they were doing and Hayley's fits of laughter subsided. She wiped tears from her eyes with her sleeve. "What the heck? What does that even meeeen?"

Lucas opened his mouth, but didn't know what to say. He turned to Seamus and raised his eyebrows.

Seamus leaned in close and his voice went cold as steel. "It means, brother... if anyone harms you, let the devil harm them." Then he brightened and said, "Well, time for me to get back to my gig." He gave a quick bow and went back to play another set of music.

Lucas and Hayley looked at each other, then laughed. What kind of blessing was that?!

Hayley still had her hand on his arm and let it slip down onto his leg. "Oooh… is that a phone in your pocket or are you just happy to see me?" She laughed at her own joke, but then the phone vibrated and her hand shot up in the air. She froze for two seconds, then fell into another fit of laughter.

Lucas yanked the phone out of his pocket and checked the caller. Uh oh. He'd better take it. He brought the phone to his ear and stuck a finger in the other as he turned away. "Hey, Alice—"

"Luc, you need to come home. Now. It's Abigail."

CHAPTER 35

After school, Abigail went straight to the front window to look for the little bird. She didn't see him, so she waited for a minute to see if he would reappear. When he didn't, she turned to walk away. Abigail had taken three steps when she heard it. *Tap.* Like someone threw a small pebble at the glass. She turned back and saw the junco fly at the window again.

"Mama! He's still here! The dark-eyed junco is still tapping at the window."

Her mama walked in from the kitchen and glanced at the bird. "I know, honey. He's been doing that all day and it's about to make me lose my mind."

"How can you lose your mind, Mama? Your mind is in your head. You can't lose it."

"It's a figure of speech, Abigail. That tap-tap-tap all day long, it's like Chinese water torture. It's driving me crazy." She gave the bird a long glare, then returned to the kitchen.

Abigail sat and watched the bird for a while. "What are you trying to do, little guy?"

The twins bounded down the stairs and came up to Abigail with grins on their faces. "Hey, Abby," Sarah said. "Guess what we heard at school today?"

They smiled at each other and narrowed their eyes. What did that mean? Their mouths looked happy, while their eyes looked mad. They both looked at Abigail again, their faces unreadable.

Sydney said, "We heard a bird tapping at your window is a sign someone in the house is going to die!"

"It is not!" Abigail insisted. "He's just confused."

"It's a bad omen, Abbsters," Sarah said shaking her head slowly side to side.

Abigail flapped her hands. That couldn't be true. She had to calm down. They were probably just teasing her.

"Well, it is only a sign," Sydney said. "Doesn't mean it will happen. It's not like a dead bird outside the house. That would mean someone's about to die for sure!" She let the statement hang in the air, then she and Sarah walked away, whispering to each other.

Abigail continued to watch the bird while she considered what her sisters had said. *If they aren't right, what are you doing, little birdie?* Abigail thought about the angel who had been to their house and what it said about her daddy. It said wolves were after him. Is that what this bird was saying too? That her daddy might die?

Abigail decided she couldn't take any chances. She went to tell Mama her Daddy was in danger and found her in the kitchen talking on the phone.

"You owe me big time, mister." Her mama slammed the phone down, then jumped a little when she noticed Abigail standing there. "I'm sorry, honey… your father won't be home for dinner tonight."

This did not make Abigail feel any better. She told her mama about what her sisters said the bird tapping at the window meant. Her mama assured her the twins were merely trying to scare her and there was nothing to it, that it was nothing but a superstition. Abigail didn't buy it. Some people thought the idea of guardian angels were a superstition, but Abigail knew they were real. But then, her sisters didn't seem at all worried about the bird tapping at the window, so maybe Mama was right.

All through dinner, Abigail pushed her food around her plate. She had lost her appetite.

"Girls, do you see how much you've upset Abigail?" Mama said. "I'm very disappointed in both of you. Your father's not here tonight and I don't have the patience or the energy to deal with you. I want you to clear your dishes then excuse yourselves to take your showers and get ready for bed."

"But Mom—" they started to protest.

"No. No buts. I suggest you don't push your luck right now and do as I said."

The twins grumbled and scraped their chairs back noisily, making a dramatic exit from the table. Abigail helped with the dishes while her sisters were supposed to be getting ready for bed. She could hear laughing and horsing around upstairs.

"Excuse me, Abigail, it does not sound like those girls are doing what they are supposed to be doing right now. I'll be right back."

As soon as her mama left, Abigail heard a tap at the dining room window. She went to see and there was a junco tapping at this window now. Was it the same one? Abigail listened carefully for a few seconds, then she heard the tapping coming from the front window still. No, this was another bird. She went right up to the window to try to shoo the bird away. It just sat on the window ledge turning its head in short, quick movements looking back at her.

Abigail turned her head away from the window to holler at her mama about the second bird when a loud smack made her jump. She whipped her head back and didn't see the bird, but there was a small smudge on the window. Abigail leaned in close to look at it. Blood? Out of the dark the bird flew back, right toward Abigail's face and hit the window so hard, it shook. Abigail jumped back and cried out in surprise.

"Abigail?" her mama called from upstairs. "Are you OK down there?"

Abigail didn't reply. She just watched and listened. There was nothing for a minute so she hesitantly returned to the window and looked down. The junco limped around in circles on the ground, stunned. Sooner than she expected, it was able to take flight again and flew off, away from the house. Abigail let out a sigh, relieved the bird was alive. A second later, it flew back at the window, harder this time. Abigail again recoiled in surprise at the loud impact. She could see a tiny crack in the glass. Could he break through it? There was a larger patch of blood this time.

Abigail tried to look down to see if he was going to get up this time, but she was met with a mass of feathers as the junco beat its wings against the window while it climbed once more into the air. This startled her so much she fell back onto the floor. She couldn't take any more of this. As she started rocking, Abigail closed her eyes and pressed her hands over her ears. She tried to hum, only what came out was more like a whimper. She could still hear repeated banging against the glass, but she dared not look. Louder and louder, the attacks became more furious. Abigail was sure this would end in a resounding explosion of glass and feathers.

Just when she was certain the window had reached its breaking point, there was an abrupt silence. Tears streamed down her face as Abigail forced herself to stand and look out the window again. Her lips trembling, she slowly stepped forward until she was up against the blood streaked glass.

She heard Mama run in behind her. "Abigail? What's happening? Are you all r—" She stopped short when she saw the cracked and bloody window. "Oh my…"

Abigail peered down and saw the junco lying on the ground. It wasn't moving. A dead bird outside the house! Fear infected her like a virus. It wasn't just in her head, she felt the fear in her blood. "Noooooo! Daddy, no! NoDaddynoDaddynoDaddyno…" She couldn't stop herself.

"Alright, Abigail. I'll call your father. I'll get him home right away. It's all going to be OK."

She continued screaming her daddy's name. It was not going to be alright. The dead bird was a sign.

Abigail was convinced her daddy would not come home… ever.

CHAPTER 36

What surprised him was the amount of blood. Lucas inspected the crack in the dining room window. It would have to be replaced. Just what he needed. Lucas knelt and gently lifted the dead bird with a gloved hand.

Serves you right for all the trouble you've caused me.

The creature was almost unrecognizable. The head had been pulverized into a soft, bloody mass that hung limply from the tiny winged body.

"How could he have hit hard enough to do this much damage to himself and the window?" He looked up at Alice, who illuminated the gruesome scene before him with a flashlight.

"Abigail insists he flew at the window repeatedly. Like he was suicidal."

"That doesn't make sense."

Lucas stood and looked back at the window. The twins, now

in their pajamas, desperately tried to get a look at what happened, their faces pressed up against the glass. Abigail paced back and forth behind them with her head down, flapping her hands. Every few turns she would move back to the window, then shuffle away from it without ever glancing up. She had calmed down significantly since Lucas got home. She was about as far gone as he had ever seen her when he walked in the house, but on seeing his face, she almost immediately regained some control of herself.

Lucas looked down at the dead bird in his hand.

"What are you going to do with that?" Alice looked at him expectantly. "You *are* going to bury it aren't you?"

That was not his plan at all, but Lucas decided this was not the time to argue. There was only one correct answer to Alice's question. "Yeah… I'll go get my shovel."

"Do you need me to hold the flashlight for you?"

"No, I got it. You go on back inside with the girls."

Lucas plodded off to the garage to get his shovel. He found a spot in the garden as far away from the house as possible and buried the junco in what he hoped was a deep enough hole that it wouldn't be dug back up by Abigail's cat.

When Lucas returned to the house, he found the girls in the family room watching *The Secret Garden*, Abigail's favorite movie. Abigail was mouthing every line. She seemed relaxed. This movie always seemed to have that effect on her for some inexplicable reason. Probably why Alice put it on. Scratches was nestled up next to Abigail as close to her as he could get while staying as far away from the twins as possible.

Sorry, Scratches, no late-night snack for you tonight.

"What's with the grin?"

Lucas popped his eyes up to Alice, who was half paying attention to the movie while she perused catalogs, but now stared at him. He didn't realize he was smiling at the cat.

"Um, nothing. I'm going to go take a shower. I'm feeling… just… I need a shower."

Lucas trudged upstairs. What a bizarre day. A nice hot shower would hopefully wash some of the weirdness away. He stripped off his clothes and turned on the tap.

When the water reached nearly scalding, Lucas stepped in and the spray felt like needles until his body acclimated to the temperature. Lucas dipped his head and let the hot water beat down on the back of his neck.

What happened with that bird and Abigail? She had rambled about how birds tried all day to get in, tapping at the windows and something about signs and omens. She was still too upset; it was hard to follow her. Why did things like this always happen? He was having such a good time with his co-workers. With Hayley. Then yet another family emergency cut it all short.

Lucas thought he heard a commotion downstairs. Were the girls screaming? Couldn't he have 15 minutes of peace where he didn't have to think about Abigail's issues, or fighting kids, or windows that needed to be replaced? He wanted to escape. He closed his eyes and thought about Hayley again.

A sickening feeling boiled in Lucas's stomach. He tried to listen more carefully to what was going on downstairs. Paranoia crept in and perched on the edge of his consciousness. Lucas quickly shut off the shower.

Something was definitely wrong.

CHAPTER 37

Now that it was actually happening, Nikki was having second thoughts. What seemed like a good idea when they talked about it, didn't feel right now that it was reality. She looked over at her boyfriend who drove slowly down the street, squinting to read the house numbers on the dark street. She stared at the back of his shaved head until he turned to look forward again, then she focused on the pentagram tattooed on the side of his neck. Nikki bit her lower lip. Did she dare say something?

He turned and caught her looking at him. "What!" he barked as he continued scanning.

"JD, I don't know if I still want to do this."

"Shut up. We're doing it." JD pulled the car over and put it in park. He pointed at the house across the street. "That's the one."

Nikki noticed the car's single headlight shining on the car parked in front of them. "Shouldn't you have replaced that headlight? I mean, driving around with one headlight sorta draws attention to ourselves, doesn't it? Cops love to harass people for that kind of thing. We shouldn't give the cops a reason to pull us over. Don't you think?"

"Did I ask for your opinion?" JD glared at her, anger burning behind his eyes. "I'll give the opinions around here, you got that? Now stop trying to use that tiny little brain of yours and shut your hole!"

Nikki dropped her eyes and nodded. She had gone too far. JD was jacked up tonight and she needed to be careful. He had a mean streak. Smacked her around sometimes, but she tolerated it because—face it—who else would love her? She was fat and ugly and nobody wanted her. Not even her own parents. She ran away when she was 17 to live with JD, who was two years older and had finished high school. Barely. He looked out for her, made sure they always had something to eat and some means for getting high. He was the smart one, not her. Why did she question him? She was just stupid, stupid, stupid. No, she didn't blame him for hitting her sometimes. She deserved it.

JD shut off the engine. "Do we need to go over the plan again?"

"No, JD. I got it."

He looked at her a moment as if trying to decide if it was conceivable she actually got it. Then he reached over and opened the glove box, took out his Browning .40 caliber semi-automatic pistol and set it in his lap. His pride and joy. He called it "The Breadwinner" because it was what got them most of their money. JD worked odd jobs here and there which brought in a little extra cash, but he never seemed to hold anything down for long. He was often too high to show up for work, or just didn't care.

"I've got something for you. I picked it up for tonight's occasion." JD reached back into the glove box and pulled out a small revolver.

Nikki's eyes widened. "Where did you get that?"

JD was grinning now, like a little kid who just gave his mother a Christmas present he made all by himself. "It's a Smith & Wesson .38 special. Just the right size for your tiny little hands."

Fear clutched at her chest like a vise. "I'm not so sure about th—" Her words were cut short by a swift smack from JD's hand.

"Bitch, don't you show no gratitude when someone gives you a gift?"

At least he didn't use the back of his hand this time. "Sorry, JD. Thank you." She rubbed her cheek with one hand to ease the sting and accepted the gun with the other. It was heavier than she expected.

"There's nothing to it," JD said. "Just point and shoot."

Shoot? There wasn't supposed to be any shooting tonight.

As if he read her mind, JD added, "Not that it will come to that. It never does. Flashing a gun is usually all it takes. It's a very powerful motivator." The twisted smile had returned to his face.

Nikki slipped the gun into her sweatshirt pocket. JD looked at her like she just kicked a puppy. No, not like that. JD would get off on kicking a puppy. His look was more like she had gathered all their cash and lit it on fire.

"What?"

"Are you a complete moron? You don't go up to someone's door with a gun bulging out of your front pocket. One look at that and you'll find the door slammed in your face and the cops on the way. We need to be invited in first, then we show the heat."

"Well... where am I supposed to put it then?"

"Stick it in the back of your pants."

Nikki slowly took the revolver out of her pocket and leaned forward to tuck it into her waistband. The cold steel pressed against her low back and sent a chill all the way up her spine.

JD reached into his own pocket and pulled out his crack pipe and a lighter, took a hit and offered it to Nikki. "Here, take the edge off."

Nikki accepted it gratefully. She brought the glass pipe to her lips and flicked the lighter on underneath the rock. As she inhaled, warm vapor filled her throat and lungs. Nikki felt her blood vessels open up, adrenaline pumping through her veins. The effect was almost instantaneous. Everything came into sharp focus. She was alert and feeling good about the plan again. This was just what she needed.

"Ready to do this?" JD's eyes moved rapidly, making him look slightly crazy. He was definitely flying high.

They got out of the car and JD tucked his pistol in his pants and pulled the hood of his sweatshirt over his head, enveloping his face in shadows. They trotted to the house directly across the street and stepped onto the front porch.

JD pointed at a spot directly in front of the door. "You stand right here."

He moved under the porch light to the right of the doorway,

turned and pressed his back against the siding. He brought an index finger to his lips, which were curled into a grin that made Nikki shiver. With his other hand, he reached up and slowly unscrewed the light bulb, just until it went out and he disappeared into darkness.

Nikki reached out with a trembling finger and rang the doorbell.

CHAPTER 38

Abigail heard it first.

"Mama... someone's at the door, Mama."

Her mama looked up with a sort of pinched face. Abigail tried to think what that look meant. Confused? Irritated? Trying to remember something, maybe.

Abigail followed her mama to the door. She always had to be there when someone answered the door. Visitors disrupted her sense of order at home and it was always best to witness changes to her environment as they happened. Her mama opened the door, then reached for the light switch on the wall and flipped it up and down a few times. Nothing happened. The front porch was still dark except for the light that poured out from inside.

Abigail could see a young woman standing there. She was short and kind of big and had jet black hair down to her chin. Abigail looked at the girl's face then quickly had to look down.

Too much to process. The girl had a ring through her left nostril and one in her lower lip, a mole on her right cheek, hazel eyes, eyebrows which weren't nearly as dark as the inky hair on top of her head, beads of perspiration on her forehead—the details were overwhelming. When Abigail looked at someone's face it was like her mind took a thousand pictures of it, turning it into something like one of those photomosaic puzzles. One thousand tiny photos that, put together, made one large picture. Most people, when they looked at someone, only saw the big picture. But Abigail saw all the little ones that made up the whole. It was why she found eye contact very hard and generally avoided it.

"Sorry, our porch light seems to be out. Can I help you?" her mama said.

"I'm Margaret."

"Margaret... Oh! Margaret, from Craigslist. You're here about the ring. You are... younger than I was expecting. I apologize, it's been a crazy day and it completely slipped my mind you were coming tonight."

"So, do you have it?" The girl seemed nervous.

"Yes, of course. Did you bring cash?"

The girl pulled out a wad of bills from her pocket and held it up. "Can I see the ring first?"

"Of course, wait here one second."

Abigail stood there and watched the girl while her mama stepped over to the entry cabinet and dug something out of a drawer. She risked a glance back up at the girl's face. Something was going on with her. Her eyes kept glancing to the side and she fidgeted a lot. Abigail fidgeted a lot and her own eyes often moved around looking for a safe place to land. Maybe this girl was like her.

"Here it is." Her mama was back and held out a small box that was open, revealing a shiny diamond ring inside.

"I'll take that." A male voice said.

A rail thin man stepped out of the shadows, causing her mama to scream and jump back from the door. The man took this opportunity to step into the house, forcing her mama farther back, as he drew a gun from his pants. The girl followed him in as she reached behind her back, tugging awkwardly at something. She finally got it free and brought her hand around. She had a gun too. Why were there strangers in the house with guns? Abigail started blinking and flapping her hands.

The twins appeared. "What's going on?" They saw the two strangers with the guns and screamed in perfect unison as they grabbed each other's hands.

"Everybody shut the hell up!" The man pointed his gun at them and ripped the hood from his head with his free hand. "Now, we'll take that ring and anything else of value you have around here. Cash, jewelry… small stuff we can carry out of here."

The twins were whimpering, hugging, trying to comfort each other. Abigail stood by her mama's leg and rocked on her feet. Back and forth. Back and forth. The man glanced around, craning his neck to see into the other rooms. He wrinkled his face up like he'd eaten something disgusting, like baked beans.

"Doesn't look like you have much worth taking." He spat the words out like they were the source of distaste in his mouth. He looked down at Mama's hands, which gripped the now closed ring box. "That's a nice rock on your finger. I'll take that too."

Her mama gasped. "No, please…"

"Shut up! This isn't a negotiation! Anyone else in the house?"

"My husband. He's up in the shower."

Daddy! Was this man a wolf who's come for him?

"Margaret, go watch the stairs. Make sure the dude doesn't come down and surprise us."

The girl didn't move.

"Margaret. Hey! I'm talking to you! Go watch the stairs."

The girl hurried over to the bottom of the staircase and raised her gun, pointing it at the empty stairs with a shaky hand.

The noise in Abigail's head got louder. Too much was happening. The inputs were impossible to process. Everything was coming at her and the sensory noise was becoming too much. It was like having headphones on full blast with different music pumping into each ear. It was not discernable, just noise that hurt her head. She put her hands to her ears and hummed, but the pressure soon built up in her hands and she had to let go of her ears to shake them out. She continued the cycle of covering her ears and flapping her hands, humming the whole time in an attempt to block the external forces that attacked her.

"Hey. Hey!" The scary man pointed his gun at Abigail. "What the hell is she doing? Is she some kind of retard or something?"

"No, she… she has Asperger's."

"What the hell is that?"

"It's a form of high functioning autism. Please, she can't handle—"

"Shut up! Just shut up!" The man pressed the back of the hand holding the gun to his forehead and squeezed his eyes shut for a second. Then he threw his hand forward again, pointing the gun at her mama this time. "Make her stop. She needs to stop. Now!"

"You don't understand, I can't just—"

"No, you don't understand. I said make her stop doing that, now! Do it, or I will." He swung the gun back in Abigail's direction.

The twins suppressed their screams and held each other tighter.

"OK, OK! Abigail, honey… Mama needs you to calm down, OK? Please, honey, I know it's very hard, but I need you to do this for me." Her voice was shaky.

As her mama spoke, Abigail felt herself being wrapped up in her mother's arms. She could hear what Mama was saying, understood why she was saying it, but Mama knew better. She knew Abigail was no longer in control of her body. Now the embrace made her skin feel like it was on fire.

She struggled wildly to get the heat off. Abigail twisted her entire body side to side and pulled against the fiery embrace which made her body ache with a million hot pinpricks. She managed to get one arm loose and flung it around like she was swatting away a bee attack. Her hand made contact with something hard. Mama's cheek. But Mama held on. The pressure was building and Abigail's body felt like an already-full tire still being inflated with an air compressor. If it didn't stop, her body would explode.

With a desperate effort, she finally broke free and fell backward, hitting her head on the floor. For one second, the noise, the pain, the overstimulation, it all stopped. Then, just as quickly, the pressure and the fire and the noise all returned full force. Abigail lifted her head off the floor and threw it back down. Ah, beautiful peace. Except it only lasted as long as the initial shock of striking the floor. She would have to keep banging her head if she was going to stop herself from exploding.

Abigail continued to repeatedly slam her head back into the floor. She moaned, partly from the pain of the impact and partly from the pleasure of the silence it created. She wouldn't stop. Couldn't stop.

Not ever.

CHAPTER 39

Never use your real name. That's what JD had told her. The truth is, Margaret *was* her real name, but she changed it to Nikki when she ran away to be with JD. She didn't just leave home back then, she left her whole life behind. She always hated the name Margaret, anyway. She liked the sound of Nikki and JD thought it was cool, so that was that. She was Nikki.

Except tonight.

When she answered the Craigslist ad for the wedding ring, she used her old name, Margaret. The whole plan was JD's idea. He suggested they search Craigslist for a valuable item. He explained if someone was selling one valuable item, they probably had a lot more valuables around the house. So the idea was to answer the ad and when they went to pick up the ring, they would bust their way in and take whatever they could carry out with them. No one had to get hurt. It was a great plan. What

DARK ANGEL

could go wrong?

Now, here she stood guarding the stairs, watching their plan fall to pieces. There was a man upstairs they had to worry about and there were so many kids. She hadn't considered there might be kids. What were they thinking? And now something was wrong with the youngest girl.

Nikki risked a peek at what was going on, keeping her gun pointed at the stairs. The mother was trying to hold the girl, get her to calm down, but the girl was going berserk. All the screaming made Nikki nervous. It would draw attention to the house.

Nikki looked back at the stairs, doing what JD told her. This isn't the way the plan was supposed to go. Maybe she shouldn't listen to JD so much. This whole mess was out of control. He was out of control. She could feel the effects of the crack already wearing off. Her euphoria was fading, leaving her jittery.

There was a loud smack and Nikki heard the mother cry out. Then a loud thump.

Please, JD. Please don't hurt them.

Nikki turned to see what happened. She watched in disbelief as the girl slammed her head repeatedly into the floor. Like she was having some kind of seizure. This was bad. She stood open mouthed, unable to look away. Like seeing a car wreck.

"What's going on down there?"

She had been so wrapped up in what was going on with the young girl, she didn't hear the man coming down the stairs. The voice caught Nikki off guard and she jumped at the sound of it. When she started, her finger jerked the trigger and the gun went off.

The sound was earsplitting. Nikki stared at the gun in her hand, horrified. What had she done? Her thoughts were disrupted by the pounding coming down the stairs. She looked up just in time to step back as a man wearing nothing but a towel, which came loose as he tumbled toward her, landed face down at her feet.

Nikki could no longer hear the chaos behind her. Her head was filled with her own screams. She looked down in shock at the naked man sprawled on the ground. He wasn't moving. There was Blood. Lots of it. Spreading from underneath his body.

Something let go inside Nikki's mind. She felt detached from the world, from herself. Everything around her became surreal. Her reality was crumbling. But there was one thing she was sure of.

She had just killed a man.

CHAPTER 40

Dante's eyes flew open. *No!* He could not allow Lucas to die. Not yet. His visions gave him mere seconds to react before they happened in real time. Fortunately, his kind didn't rely on the physics of this world to get around. He vanished in a wisp of black smoke, into the spiritual realm. Able to cross great physical distances in the blink of an eye, Dante reappeared almost instantly in Lucas's house, completely undetected by the inhabitants.

The scene before him was every bit the madness he had watched play out in his vision. The girl, Abigail, was beating her head into the floor, a crazed young man with a gun was yelling and everyone else was screaming. The man, a kid really, had no glow about him whatsoever. The air around him was like a dark void. Dante was quite pleased with this new development. He had come to save Lucas, but instead found an empty soul, served up on a silver platter, ready to hand over to the dark master.

"What's going on down there?"

Dante whirled around. *Lucas!* The girl with the gun was already turning back in surprise and Dante was not within reach to stop her. He arched his right wing up and brought it down with a single, powerful, swoop. The rocket of air it produced shot out toward the girl and caused her to lose her balance and readjust her footing as she spun. The gun still went off. She seemed to move in slow motion as she looked down at the smoking hunk of metal in her hand. The screaming behind him doubled with new life.

Lucas's body tumbled down the stairs and landed at the stunned girl's feet. Dante felt something wash through him. A feeling he wasn't used to, what humans might call fear. He screwed up. How did he let this happen? He was distracted by his own needs and desires. Dante knew he had very little time to stop this event and he wasted precious time thinking about shredding a punk kid's soul.

What was he going to do? His master would not be pleased. Lucas was still a loved child of God, not yet destined for hell. This was not his time. Dante looked at the motionless body on the floor. Something was different this time... the blood! There was no blood.

Lucas moaned and rolled over onto his back, naked and exposed. The bullet had missed!

"Margaret! What the... do you have any brains at all?"

"JD, I'm sorry! I don't know how it... it just..."

"I told you, no real names, you dumb bitch!"

Dante turned his attention back to the boy with the black soul.

JD is it? Nice to meet you, JD. This is not your lucky day... It's mine.

The room went immediately quiet, as if the whole scene was so incomprehensible it took every ounce of concentration to figure out reality. Even Abigail stopped banging her head, but she wasn't trying to figure out what just happened. She was staring right at him. Studying him. She appeared completely calm now. Not afraid, curious maybe.

Margaret was crying now. She brought her hands to her face, still holding the gun, and wiped at her tears.

Violence screamed in his eyes as JD marched over to her and grabbed the gun from her shaking hand. "Give me that before you shoot yourself, moron."

Dante decided to have a little fun with these two. As soon as JD walked off to deal with his girlfriend, Dante stepped up to Alice. She was completely unaware of his presence as he paused in front of her, then turned to Abigail. Even though she clearly saw his dark form as it towered over her, she didn't shrink away. She just looked up at him with intelligent brown eyes. Dante gently placed something in Abigail's hand and closed her small fingers around it.

"This whole thing has gone to hell. Let's get out of here." JD stormed back to the front door and as he passed Alice, he reached down and yanked away the ring box she still clutched in her left hand. "I'll take that now. I'm not leaving completely empty-handed."

As he passed through the spot where Dante stood, he stopped, shivered, and then ran out the door. Margaret followed him. There was a siren in the distance. The police were coming. A neighbor heard the gun go off and called it in, no doubt. But the cops would never catch them. Dante would make sure of that. They belonged to him.

You and your little girlfriend nearly ruined my day, so I'm going to take my time with you. And I'm going to savor every minute of it. You will feel pain, like you've never felt before. You will feel terror, like you've never imagined.

Then you will die.

CHAPTER 41

He couldn't breathe. The wind had been knocked out of him. Lucas moaned and rolled himself over onto his back. It felt like an entire law library was on his chest. Then slowly the pressure on his lungs relaxed and the air started to flow again. Lucas became aware of his nakedness, but he didn't care. Still disoriented, he closed his eyes and focused on piecing together what just happened.

Lucas remembered throwing on a towel and rushing to the stairs, where it became clear everyone was in a state of fear over something. It was coming back to him, now. He had called out, "Is everyone all right?" as he descended the stairs. No, that wasn't right. He was annoyed at having his shower interrupted. He said, "What's going on down there?" Then the room exploded in a burst of sound which made his ears ring. He had heard a sound just like it a few weeks ago.

Something whizzed past his cheek as he was rocked by a blast of air so powerful he lost his balance as his forward momentum pitched him down the stairs. Could a passing bullet produce enough force to knock a man over? Or had he felt something else? Maybe the noise from the gun had rocked his equilibrium.

Lucas had been moving so fast he hadn't quite processed what he was seeing yet. As he tumbled down the stairs, he barely registered a young woman standing at the bottom. Then his world went black.

Now he lay there, attempting to catch his breath. How long had he been out? Probably only a second or two. He opened his eyes and saw a heavyset girl with short black hair standing over him, looking back. Lucas didn't recognize her. Who was this? Then he realized there was someone else in the house too. He heard a male voice he didn't recognize. The man was yelling and swearing at the girl.

Lucas closed his eyes again and pressed the palms of his hands to his temples. He tried to sit up. Could he sit up? A brief fearfulness gripped him as he considered he might have broken his neck in the fall. No, he had rolled himself over. He wasn't paralyzed. As he pushed himself up to a sitting position, he turned and saw a skinny kid with a shaved head and crazy eyes stomp over and grab the gun from the sobbing girl. He was holding his own gun too. *What had he walked into?*

The intruders quickly walked away. He should have grabbed the girl. No, maybe not. Too many guns. What would he have done if he had gotten ahold of her? Lucas watched helplessly as the male pulled a small box from his wife's grip and said something about not leaving empty-handed. Then they ran out the door.

The house was deathly silent. Lucas made eye contact with Alice, who asked, "Luc? Are you alright?" He saw fear in her eyes, then he glanced at the twins huddled behind her, their faces buried in her back, arms around each other. They looked absolutely terrified. Abigail sat on the ground and oddly, she looked completely at peace. Her eyes shifted briefly to the open doorway, then back to him. She should be a disaster at this point. How is it she's just sitting there, calm as can be?

Suddenly feeling self-conscious, Lucas now had the presence of mind to cover himself up and scanned the area for his towel. It lay rumpled on the bottom step of the staircase. He slowly stood and shuffled over to pick it up. He felt a tightness in his back as he straightened up and wrapped the towel back around his waist. He would be sore from the fall, but everything seemed to be working fine.

"Lucas?" Alice persisted. "Are you OK?"

Lucas spun around. "No! No, I'm not OK! I come out of the shower to find two armed strangers in my house, I get shot at... again, I take a fall down the stairs, and... And! To add insult to injury, I find myself lying completely naked on the floor, humiliated and helpless as these people steal from you and run! What was that, anyway? What did they take?"

Alice dropped her eyes and fumbled for words.

"Alice... what did they take?"

"It was my mother's diamond ring. They were answering my Craigslist ad and, when they showed up, demanded more. They came in with guns, Luc, and then Abigail started... and they..."

Alice broke down and buried her face in her hands.

"Why would you still have that ring posted? I have a good job now; it wasn't necessary anymore."

She dropped her hands and looked back up at him revealing bloodshot eyes and wet cheeks. "Lucas, we are so behind in our bills and you took an advance on your salary to buy new clothes and pay off your lease on the old office space. We aren't catching up fast enough. We've got Abigail's therapist bills, her medication, and special needs aids to pay and we have barely been able to keep up with the mortgage and everything else. Oh, Luc, I'm so sorry. I never imagined something like this would happen."

Lucas stared at her a moment then closed his eyes as he ran a hand roughly through his hair and gave it a tug.

"MamaDaddy," Abigail spoke up for the first time. "Something happened tonight."

"Yes, sweetheart," Alice said. "Something very bad happened tonight."

"No, Mama, that's not what I mean. I think the wolves were here tonight. I think Daddy was supposed to die, but he didn't because—"

"Stop!" Lucas had had enough. "I don't want to hear talk about angels or spirits or wolves or God. If God exists, why does this kind of stuff happen to me? To us. I can't think of a worse situation. This is how God watches out for us? This is how He rewards his faithful? I don't know what I'm being faithful to anymore, to be honest. There were no angels here to protect me tonight. The only thing here was evil. Now that is something real. Something I can believe in. So don't you tell me I have angels watching out for me. No, my life couldn't get any worse."

"Well, you could be dead," Abigail said. "That would be worse."

"Abigail..." Alice gave her a sharp look, knowing it was lost on her.

"Look, we've got guns going off in our house, kamikaze birds braining themselves on our windows, and precious jewelry was stolen. If this is how God treats those who believe in Him, then if He does exist, I don't want anything to do with Him. I've got a real chance at a good career now and I think it's time to stop trying to always do the so-called right thing. It's time to do what it takes to be successful. The world is obviously against me for some reason, so it's up to me and no one else to make it work for me. Believing in God has cost me too much and there's no return."

"You're wrong, Daddy."

"Abigail, now is not the time to argue theology with your father."

"OK, Mama. He's wrong about that too, but it's not what I meant."

"What *did* you mean?" Lucas asked, daring her to challenge him. He was so fired up, he had to fight to stop himself from ripping into his own daughter. If she wanted to push his buttons right now, he wasn't sure he could control his words.

"I mean, no jewelry was stolen. The bad people. They didn't take anything. Well, they did take something. They took the box. The box is something and they did take that."

"Abigail, what in the world are you talking about?" Alice asked. "The ring was in that box. I showed it to them when they first got here."

Abigail slowly opened up her hands and held them out for inspection.

Sitting in her small palms was the diamond ring.

CHAPTER 42

The angel was torn. What should he do? He had arrived just in time to make sure Lucas was safe. Things didn't play out the way he would have liked, but Lucas was alive. He had not expected the demon to be there, but right now they had a common goal; keep Lucas alive until the battle for his soul was complete.

Lucas may be alive, but he was not well, spiritually. No one was seriously harmed and they lost nothing. Still, the man's spirit had taken a crushing blow. The demon had the advantage now and Lucas's soul was in grave danger. What was he supposed to do? He couldn't simply reveal himself; it didn't work like that. This was a matter of faith and you don't restore a human's faith with solid proof. Indeed, seeing is believing, but that's not faith. That is simply understanding and accepting truth. Strengthening faith is a subtle matter and that was not his job. His job was merely to protect. The best he could do to save Lucas's faith was to keep the demon at bay. The rest would be between God and Lucas to work out.

The two drug addicts were fleeing into the night. The demon looked at him with a smile that said, "He's mine now," and then he was gone. The girl, Abigail, was watching him. This child was special. Maybe she will get through to her father. Probably Lucas's best hope.

What did he care? This was not his concern. Lucas was safe enough for now. He would rather be doing what he was created to do. It was decided. The angel turned and raised his great wings, then was gone, leaving Lucas to his own thoughts. He knew that was probably a mistake. Lucas was extremely vulnerable right now. The demon had him in his grasp. A compassionate angel would stand watch by him every second of every day with concern for his soul.

Too bad for Lucas, he wasn't that kind of angel.

CHAPTER 43

Dante watched from the shadows. The two drug addicts were home now. Home was a generous term. The place didn't look fit for a stray animal. Windows had rock-sized holes in them, the paint curled up on the siding like rough blue eyelashes, and a roof of moss sat atop a frame which sank back and to the left, twisting the house so the front door hung at an odd angle. The front yard was a lawn of knee-high weeds, giving the appearance of an abandoned property. It probably should be.

JD cursed in fits at Nikki the entire drive back for how she had screwed everything up. The more he yelled, the angrier he became, his voice rising to a ballistic scream. Nikki had pressed her hands over her ears and whimpered, "Stop, JD, Stop it. Please, please stop." Tears ran down her face, a salty stream of shame and fear.

This had only spurred him on further. His anger seemed to

feed off the intimidation he caused her. JD could barely control the car in his rage. It was a miracle they made it here alive. Not that Dante would have allowed anything to happen to them. Their lives would be his and his alone to take.

Inside now, Dante observed the sparse furnishings, most of which looked like they had been acquired from curbs where people left them out to be picked up with the trash. JD was going on about how Nikki almost killed a man and all they got out of there with was a ring that wasn't worth the risk and trouble it took to snatch. Then it happened. JD opened the ring box and got Dante's little surprise. He stared down into the empty box, his mouth hanging open. "What the f—" His outburst was cut off by the sound of his fist smashing the box into the card table he had set it on, which buckled under the force of the blow.

Something in JD must have snapped. He went completely off the rails and beat on Nikki without restraint. Her arms flew up like wet noodles to block his punches, but he still landed every one. Something cracked and blood splattered him in the face. Nikki went down then pushed herself up on her hands and knees, spittle mixed with snot and tears dangled from her lips. She slowly attempted to crawl away, but JD slammed the heel of his black boot down on the middle of her back, flattening her to the rotting hardwood floor. A squeaky gasp of air escaped her lungs.

"What's that?" JD yelled. "You want more, you dumb bitch?" Then he kicked her in the side with his reinforced steel toe. Blood trickled from her mouth. JD gave her another kick then jumped on top of her and continued to pound away even though she gave up all resistance.

Nikki lost consciousness and JD finally seemed to be tiring.

He stood, panting, and looked down at her. Dante's eyes burned wildly, illuminating the space around him with a red glow.

JD had had his fun. It was time for Dante to step out of the shadows and have his.

CHAPTER 44

JD never saw him coming. Dante laid a cold, heavy hand on his shoulder and JD spun around, his eyes wide. The surprise quickly gave way to anger as JD registered the fact there was an intruder in his house. The kid had no fear. That was about to change.

"Yo, man. What the hell?" JD reached back and pulled his gun out. He tried to step away, but Dante's iron grip held him fast. Unable to get away, he shoved the barrel into Dante's abdomen, but found himself unable to pull the trigger. For the first time Dante detected a hint of uncertainty on his face.

"What the hell is right," Dante said as he moved JD up against a wall. "You're about to see it up close and personal." He looked down at Nikki's unmoving form and almost felt sorry for her. "So you think you're a tough guy, JD?"

"Hey, how do you know my name? Who the hell are you?"

"Do you believe in the devil?"

"I don't believe in nuthin', asshole."

Dante grunted. "And that was your mistake. I'm about to make a believer out of you." With that he released his grip and watched with grim satisfaction as JD experienced every blow he placed on Nikki. His body jerked and twisted as if an invisible copy of himself reenacted his attack on Nikki, only this time he was the victim. He felt every punch just the way Nikki did. Every cut, every crunch of bone she incurred were now his.

JD's smaller frame took the hits with a little more impact without the extra flesh to absorb them. His body was knocked around more wildly, receiving serious damage. Dante considered backing off a little. It would be a pity if JD died too soon from his own beating. No, he would take the chance and let JD experience the whole thing exactly the way Nikki did. If she could take it, he could take it.

JD was on the ground, his body bouncing with each impact, but still breathing and staring at Dante with a fire of hatred in his eyes. Dante doubted he could cast a glare of such evil himself.

When the reciprocated beating finished playing out, JD lay on the ground looking slightly the worse for wear than his girlfriend. Turned out he *was* a pretty tough guy. He took his beating with hardly a sound. It was like his brain was completely disconnected from his body, shutting off all sense of feeling. Perhaps all the drugs in his system made him numb to the pain. Or maybe his stone cold mentality refused to acknowledge pain. Whatever it was, he took as well as he gave. Regardless, the human body can only take so much and when it was done, even though he remained conscious, JD was barely able to move.

Normally, this would be the point where Dante's victims would beg for mercy, not that he was in the business of mercy, but not JD. Rather than show any sign of resignation, JD spat blood as he said, "Fuff ooo." The lack of teeth and a mouthful of blood impaired his speech, but Dante got the gist.

"Me?" Dante replied. "It's not me that's about to get fuffed."

Dante heard a sound behind him and turned to see Nikki stirring. She was starting to regain consciousness. Dante studied her for a moment then turned his attention back to JD. She wasn't going anywhere.

Throughout the beating, JD never lost his grip on his pistol and once again tried to point it at Dante. When it still wouldn't fire, JD tried to throw it at him, but his arm didn't work right and the gun didn't make it six inches before it clattered uselessly on the floor. JD's lack of fear and distress at his situation was denying Dante some of his pleasure.

He would have to try harder.

CHAPTER 45

It had been a long time since he'd done this. Too long. Lucas finished stretching at Jack Hyde Park on Commencement Bay. It would be about a four mile run down and back along the Tacoma waterfront. That was all he needed. He wasn't in marathon shape anymore, not to mention a little stiff from his tumble down the stairs last night. He probably shouldn't run at all, but Lucas needed to do something to clear his head and running always brought him a sense of inner peace.

The sun hadn't yet risen as he started a slow jog down the pathway. Why had he ever stopped running? Something whispered in his mind this morning to come down here and run. He missed the fresh air, the endorphin rush, the time to let the world slip away and be alone with his thoughts for a while. And he had a lot of thoughts to be alone with right now.

Lucas passed an elderly couple, hot beverages steaming from

paper cups in their hands, walking a Yorkshire terrier which immediately went for his ankles as he passed. He scowled at their smiling faces as he dodged the little rat with fur. With no one else in sight, Lucas picked up the pace and let his legs fall into their natural gait. His body moved in perfect precision, arm and leg muscles working together in a fluid motion to maintain a comfortable stride while his lungs and diaphragm kept his breathing in pace. It all came together automatically from years of training, even after all this time. Lucas felt no pain. He was in the zone.

As he moved down the path, he let his mind wander. What if there wasn't a God? He was raised to believe in God, but he didn't see any trace of Him in his life. Was he holding back from doing the things he really wanted to do, the way he wanted to do them, for no reason? Living by some moral code based on nothing but lies? He couldn't think of one way being a believer had benefited him. He had an autistic child, whom he loved more than anything, but who was also a drain on his finances, his marriage and his energy. Sometimes it felt like more than he could handle. He has struggled with his career, which seemed to be on the rise, but he still had to prove himself to keep this job and was still barely keeping his head above water with the bills. And even though his livelihood seemed to be improving, since he took the new job he'd been burglarized and shot at. Twice. Where was God in all this exactly?

Lucas had always imagined a God-loving family as this picture-perfect unit who only said nice things to each other, who didn't have struggles or fights, who always smiled, and things always went their way. His family loved God, but their household was total chaos. It was far from perfect and filled with pain. Right now his life felt like an absolute mess. What was he missing? Was the Christian lifestyle just so much propaganda designed to suck you in with images of a trouble-free life where nobody has real problems, only to conform you to some ulterior purpose and ask you for money?

Maybe this life was it. Maybe there was nothing else when you died. If that was true, he was not getting the most out of living. There were so many things he didn't do, trying to live his life as a faithful believer so he would go to heaven when he died. But if there was no heaven…

"Nice form, Daniels."

Lucas was jarred from his thoughts by the sudden sound of a woman's voice. He hadn't heard the approaching footfalls. He turned his head and saw Hayley jog up next to him, keeping pace. His blood moved faster at the sight of her, causing a tingling in his chest. He couldn't think of anyone he'd rather see right now. Why did he feel that way? He knew he shouldn't, but he did.

"Hayley?" There was no disguising the surprise in his voice. "Do you usually run here?"

"Yeah, I live close." She tipped her head toward the Old Town district up on the hill. "It's my morning routine."

"I figured after last night, you'd be in bed most of the day." As soon as he said the words, an image flashed in his mind of Hayley lying in bed. He immediately shook the thought, but the fact his mind even went there caused him to flush slightly. Hopefully she wouldn't pick up on that. His cheeks should already be red from the cold morning air anyway.

"Every morning. No excuses. Besides, I find running to be a great hangover cure."

Lucas was silent for a moment, not sure what to say, but enjoying her company.

"I'm sorry, Lucas. You probably want to be alone. I shouldn't have intrud—"

"No!" Lucas cut her off a little too enthusiastically. Then quieter, "No, I'm glad for the company. I… let's just say it was a rough night last night, but I don't want to go into it right now."

"Fair enough. We'll just run. But if you want to have company, see if you can keep up." With that, Hayley flashed him a smile that made his heart bounce then boosted her pace and pulled ahead of him.

Lucas quickened his pace, but held back enough to admire Hayley in her form-fitting running pants. He could see every curve held perfectly in place by tight, black spandex and found it hard to tear his eyes away. Why was he looking at another woman like that? He had a beautiful wife at home. He considered himself lucky he had such an attractive woman to call his spouse. Alice seemed to get better looking with age. She still cared about how she looked, although he wasn't sure it was for his benefit so much as out of personal need for her own self-esteem. Yet here he was drooling over a girl 10 years his junior. Was that such a bad thing though? He was just looking. Like admiring a beautiful painting. Nothing wrong with that. And she was definitely a fine work of art.

His daydreaming was cut short when she called over her shoulder, "You gonna keep checking out my butt or are you going to keep up?"

Lucas was seized with shame and almost tripped from the jolt. How could she have known he was checking her out? "I wasn't, I was just…" He fumbled his words trying to cover up with some excuse.

Hayley laughed. "Relax, I'm just messing with you, Lucas."

Lucas was overcome with relief. Almost busted that time. Or did he actually get caught and she was just playing it off? He needed to be more careful.

They continued running in silence, side by side now. Lucas tried to keep his mind clear and not think about last night and especially not about his beautiful running partner. He needed to focus on his breathing and keep pace with Hayley, which he struggled to do. He was more out of shape than he thought.

As they neared the end of the two-mile pathway, Lucas slowed to turn around.

"Do you need to rest?" Hayley slowed with him.

"Were you going to keep going?"

"Oh yeah, I follow Ruston all the way to the end to get a full six miles in."

"Sorry, I'm not up for that yet. Today is my first day out in I don't remember how long. I don't want to overdo it. I'm going to turn around and head back."

"Sure. Totally understand. I'm gonna keep going." She paused. "It was so nice running with you, Lucas. Maybe someday we can do the whole route together."

As she continued down the road, Lucas felt a slight disappointment she wasn't turning around with him, but encouraged by what sounded like an invitation to go running again. It would be nice to have a running partner. Maybe it wasn't a good idea though. Alice might not like the idea so much. And he might like the idea a little too much.

As he ran back along the path alone, Lucas noticed he was feeling a distinct sense of loss. Not the feeling something precious was taken away, but more like an actual part of him was missing. He realized when he was with Hayley, there was an energy there. Something electric that charged his soul whenever he was in close proximity to her. Did she feel it too, or was it just him? The energy was so strong that once he was apart from her, he felt the loss, for a while at least. Like an addiction, his body craved that feeling. He didn't remember anyone ever making him feel this way.

What was that feeling? That electricity? Maybe this was what it felt like to find what some would call your soul mate. Was there such a thing? Lucas loved Alice with all his heart, but he never considered her his soul mate. She was his high school sweetheart and the only love he'd ever known. Perhaps it was only a crush and he was now too old to remember the power of hormones and the excitement of lust. Maybe the feeling wasn't so special, just forgotten. But he was not a teenager anymore. His hormones weren't raging. Maybe there was actually something special here. Something magical. Lucas knew he was getting into dangerous territory.

As he neared the park, Lucas picked up his pace to push himself to his limits in that final stretch. Then something caught his eye, a dark shadow bearing down on him which caused Lucas to jerk his head to the side. But when he looked, whatever it was seemed to have vanished. When he shifted his focus ahead again, he noticed the same shadow approaching, slower this time, like a giant black bird targeting his head, moving in on him swiftly and silently. When he raised his chin to look at it directly, it was gone. There was nothing there.

Panic gripped at him like a seizing muscle. He had the distinct awareness of a presence that was after him. That meant to do him harm. But there wasn't a single person on the path in either direction. Only the occasional car driving down Ruston Way. Lucas was being paranoid. He'd been the victim of too many violent crimes lately. He needed to relax. Wasn't God supposed to bring him a feeling of peace? All Lucas felt was stress and unrest.

When he reached the park, the sun was barely peeking over the horizon in the east, its light bounced off the water like a thousand flashing beacons. He breathed in the salty air, which was filled with the pungent smell of seaweed and rotting crab. Lucas now noticed the sound of the water lapping against the bulkheads and the cry of seagulls piercing the air. It was as if someone had just taken the world off mute. He had completely detached himself from his surroundings for a while. Nothing took him away like a good run.

Back to reality, Lucas stretched out his muscles. He absolutely needed to run on a regular basis again. And maybe he had a running partner now. But why did the idea make him feel so guilty? It's not like he was going to have an affair with Hayley. He would never do that to his wife, to his family, to his own reputation. He just wanted the feeling he had when he was with her.

What was the harm in that?

CHAPTER 46

She thought she was dead. When she opened her eyes, all Nikki saw through a hazy lens, tinged with blood and obscured by swollen flesh, was a set of giant wings. An angel come to take her to heaven. Heaven. There was a concept she hadn't thought about for a long time. A Sunday school fairy tale from a childhood so distant and foreign, she wasn't sure it was even hers. That was another life, one lost to drugs and violence. A life where she was still Margaret. A life she didn't deserve.

As her vision cleared, she saw JD lying on the ground. A frightening creature stood over him, silhouetted by the morning sun slashing through dirt-caked windows and poorly hung sheets that served as curtains. She was still alive. But if she was going to be its next victim, maybe that wasn't a good thing. Whatever this being had been doing to JD, it had been doing it all night. This couldn't possibly be an angel.

The dark creature dragged the barely-conscious JD into the next room like he was nothing more than the shirt he wore. As he passed through the doorway, the monster paused and turned toward her. She felt a cold hand, like death, grip her chest as he looked at her with his red eyes, which exhibited a glow like hellfire. She shut her eyes tight, as if he might not see her if she squeezed really hard. When she had the courage to open her eyes again, she could see JD lying on the soiled, bare mattress on the floor which served as their bed. She could only see him from the waist up, the rest of him obscured by the wall. She couldn't see the creature anymore.

JD's arms were wrenched above his head and held rigid as if tethered to invisible posts. His eyes were half open, his head rocked slowly from side to side. He seemed too out of it to have made such a rapid movement himself. Then he arched his back and his eyes bulged as if the mattress had become electrified. It only lasted a second then his body went limp except for his arms which were held fast by something she couldn't see. She thought she caught a whiff of burning flesh.

At first she tried to convince herself what she was seeing couldn't be real. That it was a hallucination. She attempted to roll away so she wouldn't have to watch, but something was wrong with her right arm. Probably dislocated. She couldn't seem to move. Nikki resigned herself to watching, wondering why she wasn't in more pain. Was it the drugs in her system doing what drugs are supposed to do and made her feel nothing? Was she so bad off from the beating JD had given her that her body had gone into shock? Maybe the creature had done something to her. She was so tired. So very tired. Nikki closed her eyes and slipped away.

When she opened her eyes again, she wasn't sure how much time had passed. The stench of vomit, seared flesh and something else, like metal, filled the air now. Nikki went into a coughing fit and couldn't stop until she threw up. The bile burned her throat like sulfuric acid. As she wiped her chin with her left sleeve, she raised her eyes and forced herself to look at JD, who was now lying with his arms limp at his sides. He was panting as he stared back at her. He glanced at something in front of him then looked back at her. The giant, black creature must still be there.

As she looked into his eyes, she saw something there that surprised her. The anger was gone. He looked defeated. His eyes seemed to plead with her to do something, anything to make it stop.

Something stirred inside her, and she felt a lightness, as if she had been carrying around a burden that physically weighed her down all her life that suddenly was not there. There was a clarity in her mind now and she saw for the first time where her life with JD had led her. Nikki was a smart girl; she could have made something of her life. Instead she lay here in a pest-infested, rotted old house, beaten and near death, which she was sure would come soon. As soon as that thing was done with JD, she knew she would be next.

Was this it? She was about to die and had nothing to show for her life. What was next? If there was a heaven, she certainly wouldn't be going there. The thought made her cry. Nikki deserved to die. Nikki *would* die. She would be her old self again, if only for her last moments, because at least that girl had a family. That girl had people who loved her, once. Nikki didn't. JD never loved Nikki. JD had robbed her of everything; she saw that now. She looked back at him with contempt, her eyes narrowed to slits. She mouthed her words slowly so he would be able to read her lips, "Go to hell, JD."

As if on cue, the mattress JD was lying on burst into flames. JD was engulfed in fire and unable to move. His screams made Nikki cringe, but she would not look away. She was going to watch him get everything he deserved. She probably deserved the same, but she remembered the God from her childhood who was forgiving and had to put some hope in that.

The fire grew and completely obscured her view through the doorway. The screams stopped. JD was gone now, she knew. Then, through the flames stepped the black-winged beast, coming for her. It was more frightening than she remembered and she almost passed out again from fear. But she wasn't so lucky. She would have to suffer her fate awake and alert, so she did the only thing she could think to do in this moment.

She closed her eyes, and she prayed.

CHAPTER 47

Dante stepped through the fire and stopped, completely baffled. How could this have happened? Before him lay the girl, still immobile on the ground, but something had changed. She had the glow. Had it been there before, so faint he didn't see it? The other one, the boy, he was so dark his absence of belief must have sucked her light out like a black hole.

Her eyes were closed and her lips were moving. What was she doing? Then she crossed herself awkwardly with her left hand and he knew. She was praying. Dante roared in frustration and she kept her eyes shut, but she trembled at the sound. He had so very much looked forward to sending two souls on their journey to hell and now this.

Where did her faith come from? It must have been buried so deep, it was a miracle she was able to revive it at all. Dante wasn't sure he could stop himself now. He was in killing mode and when he was in killing mode, he let himself go completely to his passion. He let his need take over and his bloodlust drive him. He never held back because that would only take away from the pleasure. Once he settled on a target it was like the shackles were off and he was free. Free to do what he was meant to do. Free to be true to his purpose and there was no stopping him.

But if he didn't stop himself now, there would be hell to pay, only for him this time. His master would not look kindly on this. If he killed the girl now, she would likely get the grace and forgiveness God inexplicably offered to humans, even when they didn't deserve it. Then she would be dead and in God's realm. He had license to send people's souls to hell, but not to heaven. That was an unforgivable act and, unlike the human, he would not be offered any grace. Once he crossed that line, he could never step back over it. He didn't walk near the line, he fearlessly stomped directly on it and when he was consumed with his desires, he was just off balance enough he risked falling on the wrong side. His anger flared at the girl for putting him in this situation, which made it harder to hold back. He roared again and launched himself into the air, crashing through the roof into the early morning sky. The only way out of this for him was to remove himself from the situation as quickly as possible.

As he looked down through the enormous hole he created and saw the girl lying there, something occurred to him. She would not be able to get herself out of the burning house that now threatened to collapse on itself. If she were to die as a result of his actions, directly or indirectly, he would suffer for it. If he wasn't going to experience the pleasure of her death, he certainly wasn't going to suffer the consequences for it.

The distance he had put between himself and the girl had helped some. He was more in control now and flew back down to her. She had stopped praying, distracted by his ferocious exit. When she saw him coming back at her, she quickly closed her eyes and resumed her prayers with renewed effort. Dante grabbed her by an ankle and not the least bit gently dragged her out the front door and a safe distance away from the house.

The moment he touched her she screamed, "No! No no no no, please no. I don't want to die."

Dante released her and said, "You will not die today, Nikki."

As if she had a sudden understanding he couldn't harm her, she regained some confidence and dared to look directly at him. She said with surprising force, "Nikki did die today. My name… is Margaret."

CHAPTER 48

"So that's it." Lucas spread his hands wide. "That's what happened."

Hayley sat across the table from him at Legal Grounds, her hands wrapped around her cup of chai tea, which she hadn't touched since Lucas started telling her about the events of Friday night. "Wow, no wonder it took you a few days to talk about this. I'm glad you did, though. You've been out of sorts all week, Lucas. I was beginning to think it was me."

"I'm sorry. Of course not, you're perfect." Lucas stopped short. He didn't mean to say it like that. Hayley was grinning like a shy little girl. "What I mean is, you are doing everything perfectly. Matter of fact, I should thank you for carrying a little of my workload these last few days."

Hayley nodded. They both sat there in silence for a few minutes. Lucas picked up his coffee and swirled it around, watching the liquid slosh up against the side of the cup.

Hayley finally broke the silence. "So, I'm in this band..."

Lucas's eyebrows shot up. "Really? What kind of band?"

"It's hard to put a label on it, but if I had to, I'd call us gothic metal, although that means different things to different people."

"Now you're just messing with me."

"Why do you say that?" Hayley smiled like she was amused.

"Come on. You? In a metal band? You don't exactly fit the image. You're too sweet and pretty." Lucas immediately wished he could take back the words. Slightly embarrassed, he tried to recover. "I mean, you know... you're not all ugly and mean and tattooed and pierced."

This made Hayley laugh. "Some like to call us a beauty and beast band." She slipped into a British accent. "I, dear sir, am the beauty." She tossed her hair back with dramatic flair. "I'm the singer."

"Wow. What's your band called?"

"Epic Storm. Do you like music?"

"Very much. I used to play a little guitar myself. I was pretty good, I guess, but I gave it up in college to focus on getting a real job."

Hayley frowned. "That's sad. If music is a passion, you should never give it up completely. It would be like giving up a part of yourself, like the small toes on your feet. You may not think you need them, but without them, you are off-balance. You're incomplete."

Lucas bobbed his head slowly while he thought about what she said. The more he thought about it, the more he agreed. He nodded more vigorously then smacked his hand on the table.

"You're right. I've been denying something that is a part of me for a long time. I don't think I realized how much I missed it until now." He looked deeply into her eyes. She was amazing. One surprise after another. They were alike in so many ways. She really understood him.

Lucas shook himself from his straying thoughts. "So gothic metal, what is that?"

"Why don't you come see for yourself? We're playing a show tonight up in Seattle."

"Tonight? I don't know…" Lucas thought about this for a moment. He was curious to hear Hayley sing, but had family obligations. He hasn't been around much at home lately, how would he swing this?

"Hey, guys, mind if I join you?" Kevin walked up to their table dressed in full uniform.

"Of course, Kevin." Lucas pulled out a chair for him. "What are you doing over here?"

"I'm on break and this place serves the best coffee this side of heaven."

Lucas and Hayley just stared at him.

Kevin shrugged. "What? At least it's not the muck they serve in the courthouse. I swear they make their coffee using dirty laundry water. So anyway, what are you two discussing here? Big case?"

"Actually," Hayley said, "I was trying to convince Lucas to come see my band play tomorrow night. You should come too."

Kevin gave Lucas a questioning look, like he was trying to figure out exactly what was happening here.

"We're playing at El Corazon," Hayley continued. "It's off

Eastlake Avenue in downtown Seattle. Do either of you know the place?"

"I know it well," Kevin said. "I'm not sure that's your type of scene, Lucas."

"I don't think I can go on such short notice, anyway." Lucas said it like an apology. "I really want to go, though."

Hayley smiled at him expectantly. She was so beautiful when she smiled. Lucas sighed and shook his head, trying to look exasperated, but he smiled too. "Hang on." He pulled out his cell phone and called Alice.

She answered on the first ring. "Hey, Luc. Everything alright?"

"Yeah, yeah. Everything is fine. I was just wondering… someone from work is performing in a metal band up in Seattle tonight. I know it's last minute, any chance I could go check it out?"

"A metal band? What are you, 16?"

Lucas lowered his phone and covered the microphone with his other hand. "Can I tell her you'll come with me, Kevin?"

Kevin considered this a moment. "I wouldn't let you go alone."

He put the phone back to his ear. "Kevin is going too." Had he really reverted to playing the Kevin card? He knew she had a soft spot in her heart for him. "He doesn't want to go alone."

Kevin laughed. "That's not what I said."

Lucas wasn't proud of himself and turned his back to Hayley and Kevin so he wouldn't have to see any judgmental looks.

Alice's tone lightened immediately. "Kevin's going?" She paused.

Lucas could tell she was almost onboard. She just needed a push. "With everything going on lately, I could use the chance to blow off some steam."

Alice sighed. "You're right, you should go. Spend time with Kevin. Will you at least be home for dinner before you go?"

"Yes, definitely. I'll see you then." Lucas hung up and turned back around. "I'm in."

Hayley laughed and clapped her hands, like a young girl who was just given a puppy.

Lucas looked at his watch. "Hayley, we'd better get over to the courthouse." They stood to leave.

"I'll see you guys at the show," Kevin said. "What time?"

"We go on at 8:30. I'll put you guys on the list so you don't even have to buy a ticket."

"Cool. Lucas, I'll find you there."

As they walked across the street to the courthouse, Lucas felt an excitement stir in him he hadn't felt in a long time. He couldn't wait to see Hayley perform.

Something told him tonight would be magical.

CHAPTER 49

Maybe this was a mistake. After driving around the area for nearly 20 minutes, Lucas eventually found El Corazon. It was right next to I-5. You could see the midnight-blue, concrete building from the freeway, but getting to it was no easy task. After a couple wrong turns and one-way streets which took him the opposite direction he needed to go, he finally found his way there and parked a block and a half away in front of the REI building.

Lucas sat in his car, contemplating the questionable crowd lined up outside the entrance. When he had driven past, he saw a lot of hair, leather, makeup, and tall boots, all of it black. What was he doing here? Maybe his wife was right. He wasn't a teenager anymore.

A knock on his window jolted him nearly out of his seat. He turned and saw Kevin standing outside his door smiling and moving a loose fist around in circles, indicating he wanted him to roll down his window. Lucas did.

"Having second thoughts?"

"Geez, you scared me. Where did you come from, Kevin? I didn't see you."

"I saw you drive by and park, so thought I'd come get you."

"You might have been right. I'm not sure this is the right scene for me."

"What, them?" He gestured toward the line with his chin. "They're a harmless bunch. Besides, you're with a cop now, right?" Kevin smiled his most brilliant smile.

He did drive all the way up here. "OK," Lucas said. "For Hayley."

When they got to the entrance, a very large bouncer instructed them to empty their pockets and hold the contents above their heads while they were patted down. They were then allowed just inside the opening to a beat up host stand covered in stickers. They were greeted there by an angry looking young woman with dyed black, bobbed hair, smoky eyes, black painted fingernails, and piercings all over her face.

"Tickets?" She said it like it was an inconvenience to do her job.

"Um, we're supposed to be on a list of some sort?" Lucas said.

She looked up at the bouncer and made eye contact with him. "Names?" She looked down at a sheet of paper on the counter.

"Lucas Daniels and Kevin Stiev." Lucas hoped they were on that piece of paper because he sensed there would be pain involved if they wasted her time.

She studied her list for a moment then called out, "Next." She was already looking past them at the next person in line.

Lucas wasn't sure what to do. Were they on the list or not? Kevin grabbed his arm and pulled him the rest of the way inside.

"Come on," he said laughing. "Before Miss Congeniality changes her mind!"

Lucas was surprised at how small the place felt. Where they came in was an open entry area. To the right was a coat check, bathrooms and the entrance to the bar, where another sullen girl stood to check IDs and probably kill you if you didn't have a valid one. To the left was the stage, though not much of one. He couldn't wait to see how they would fit an entire band up there. In front of the stage was a circular space about the size of a dime where the crowd stood, crammed shoulder to shoulder, and waited for the show to start. The back part of the room was raised up a few steps with a short wall that separated it from the pit area below. Along the back wall were the concession stands, that sold t-shirts, CDs, and posters for all the bands performing. Even though the back section was intended to allow an open walkway in front of the concession tables, people stood there too, watching the stage from a higher vantage point.

While Lucas looked around, trying to figure out where they could squeeze in to get a decent view, he heard his name being called. He looked up by the concession tables and there was Kevin, standing right up against the waist-high wall, waving him over. How did he get that spot? It was probably the best one in the room. There wasn't an opening there a minute ago. There couldn't have been. He must have flashed his badge or something. Lucas didn't care how he did it, he was just glad

Kevin got him here.

As soon as Lucas reached Kevin and looked out at the stage, which even from back there was less than 30 feet away, the lights went down and the crowd roared in anticipation. Before anyone walked out on stage, the music started up. It was some sort of orchestral interlude that sounded like something from a horror movie soundtrack. Then choral voices came in that reminded Lucas of Carl Orff's *Carmina Burana*. As the musical tension was building, he could barely make out the silhouettes of people walking to their places on the stage. When the pre-recorded intro climaxed, the lights came on and the band joined in with loud guitars and pounding drums. The music was like heavy metal accompanying a movie score. It was fantastic, but Lucas didn't see Hayley anywhere.

After a couple minutes of instrumental intro, the lightning fast beats slowed down to a low, steady rhythm. Then he heard the most angelic female voice pour from the speakers. Moments later he saw Hayley saunter on stage from the back, singing operatic style vocals. Not what he was expecting. She looked amazing. Hayley moved along the front of the stage as she sang into the microphone held in one hand and waggled her fingers at the crowd with the other, to which they cheered their approval.

She was dressed in tight black leather pants and a red and black leather corset that accentuated her pale breasts. Her cheeks were highlighted with glitter and she had these expressive, Nicole Kidman eyes when she sang. When she reached center stage again, she looked directly at Lucas and he was hypnotized. Lucas became aware of what must have been a stupid childlike grin on his face, but he didn't care. Hayley was an incredibly engaging performer and she had him charmed with a spell he hoped would never break.

The music was interesting, a combination of heavy metal and bombastic symphonic music topped with classically trained vocals. Lucas had never heard anything like it before and he was hooked. The band was very good. He could tell they were all incredibly talented, but he couldn't tear his eyes away from Hayley. She may as well have been the only one on stage. Abigail had talked a lot lately about seeing angels. Maybe he was seeing one now.

Lucas wished the music would never end, but after a short 35-minute set, it did. Way too soon. Lucas hadn't paid attention to Kevin the entire time, he was so fixated on Hayley. He turned to ask him what he'd thought of the band.

But when he looked, Kevin was nowhere to be seen.

CHAPTER 50

Lucas was going to have to wait. While the next group got set up on stage, Hayley sat at her band's concession table signing autographs and chatting with fans. Lucas didn't care about any of the other bands that were going to play, so he figured he'd have his chance to see her once the music started up again. He tried to nonchalantly check out the other bands' merchandise, but kept glancing over to see how busy Hayley was.

She was very popular here. Apparently he was not the only one infatuated with her. Is that what he was? He definitely felt differently about Hayley now that he'd seen this whole new side of her. Maybe infatuated was too strong a word. In awe, certainly. Lucas was staring and realized she was looking back at him. She smiled and waved at him to join her.

"Hey, Lucas! I was so glad to see you out there in the crowd tonight. I've been waiting for you to come find me back here.

Where's Kevin, didn't he come tonight?"

"I don't know what happened to him. He was standing right next to me, then when the lights came back on, he was gone."

Hayley scrunched up her face. "I didn't see him with you."

"I don't know why he'd leave without saying something to me. He was just gone."

Hayley shrugged it off and turned to the crowd gathered in front of her. "Thank you so much for coming to see us tonight. I hope to see you all next time. Bring your friends." She flashed a conspiratorial grin. "Oh, and buy lots of stuff, it's how we make our money." She grabbed Lucas's hand and pulled him toward the far side of the room. "Come on, I want to introduce you to the boys."

As they walked away Lucas could hear the disappointed groans behind them. Hayley led him along the far wall, past a roped-off area, and to a doorway that led backstage which was blocked by a considerable man with ruddy cheeks and a black security t-shirt that didn't quite cover his belly. "Hi, Reid," she said to the bouncer as he stepped aside. Reid was quick to give Hayley a boyish smile that contradicted his imposing frame and just as quick to drop it for Lucas as he followed her through. The rest of her band was there, packing up their instruments.

"Hey guys," Hayley said. "I want you to meet my friend, Lucas."

They all stopped what they were doing and came over. The one who played lead guitar stepped a little too close for Lucas's comfort and gave him the evil eye. He was bigger than he looked on stage, about six foot two, and had strawberry blond hair. Hayley stepped up to him and hooked her arm in his.

"Lucas, this is my brother, Christian."

Lucas extended his hand, but Christian ignored it and turned to Hayley. "Who is this guy?"

"I work with him, Chris. He came to support me. Be nice." She gave him a little shove and he went back to packing up his gear. She put her hand on Lucas's shoulder and introduced the rest of the band. "This is Mike, our drummer. We call him double-tap because he's an animal on the double bass pedals. On bass guitar and rockin' the metal shirt is Greg." She gestured toward a tall lanky guy in a ridiculous black netted shirt. The guys all laughed. All but one. Clearly the shirt was some sort of joke. "And that's our band leader and keyboard player extraordinaire, Austin." She pointed at the one who didn't laugh at the shirt. "Austin does all the orchestral and choral arrangements."

They each shook his hand then asked him what he thought of the show. Hayley left her hand on his shoulder while they talked and he made no attempt to move away. It felt nice there. No big deal, it was only a hand on his shoulder. But then why was he so focused on the fact it was there? He tried to ignore it.

The next band began their set and it was instantly too loud for conversation. Hayley suggested they move over to the bar on the other side where they could talk more, so they left the band to finish packing their equipment.

The way the bar area was set up it was surprisingly effective at blocking out the live noise in the next room. They had TVs mounted on the walls all over the bar where they showed what was on stage so you could still watch the bands and have a decent conversation at the same time.

"So what's up with that Austin guy?" Lucas asked as they sat. "What is he so angry about?"

Hayley laughed. "He's not angry, that's his metal face. He was staying in character for you. He's the funniest guy in the band, believe it or not. I don't think I've ever seen him angry."

"What about your brother? He didn't seem to like me much. Was that metal posing too?"

"Chris? He's just being protective. He acts like I'm still a little girl who needs her big brother to watch out for her. It's kind of annoying sometimes, but actually, it's very sweet. So tell me really… what did you think?"

"I thought you guys were amazing. Truly. I've never heard anything like that before. Your stuff has all the complexities of jazz and classical music, but with the catchy hooks of pop and the energy and rhythms of heavy metal. After hearing this, it makes all other music seem kind of… boring. And you were incredible, Hayley. I am impressed."

"Thanks, you're too kind. But we're just the opening band. We haven't made it yet." She made air quotes with her fingers.

"Is this what you want? To be a professional musician?"

"I don't know, it means a lot more to the guys. This is all they care about. I have a great career outside of this. They don't have that."

They continued to talk about music and career choices for almost an hour until Christian walked in and interrupted them. "There you are. We need to get going, Hayley." He never acknowledged Lucas.

"OK, Chris. I'll be right there."

Christian stared at her for a couple seconds then stormed back to the stage area.

"Well, I guess that's my cue," Hayley said as she stood. "I'm so glad you came to see me, it means a lot."

Lucas stood with her. "I hope I get to see you again soon."

"Won't you see me at work tomorrow? You're not calling in sick because of a little late night are you?"

"No, I meant see you perform ag—"

"I'm teasing." Hayley batted her hypnotic blue eyes at him. "See you tomorrow, Lucas."

She stepped up and gave him a hug. Lucas hesitated for a second then hugged back. Then she let go and bounded away with a wave.

Lucas just stood there, still trapped in her magic spell.

CHAPTER 51

His head pounded, his mind was in a haze. Lucas sat in his office and rubbed his temples. He felt hung over though he hadn't had a drop of alcohol the night before. His eardrums didn't appreciate the loud music they had been subjected to and were making him pay. Everything sounded muffled and his equilibrium was off, which caused a feeling of drunkenness. His body ached from only five hours of sleep. When did he become so geriatric?

The way he felt made it hard to concentrate and his mind kept drifting back to his experience the previous night. The music. His talk with Hayley. Her voice. He couldn't focus on work and trying gave him a headache. Lucas gave up and dropped his head to his desk in hopes of two minutes of peaceful bliss. But right as his head hit the cherry veneer, there was a knock at his door.

"Morning, Lucas!"

Hayley stood there like a bright ray of sunshine on a dew drop, looking full of energy. Lucas groaned. He was definitely getting old. How did she do it?

Hayley sat across from Lucas and studied him for moment, then let one side of her mouth curl into a smile. "I take it you didn't make it out for a morning run today."

"Oh, and you did?"

Hayley didn't say anything. She just smiled at him with a direct stare that said, "of course."

Lucas dropped his head back down on the desk. This was ridiculous. "Are you even human?" Lucas said to the floor

This prompted a laugh from Hayley. "Your body gets used to it, the crazy schedule. Speaking of which, are you ready to go?"

"Go?" Lucas looked back up at her.

"We have those depositions to give at the courthouse."

"Oh right, right. Yeah, just give me a few minutes to gather my files." Lucas was not at all ready. He didn't put a tie on today. He hadn't even shaved. It completely slipped his mind he had to be at the courthouse today. He was slipping. Falling behind, and getting disorganized. He really needed to pull it together.

After Lucas frantically gathered everything he hoped he'd need, a quick search of his car produced an abandoned tie he could put on. The green diamond pattern on maroon didn't exactly match the blue striped shirt he wore, but at this point he wasn't going to question Lady Fortune. Nothing he could do about the shaving.

When they arrived at the courthouse, they were greeted by Kevin at the security checkpoint, who also looked ridiculously refreshed and chipper.

Lucas hated him right now. "Kevin, what happened to you last night? I thought you were standing right next to me the whole time, but after the show, you were gone."

"Yeah, sorry about that, man. The boss called and I had to go. I tried to tell you, but you were a bit," he grinned at Hayley, "entranced."

"Awww." Her voice pitched down then back up as she gently pushed Lucas's shoulder with her fingertips.

"Enough!" Lucas held his hand up as if it would stop the embarrassment.

Kevin slapped him on the shoulder. "I'm just messing with you, man. You might be married, but you're not dead, right?"

Lucas tried to laugh it off, but the words stung a little. Was he dead? Half the time he only felt half alive, going through the motions just to make it through each day, like he was sleepwalking. The only time he'd felt awake lately was when he was with Hayley, who at the moment made him uncomfortable by being present through this whole exchange.

"We really need to get going, Kevin. We're running a little behind today."

"Well then let's get you two to your business." Kevin beckoned them through.

Was he making a double entendre? That didn't seem likely. It was probably Lucas's own mind going to the wrong places.

Lucas and Hayley got through the depositions, but they were both very aware of the fact she was carrying him a bit today. As they were about to leave the courthouse lobby, they ran into Marcus Wall.

"Daniels," he said sounding gloomy as ever. He didn't so much as glance at Hayley.

"Mr. Wall, how are you, sir?"

Wall looked him up and down, his eyes narrowed in obvious disapproval. "Meet me in my office in one hour."

CHAPTER 52

It stood right there by the fence, but nobody else seemed to see it. It was recess and Abigail scanned the playground to see if anyone had noticed there was an angel summoning her over. The kids were swinging, climbing, bouncing balls, running and squealing like every other recess, as if nothing was out of the ordinary. The grown-ups were oblivious too and they usually kept a close eye on the fences, always watching for stranger danger.

Abigail sighed. Why didn't other people see angels too? Why didn't they take a good look and see what was obviously there, all around them, all the time? She walked over to the fence and immediately felt different. Her body relaxed, the prickling she felt all over her flesh when she was in chaotic settings like recess stopped, and her mind, which usually ran too fast to keep up with, slowed down to a more manageable pace. Abigail always felt at peace when in close proximity to an angel.

"You do see me," the angel said, the words like a gentle echo in her mind.

"I know you. You're the angel who was at my house. Twice."

"Yes, Little One."

"You're here to see me?" Alarm swarmed at her and the calming effect of the angel's presence started to lose its hold. Abigail felt the uncontrollable need to flap her hands. "Did something happen to my Daddy?"

"Physically, your father is fine. It's his soul that is in trouble. He has headed down a dangerous path, but the problem is, he doesn't know he's following the wrong road."

"Where is he? Do we need to find him? If he's lost can't he stop and get directions?"

"No, Child, I mean the road his life is taking."

Abigail scrunched her eyes closed and tried to concentrate. That made no sense. It must mean something else. A metaphor, maybe. She struggled with those, couldn't connect the dots. Abigail decided to focus on remembering what he said. She could get help figuring out what it meant later.

"Your father has chosen his path, but he doesn't realize it's not the right one. He wonders why he's not getting where he wants to go when he follows the signs, but on the wrong road, the signs are meaningless and lead him farther away from his destination."

Abigail felt like her brain was going to explode trying to comprehend this. "Why are you telling me this?"

"He needs help realizing he's on the wrong road. You can get him on the right path before he gets too far down the one he's on and can't turn back."

"Why can't you just tell him?"

"Because, I can't interfere like that. In matters of faith, revealing myself would be counterproductive. My job is to keep him from physical harm, that's it. There is a demon following him and is blinding him from being able to see the right path. If someone doesn't show him he's being deceived, the cost will be his life."

"What do you mean?" Abigail wasn't sure if the angel was still speaking in metaphors.

"The devil is battling to win over your father and has sent a demon to ravish his soul. If your father were to completely lose his faith, he will lose the one thing that is protecting his life. There are powerful forces around him who would be more than happy to send him to hell if given the chance."

This all sounded scary to Abigail. "What am I supposed to do? I'm only 10 years, five months and 27 days old. I'm just a kid."

"If you can see me, you can see the demon too. You must watch for him and warn your father when he's around to lead him astray."

"I saw him in our house. You were there too."

"Yes, but demons rarely hang out in this realm in their natural forms."

Abigail looked up in thought for a second then leaned forward and whispered, "Then what do they look like?"

"They like to take on human form and interact with people everywhere, to torment them in their day to day lives. You must look carefully."

"If your job is to keep my daddy from physical harm, why would you bother with all this? You said your job is to keep him from physical harm, that's it."

"Let's just say I'm not a favorite with God. This is important to Him and I need to stay on His good side right now. He loves your father most of all."

"He does?" Abigail felt her body flush with warmth and excitement. "What is so special about my daddy?"

"If you ask me, I see nothing special about you humans at all. But you have to understand, God loves every human being most of all."

"That's an oxymoron."

"And that's a big word for a little girl. All you need to know is, your father's soul is in particular danger and needs extra attention right now. Remember what I've told you. Watch for the demon. Be aware. Call him out, for his power comes from his anonymity. If you can reveal him, he will lose his pull on your father."

With that, the angel glowed so brightly, Abigail had to shield her eyes. Then it vanished and Abigail's precarious sense of calm left with it. She jumped at the touch on her shoulder.

"Abigail," one of the recess monitors said. "Is everything OK? You have been standing over here by yourself for quite a while and you look a little upset about something."

Abigail turned and ran away. She didn't know where she was running to; she just needed to run. She would keep on running until recess was over and they made her go back inside and sit still. She couldn't stand sitting still. It felt good to run. Running helped shut out the outside noise and stimuli that made it hard to concentrate. It brought a calm focus she rarely felt otherwise. Her daddy liked to run. He said it made him feel the same way.

So Abigail ran. She barely even noticed the mud puddles she was usually so careful to avoid.

CHAPTER 53

She needed to change her clothes. Now. Abigail was a mess, unable to calm down since she came in from recess and noticed the mud splattered on her blue leggings. She looked in her school bag for a change of clothes, because she was always prepared for just such an emergency, but today her mama had packed a pair of jeans.

Abigail felt tears coming on, felt herself losing control. She didn't like to lose control at school; it was embarrassing. But this was a catastrophe. She didn't know which was worse, the mud on her pants, the site of which made her legs all itchy, or the thought of putting the rough denim against her skin, that also made her legs itch. Abigail closed her eyes and tried not to panic. She did the breathing exercises her therapist taught her to center herself and not lose control to a tantrum. She calmed down a little and kept telling herself she could change clothes as soon as she got home. She only had to make it through the rest of the school day in her dirty pants, which was one hour and 13 minutes.

When she got home from school, Abigail was confronted by her mama.

"Abigail, I got a call from school today. Was there a problem at recess? They said it looked like you were talking to someone outside the school grounds, but they didn't see anyone. Were you talking to someone, Abigail?"

"Not now, Mama. I have to go change my clothes. There's mud on my legs."

Her mama scrutinized her clothing for a moment. "Honestly, Abigail, they aren't that dirty. I can barely see little spots of mud. Do you really need to change?"

"They're dirty. I can't wear dirty clothes, Mama, and you only packed me jeans today!"

"Abigail, you agreed we could try jeans as backup pants so that I'm not packing your everyday clothes for your emergency set."

Abigail seemed not to hear her. "I was good until I got home. I held it together at school, but I'm home now, so I can change."

"Sweetheart, do you have any idea how much laundry you create for me? You insist on clean pajamas every night and you change your clothes two or three times during the day. That's three or four outfits each day going into the laundry. I have to wash your clothes three times a week or you won't have anything to wear. It's getting out of hand, Abigail, I can't keep up."

"Mama, my pants are dirty." Was she not listening?

Her mama sighed and said, "Fine, go change." Then under

her breath as she walked off, "Pick your battles, Alice."

Abigail ran upstairs to change and puzzled over what her mama just said. Pick your battles? Why does she say that all the time? What battle? There wasn't any battle going on, except maybe the one over her daddy's soul. Was she talking about that? They weren't even talking about Daddy, they were talking about her dirty pants.

She gave up trying to figure it out as soon as she reached her bedroom and turned her attention to picking a new outfit. Abigail opened her bottom dresser drawer and pulled out a pair of pink leggings. She took off the blue ones, tossed them in the white wicker hamper in her closet, and put on the clean pair. She thought about what her mama said about how she created too much laundry, but when she looked at herself in the long mirror hung on the back of her bedroom door, she decided the top she had on didn't match the pink pants. So she threw her shirt in the hamper too and picked out a white long-sleeve t-shirt with a pink peace sign on the front that matched her pants perfectly.

Changed and clean, Abigail finally felt herself relax. The stress of being dirty was exhausting. She laid down on her bed and was immediately joined by Scratches, who purred with Abigail's gentle strokes.

In less than two minutes, they were both asleep. Abigail had drifted off thinking about what the angel said to her and now her mind processed scenes of her father like a stack of photographs. Each memory a picture she could analyze in detail and look for signs of evil.

Abigail woke with such a start, Scratches bolted from the bed, a cloud of nails and fur, and scampered out the door. Something she saw while she dreamt frightened her out of her slumber. She sat up, panting and wide-eyed.

Abigail feared she may never sleep again.

CHAPTER 54

Lucas stared at his reflection in the bathroom mirror, tugged at his open jaw, then decided. Not going to shave today. He jumped in the shower and rinsed off, then dried and put on jeans and a vintage Disneyland t-shirt. He threw on his favorite Life is Good ball cap and went downstairs where Alice was fixing breakfast. She did a double take when he walked in.

"You're not going to church like that, are you?" When Lucas didn't respond she sighed. "You're not going to church."

The disappointment in her eyes pulled at the ligaments in his chest, twisting them ever so slowly. "We talked about this. My boss pulled me aside at the courthouse the other day, remember? He is noticing I'm falling behind and expects me to work weekends if I want to make partner."

"But Luc, Sunday is family day. It's bad enough you've been working Saturdays. We don't see enough of you lately. And church is important. Couldn't you go in to the office after church?"

As much as he hated the idea of working on Sundays, Lucas was secretly glad for an excuse not to have to go to church. He wasn't getting anything out of it lately. It felt rote and meaningless.

"My boss was very clear, he expects to see me work full days on the weekends until I get on top of things. It's temporary."

"What about the example you are setting for the girls?"

"What kind of example is church? It's a gathering of some of the most judgmental, discriminatory people I know. They use the Bible to preach their high moral standards, but change the interpretation to whatever fits their own righteous agenda." There it was.

"Oh, Luc, you don't mean that…"

Lucas paused for a second to consider. Yes, he concluded. He did mean it. "What about my cousin, Stacey? She's a lesbian and the church calls that a sin. We let her watch our children all the time, but the church won't let her in the door because she's a sinner."

"That's not true, the church welcomes everyone through its doors. We are all sinners. If they didn't allow sinners in church, there would be no one there. She just can't hold a leadership position."

"So because she's a lesbian, she doesn't have something worthy to offer? She didn't choose that lifestyle, what is she supposed to do, decide not to be homosexual?" Lucas kept pushing. "Do you think she's a sinner?"

Alice dropped her eyes and slowly shook her head. "I don't

know, Luc. It's not my place to judge her lifestyle; I accept her and love her for who she is. So does God. It's a very confusing issue even the churches are conflicted on."

Lucas had her now. "Exactly my point. Churches twist the scripture to their own purposes. I'm tired of the judgmental attitudes and segregation. I can't go to a place that conflicts with my own core values."

"Lucas, what is really going on here?"

He could tell from the look on her face she was starting to take this a little personally and was feeling wounded. Lucas felt a twinge of guilt flutter in his chest like a butterfly with razors for wings. If he was being honest with himself, he wasn't sure where this was all coming from. Church was very important to Alice and he felt like he was betraying her, but he had to be true to his feelings. Was he being honest with himself though? Or just making excuses. He wasn't sure anymore.

"I'm sorry, Alice, I know church is important to you and I won't deny you that. I don't have a problem if you want to go. You should still go, just without me. Right now, I need to focus on work."

Lucas kissed Alice on the forehead, and headed out the door. As soon as he got outside, he forgot all about church. His mind shifted to a new thought.

Maybe Hayley would be in the office today.

CHAPTER 55

Alice was tired of sticking up for him. She walked across the church parking lot after services, the girls in tow, as the twins continued to pepper her with questions about their father.

"Why does Daddy have to work so much?" Sarah asked.

"If Daddy doesn't have to go to church, why do we?" Sydney added, always the one to try to get a rise out of her.

Alice didn't slow down her pace to look back. She kept walking as she answered, "Your father is very busy at work right now and has to get some things done in the office. It's going to be like this for a while, but not forever."

"Doesn't he want to be with us?" Sarah asked.

Alice reached the car and dug around in her purse for the keys, pretending not to find them at first while she composed herself. She was on the verge of losing it. Was she overreacting? It felt like Lucas was slipping away lately and she didn't know what to do about it. He seemed to fight her on everything and the more she tried to reel him back in to be a part of the family, the more he seemed to pull away. She could see now the girls had noticed it too.

Alice held back tears of frustration as she turned to face the girls. "Of course he does. He wishes he could be here too, he just can't right now."

Sarah looked up at her with big brown eyes, which swelled with moisture. Always the more sensitive one, Sarah picked up on Alice's emotions and could tell something was wrong. "He doesn't spend time with us anymore."

"Yeah," Sydney said. "He likes work more than us."

Alice dropped to her knees and wrapped her arms around the twins. "Oh, sweetheart, that's not true at all." She said the words, but part of her didn't believe them. Maybe Sydney was right. Lately it felt like work was nothing but a convenient excuse for Lucas to avoid his family.

"We'll get through this, I promise. Keep praying for your father that things will improve at work and he'll be able to spend more time with us again." Alice pushed back so she could look the twins in the eyes. "Just keep praying about this, and I promise it will get better." Then she pulled them in tight and hugged them while she silently vowed to have a very long and serious talk with Lucas. Tonight.

When Alice released the twins, a shock of realization hit her. Something wasn't right, like she had forgotten something important or something was missing. Abigail!

"Honeys… where's Abigail?"

CHAPTER 56

There would be consequences for this. It didn't matter though; this was too important. Abigail knew she wasn't supposed to go off without telling a grown-up, but her earlier pleas to speak with Reverend Cooper were met with a sharp, "Not today, Abigail." Her mama insisted on going straight home, but Abigail wanted to—needed to—talk to Reverend Cooper about what the angel told her the other day.

She couldn't talk to her parents about it. They wouldn't believe her, which was a point of frustration for Abigail. They knew she never lied. A fact is a fact and Abigail could only speak what she knew was true. Why would anyone say anything different? There's no reason, either something is true or it isn't. Yet other people, especially her parents, seemed to treat certain subjects, like God and angels, as if they weren't as absolute and real as one plus one equals two. But they were real and she couldn't make them believe until she understood what the angel said better.

Her mama was especially distracted right now as they walked to their car. So Abigail did what she needed to do. She turned and headed back to the church building without saying a word.

Inside, she found Reverend Cooper talking to some adults. There was no time for politeness or manners so Abigail just interrupted. "Reverend Cooper, I need to speak to you right now." Without waiting for a reply, Abigail headed toward Reverend Cooper's office.

Behind her, Abigail heard Reverend Cooper say, "You'll have to excuse me, this sounds very important." Then she heard laughter. Abigail had no idea what could be funny, but at least Reverend Cooper understood she had something very important to talk about.

He caught up with her on the stairs as she headed up toward the administrative offices. "Abigail, is everything all right? Where are your parents?"

Abigail kept walking and Reverend Cooper followed until they reached his office. When she got to the door, she turned her head in his direction then looked back at it until he opened the door and invited her in with a wave of his hand. She plopped herself down on his couch and he pulled up a chair so he directly faced her, his attention completely on her.

Reverend Cooper leaned forward and rested his forearms on his thighs, his hands clasped together. "So, Abigail, what is this urgent business you need to talk to me about?"

"I saw the angel again."

Reverend Cooper's expression didn't change. She may as

well have said she saw a dog, as if seeing angels was an everyday, ordinary occurrence. Abigail knew he was the right person to talk to. He would listen to her without judgment.

"I didn't understand everything it said, but Daddy is in trouble. The angel said he's lost on the wrong road, following the right signs to the wrong places and he needs help and I don't know how to help, I don't even know what this means." Abigail stood and walked five quick paces, then turned sharply around, paced back and sat on the couch in the exact same spot.

"Abigail, try to relax. Can you tell me exactly what the angel said?"

Of course she could. Abigail recounted her conversation word for word and when she finished, Reverend Cooper leaned back and pulled at his chin, but didn't say anything for a few moments. Then he stood and walked to his bookcase and ran a finger across the spines of the books on one of the shelves.

"Life is a journey, Abigail. This means each day is an adventure that leads us to be the people we are. The decisions and choices we make result in different outcomes for our lives and we call that the path. Hopefully our life's journey puts us on a path that ends with us reaching heaven. Does that make sense?"

Abigail nodded. Reverend Cooper didn't find what he was looking for and started scanning a different shelf. He continued, "There are people and opportunities in our lives that force us to make decisions. We base our decisions on what we think will give us the best outcome, so we look for indicators of what would be best for our lives and we call those indicators signs. The problem is, we don't see God's bigger plan for us and sometimes the signs that point to things that look better to us are not what God intended. When someone makes the wrong decisions, we say they are following the wrong path—one that does not lead to heaven."

Abigail's eyes became saucers. "The angel was saying Daddy isn't going to heaven?"

"He's saying your father is making decisions that seem like the right thing to do, but he's being persuaded by a demon to think that way. In reality, his decisions are leading him on a path to…" Reverend Cooper paused. "On a path that leads away from heaven. His relationship with God appears to be strained right now, leaving him vulnerable to such influence. Only when we are in a close relationship with God and we truly listen, do we hear that still small voice that tells us the right thing to do."

Reverend Cooper stopped searching the bookshelf and turned to Abigail. "Have you seen this demon he spoke of?"

Abigail stared at the carpet and bobbed her head.

"Can you tell me about him?"

Abigail got off the couch and paced and flapped her hands, keeping her eyes focused on the floor a foot in front of her. "It was at my house. But I've seen it as a human with my daddy. I think he's around him a lot. I didn't see it before, but when I looked through the pictures in my mind, I saw him. It was the demon."

"This is what the angel warned you about, that your father has a demon presence around him and he needs you to show him when he's being influenced to make the wrong decisions."

"He won't believe me." Abigail plopped back down on the couch with a huge sigh. "He never believes me."

"Don't give up on him, Abigail." Reverend Cooper

abandoned the bookcase and walked over to a tall stack of dusty old books on the floor next to his giant oak desk. He squatted and looked through the pile. "There's one thing that concerns me about what the angel said. He mentioned powerful forces that would be happy to send him to hell. Normally, demons don't take the lives of humans. They influence, torment, even possess, but don't usually end someone's life directly. Some of the angel's other statements made me wonder... aha! There it is."

Reverend Cooper pulled out a book bound in black leather and wiped the cover with his sleeve. He walked over and held the book out to Abigail. "The Nature of Angels" was imprinted on the cover in gold lettering. The book looked like it was a thousand years old.

"Angels don't always behave the way we expect, Abigail. They are more complex creatures than they are typically portrayed. They have the free will to make choices just as we do, but with much higher stakes. If they make a bad decision, there is no forgiveness. Those who make the wrong choice are cast out—"

"And sent to be a servant of Satan," Abigail completed his sentence.

"That's right. There are different types of angels too; messengers, protectors, destroyers. These angels must struggle every day to honor God, while staying true to their nature. If they slip up, well, you can imagine how bitter and angry they would be, knowing they will never get back into heaven."

Abigail took the book and flipped through the pages. The thin pages crinkled like tissue paper and tingled in her fingers. This would have answers, she knew it. "I can take this?"

"That is a very rare book, Abigail, but I know you will take good care of it. You may borrow it. Read it and watch out for the demons in your father's life, whatever form they might take. I will be praying for him."

Abigail got up and hugged the book to her chest. Then she walked out of the office without a word.

CHAPTER 57

The day wasn't turning out the way he expected. Lucas sat in his office staring at a daunting pile of briefs that teetered on the edge of his desk. He had been reviewing them all morning, but wasn't making the progress he'd hoped. He kept thinking about the way he'd left things with Alice this morning and was starting to feel guilty for being at work. But one glance at the stack of files threatening to swallow him whole reminded him he needed to be here.

Lucas was surprised at how many people were in the office on a Sunday. These guys were all workaholics. Keeping up was not as easy as he'd thought. He kept glancing out through his open door, hoping to catch a glimpse of Hayley, but of all the people who were here today, she was not one of them. Lucas now realized how disappointed he felt. He had completely expected to see her here and she was the one thing that made the idea of being at work on a Sunday bearable. Now that he thought about it, she was the bright spot in coming to work *every* day.

He was here now though, and frankly the idea of going home was no more appealing than the cases he needed to review and research. Lucas needed to dig in and focus. He refilled his coffee, then attacked his work with a renewed vigor. He plowed through it for another hour when there was a knock on his door. He looked up and saw Hayley standing there and felt a too-big smile pop involuntarily onto his face. But as soon as he registered the look on hers, his smile faded like a wave that ran out of steam. Her eyes were puffy, her hair frazzled and she wore a scowl like a bad mustache. Lucas had not thought her capable of being tired and grumpy, but she sure looked it, yet somehow she was still beautiful. Sexy even.

"Hayley, what's wrong?"

"Our band rehearsal went really late last night. We're working on some new material. Anyway, I overslept and didn't get my morning run in. I just don't feel centered without my run."

"Oh, right. You never miss your morning run, do you?"

"No." She said it a little too loud. "I brought my running clothes along hoping to get a quick lunchtime run in, but I don't feel safe running downtown by myself." She paused and looked at Lucas like she was debating asking him something.

"What is it?" he asked.

"Well you probably… it's just that… I don't suppose you would run with me? Do you have a change of clothes?"

As a matter of fact he did. He started keeping his running gear in the car thinking he might fit in a run here and there, but it hadn't happened yet. He looked out his window at the gray drizzle that seemed to suck the last thread of motivation right out of him. He hadn't planned on running today, but now...

"I actually do. I'd love to go for a run at lunch."

Hayley's face brightened and the sparkle jumped back into her eyes. "Thank you, Lucas. I feel better already. Can you break now?"

He glanced at the clock on his wall. It was barely past eleven. "But you just got here."

"I know, but I won't be able to concentrate until I do this. What do you say?"

Lucas looked again at his heap of briefs the past three hours hadn't put a dent in and shook his head. "Why not."

Hayley gave a short jump and clapped her hands together once. "I'll go change. Meet you out front in ten?" Then without waiting for an answer, she spun and was gone in a flurry of red hair.

Lucas caught a whiff of her perfume as it was launched to him on the winds of her sudden departure. He closed his eyes. It smelled wonderful. He could almost feel the sensation of it as the scent wafted over him. Like a fresh spring breeze that carried the smell of fresh-cut grass and cherry blossoms and blue sky. The scent lingered in his nostrils and reached back to some primitive part of his brain, stirring something awake. He didn't want to move and lose that smell or the feeling it brought. With great effort, Lucas forced himself up and grabbed his car keys off the desk.

Outside, the rain lightly spit at him as he reached for his duffel bag in the back seat. He realized how great it was to have someone to motivate him. He otherwise never would have gone for a run on a day like this. He simply didn't have the drive anymore. Hayley is just the thing he needs in his life right now. Running was yet another important part of his life he had given up to be a family man.

He recently came to realize how much he truly missed it, but Alice wasn't about to encourage him to take it up again. No, she'd rather have him home helping out. Of course she'd pretend to be supportive. When he mentioned how good it felt to run again after his jog along the waterfront, and how he wanted to pick it up again, she said, "Sure, that would be good for you, but do it on your own time." His own time? What did that mean? Did he even have his own time anymore? He would have to make this happen himself, but the truth was, he already felt guilty about working so much and couldn't bring himself to add yet another iron to the fire. He needed for her to support him by telling him it was OK to go for a run. But she wasn't going to say that, so he hadn't been back out again.

But now here he was, about to go running on a lousy day that only the most hardcore, dedicated runners would bother with, after a few words from Hayley. She must have quite a hold on him. That wasn't good. But yet, her influence ignited his passions, like his love for music and running. She was like an angel, sent to set him free of the burdens of his life.

Lucas realized he was daydreaming, standing next to his car getting wet and looking like an idiot. He jogged back inside, changed, then came back to find Hayley stretching, just inside the front doors.

He joined her in doing toe touches, then grabbed his right

ankle and pulled his heel to his buttocks to stretch out his quads. Hayley finished stretching and Lucas watched, transfixed, as she pulled her hair back in a ponytail. Without taking his eyes off her, he switched legs, grabbed his left ankle and pulled it back. He was mesmerized as she ran her hands over her hair, grabbing and re-grabbing, smoothing out her hair perfectly. When not a single hair was out of place, she secured the ponytail with the black rubber band around her wrist. She pulled it over the hand holding the ponytail then twisted it and pulled the hair through two more times.

Hayley turned to face him. "Ready, Lucas?"

He let go of his ankle, then nodded. "Let's do it."

Lucas let Hayley lead him down Pacific Avenue for a few blocks, but when they hit 9th Street he said, "Follow me."

They started up the impossibly steep hill, but after a couple blocks he took a right on St. Helens and followed it to 6th, which led them to Wright Park. They followed the loop trail through the 27 acre park, then retraced their steps back to the office.

As they were walking it off, cooling down, Hayley said, "Wow, that was quite a workout. Thanks, Daniels."

"Yeah, not a bad run." He played it off, but knew his body was going to absolutely hate him for this.

They stretched out again in silence, not bothering to go inside this time since they were already soaked to the bone and didn't notice the rain anymore. Afterward, when they reached their offices, Hayley remained uncharacteristically quiet. As they were about to part ways to change into their dry clothes, Hayley put her hand on his arm, gently squeezing for a brief moment. Letting her fingers linger there, she said, "I like running with you, Lucas. If you want a running partner, you're welcome to join me in the mornings before work."

She locked her eyes with his and he was putty in their magical blue spell. He would probably say yes to anything she suggested. "Yes, I'd like that. I think I need a running partner to keep me motivated."

Hayley smiled and gave his arm one more gentle squeeze before letting go. "Great, meet me at Jack Hyde Park at 5:30am tomorrow?"

"Are you insane?" is what he should have said. Instead, he said three words that would probably get him even deeper in the doghouse at home.

"I'll be there."

CHAPTER 58

He was later than he meant to be. He still made it home in time for dinner, but Lucas had promised he would be done by early afternoon. His run set him back and though it was the high point of his day, he decided against mentioning it. It would only make things worse.

Alice was stewing about something all through dinner. It had to be more than his getting home late. He knew it must be serious because she was clearly waiting for the girls to go to bed before she let him have it.

After dinner, Lucas suggested they all play a game, which seemed to brighten Alice's demeanor. Slightly. The girls decided on Clue. Abigail won as usual.

"It was Mr. Green in the study with the candlestick. Obviously."

"Obviously," the twins responded in unison and threw down

their detective pads.

"OK, girls," Lucas said. "Time to get ready for bed. School tomorrow."

After he said goodnight to the twins, he went to tuck Abigail in. He wanted to make it short and sweet so he could go find out what sort of trouble he was in now. He said, "Goodnight," from the doorway and started to close her door, but Abigail stopped him.

"Aren't you going to stay for my bedtime prayers?"

"Abby…" Lucas sighed. "Sure, sweetheart. Say your prayers."

Lucas walked in and sat on Abigail's bed. He stared at the floor while she prayed. What was on Alice's mind? They talked about Abigail's disappearing after church without telling anyone. She knows what she did wrong and how much it scared her mother, but what did that have to do with him? Was it somehow his fault? Was it something else? Lucas couldn't sort out what Alice was upset about.

"Daddy!"

"What?"

"I said, amen. You are supposed to say amen too. Were you listening? I was praying for you, Daddy. Daddy, say amen."

"Oh, sorry I'm a little distracted tonight." He turned to her. "Amen," he whispered as he leaned forward and kissed her forehead. "Goodnight, Abby."

When he got downstairs, Alice was in the kitchen washing the dinner dishes. She threw a towel at him.

"Make yourself useful."

The towel hit him in the face and hung comically on his head until he pulled it off with a snap. He couldn't tell if she was being playful or pissy, but he strongly suspected the latter.

"OK, Alice. Clearly something has been bothering you all night. Let's have it."

Alice set the pan she was washing down in the sink and dropped her head. She took a big breath, her shoulders rising and falling, before turning around to face Lucas. "I know you are working hard, Lucas, but you just aren't around enough and it's affecting the girls."

"What do you mean?"

"I mean they are beginning to think you don't *want* to spend time with them, that you don't want to be around them, and frankly it is starting to feel like you are avoiding all of us. The girls need their daddy and I need your help too." She softened. "I miss you, Luc."

"But I'm only doing all this for you and the girls. Why can't you all see that? I'm working my tail off to give you and the girls a better life."

"They're young girls, Lucas, they don't understand that. They don't care about work or money. To them, a better life is having their daddy around to play with them."

That one sliced through his heart like a Ginsu knife through a tomato. Or through a tin can, more like. What had happened to him? His heart was feeling more metal than flesh these days. But he had to stay strong, keep his eye on the big picture. "I get it, but this is only temporary. As soon as I make partner, I won't have to put in all these extra hours."

Alice looked at him, skepticism swirled in her eyes. "You've got to do better than that. I understand you have to work extra right now, but you need to find time in there for your family. You can't just abandon us."

"That's not fair." Lucas felt defensive. He also felt a little guilt. "I haven't abandoned you."

"Lucas, when the girls start to wonder if their daddy still loves them, you may as well have. Make time to be with them. Talk to them. Show them they are important to you."

Lucas had no idea the girls were being affected this way. Alice was right, they are too young to understand. He loved his girls more than anything in the world and it pained him to think they thought otherwise. Lucas stared at a speck of food on the floor as he considered his options. He had to do something.

"Maybe going forward I can bring some of my work home and do it here. Like the old days, remember?" Lucas smiled at Alice, hoping it would be returned with the memory of when they were young and he was just starting out with his own law practice.

Alice did not smile back, but her posture relaxed. "It's a start." She stepped toward him, looked deeply into his eyes and studied him as if trying to assess his sincerity. She didn't smile, exactly, but the frown left her face and she leaned in and kissed him, then wrapped her arms around him and buried her head in his shoulder. "You are going to owe us big when this is all over."

Lucas returned the embrace. It felt good to hold her in his arms. Really good. He was feeling completely disconnected from her lately. Maybe tonight they would reconnect in the bedroom. Lucas squeezed harder, then relaxed his hold and let his hands slide down to her buttocks. She pressed into him in response. A good sign. All must be forgiven. Maybe now was a good time to tell her.

"I've decided to start waking up early and getting in a run before work."

Alice tensed and pushed away from him as if she realized she was hugging a stranger and not her husband. The frown had returned to her face, her nostrils flaring. "What?"

Not the reaction he expected. Lucas thought for sure she would support this. He debated telling her about his running partner, but decided this was not the time. She was already upset and might take it the wrong way. It was innocent, of course, but the idea of him running with another woman might not sit too well with her. Not right now. He'd tell her later.

Alice's anger had reignited. "Are you even listening to yourself? We just talked about you finding more time with your family and now you are telling me you are going to take more time for yourself, off doing your own thing?"

"This isn't going to take any time away from anyone. I'll be leaving before anybody gets up, which I usually do anyway. It's not like we can get any quality time together then, you are all still sleeping."

"But if you get up so early to go running, you'll be tired and worthless when you get home. When you are here, we need you to be present."

"Why can't you support me in this? You know running is important to me. I let it slide from my life for a long time, but I need to bring it back. I should never have stopped. I need to do this to nurture my soul."

Alice jabbed a finger at him. "What you need to nurture is your family."

Lucas had had enough of this. "I'm going to bed. I need to get up early."

CHAPTER 59

It just wasn't happening today. He couldn't get in the zone. His mind raced like cockroaches running from the light. Hundreds of little thoughts skittering in every direction, looking for some dark place to hide. Lucas was usually focused when he ran, but not this time. He had been running with Hayley every morning for the past two weeks and normally they didn't say much, they just ran. Today he needed to talk.

"Hayley, do you believe in God?"

Hayley cocked her head at him and narrowed her eyes, but didn't slow her pace. "Why do you ask?"

Lucas debated telling her about Abigail's claim she sees angels, then decided against it. That would be revealing too much. "My youngest daughter believes quite strongly in God. She's been asking me a lot of questions lately. Questions I don't know how to answer, because to be honest, I'm not sure what I believe anymore."

She seemed to relax, which was good. For a second there, Lucas was afraid he crossed some line and got too personal.

"Well, I can't tell you what to believe, but here's what I believe—there is a force out there that connects us all. It connects us to the earth, to nature, to each other. I believe there are supernatural powers that we don't fully understand, things we can't explain, but a single supreme being? No. I think all religions are essentially about the same thing. They are simply different ways of explaining this life force that surrounds us. I absolutely believe you can tap into this force through meditation or prayer and experience what some would call miracles. But the idea there is one omnipotent being who can hear each and every one of us and have some master plan for our lives and who is capable of maintaining a personal relationship with us, all of us? The idea is absurd. However, there is definitely a power driving everything and there is both good and evil that comes from it. Yin and Yang. In fact, this is what a lot of my band's music is about. I write most of the lyrics myself."

Lucas didn't say anything at first as he mulled it all over in his mind. It actually made a lot of sense. He's experienced things hard to explain by any reason other than God, but other times it seemed there couldn't possibly be a God.

"What's the matter, Lucas? Too out there for you?"

"No, I was thinking about what you said. That's an interesting perspective." Did he dare bring up the subject? What the heck. "So, what about angels and demons? Do you think they're real?"

"Supernatural beings? I have no doubt. Like I said, there is good and there is evil that flows out of the force. We try to wrap our minds around the unexplainable by attaching labels or visuals to it, so we come up with ideas like angels and demons, lady luck, fate, karma, ghosts, the devil." She hesitated, then said, "And God."

"So you're saying God is a concept we have invented as a way to explain this life force that's all around us?"

"Something like that. Don't get me wrong, I have nothing against what anyone believes, because it's all the same, really. What I struggle with is religions and how they start wars. All this fighting and killing over beliefs that are just different perspectives of the same thing."

Without question, she gave him a lot to think about. Soon, Lucas felt his mind quieting. The outside world faded away as he pulled deeper inside himself, finally heading into the zone. Their talking had slowed them from their usual pace. He looked at Hayley. "You ready to do some real running?"

They poured it on, silently pushing each other faster, each taking the other's unspoken challenge. It felt good to run fast. Lucas could feel the burn in his legs, but he didn't mind the pain—it made him feel alive. They had almost reached the park where they started when Hayley cried out and Lucas found himself suddenly running alone. He stopped and turned around to find Hayley 50 feet back, limping forward and frantically grabbing at her left calf.

"Cramp! Lucas, help."

Lucas jogged back to her where she was now pounding at her leg with her fist. "Hold on, you don't want to do it like that. Come here." Lucas took her left arm and wrapped it around his shoulder and helped her off the path to a patch of grass where he had her sit. "You've got a charley horse, you have to stretch it in the opposite direction of the spasm."

Lucas sat in front of her and took her foot in his lap with his right hand and grabbed her calf with the other. "Which side is it on?" Hayley pointed to the outside, so Lucas switched hands and gripped her ankle with his left and gently pulled and stretched her leg inward with a slow, steady pressure. With his right hand, he massaged the cramp, pushing it toward the back of her leg.

Hayley threw her head back, her eyes closed, and pounded the ground with the palms of her hands. "Ow, ow, ow, ow!" Then a sharp intake of breath through bared teeth.

"Hang in there, it will pass in a second."

After less than a minute of stretching and massaging he saw Hayley's grimace replaced with pursed lips as she exhaled and dropped her shoulders, no longer beating the grass. The worst of it was over. Lucas stopped stretching her leg and used both hands as he gently massaged her calf to work out the cramp so it wouldn't seize back up again.

"Oh, that's amazing, Lucas. Thank you."

Lucas continued to work her calf, trying to be firm, but knowing it would be tender. "Do you get these a lot?"

"Sometimes. I can be prone to them when I'm nearing my time of the month."

Her frank confession took Lucas aback. She just spouted off a very personal, intimate detail like she was reciting multiplication tables. He wasn't sure how to respond, but she saved him and broke his uncomfortable silence.

"Do you know what my oma called charley horses? Ijsbeen, which means something like 'ice leg' in Dutch." She launched into an accent that sounded something like German. "Ach, Haayleeey, you should trink more vater. You're going to get ice leg."

They both laughed at her impersonation, then fell silent. Hayley closed her eyes and Lucas turned his attention back to her calf. Her skin was so silky smooth. He enjoyed the opportunity to touch her, to feel her close and soak in the smell of her while he stroked her soft, pale skin. The whole situation started to feel very intimate when he realized he was no longer massaging her, but caressing her leg from ankle to knee. He looked up to find her looking at him with a curious expression.

He stopped and patted her leg. "You should be good now. Your grandmother was right, you know."

"Right about what?"

"You'll want to trink a lot of vater after this."

Hayley laughed. "Thank you, Oma." She stood, then buckled when she tried to put weight on her left foot.

Lucas caught her and put her arm around his shoulder again. "I'll help you until your leg relaxes a little more."

They hobbled back toward the park together. Every step caused Hayley's ponytail to swish near his face and leave traces of strawberry in the air, but underneath that he could smell her sweat. It was pungent but sweet, with a hint of spice. It was not at all offensive, almost sensual, in fact. Primal. Lucas felt his heart rate rise.

As they got closer, Hayley started putting more pressure on her left leg and by the time they got to the park, she was walking on her own again. They did some quick stretching then Hayley said, "Well, see you at the office." She turned to leave, then turned back and placed a hand on Lucas's arm.

"Thanks for taking such good care of me." She held his eyes for a long moment, then smiled and gave a quick nod, like she'd just decided something. Her hand remained on his arm, her eyes glimmered with mischievousness. "I'm going to return the favor."

Before he had a chance to respond, she left with a wave and pranced to her car. Was she flirting with him? What did she mean by return the favor? It was probably innocent. She was grateful and wanted to show her appreciation. Nothing more than that, he was sure. But then there was the way she looked at him.

Lucas shook his head and smiled. He was being ridiculous and if he wasn't careful, his mind would invent fantasies that would make any actual favor nothing short of disappointing. He put it out of his head and returned to his car.

He climbed in and took his phone out of the glove box, did a quick check for messages and when he saw there were none, set it on the passenger seat. It immediately buzzed so he picked it back up. It was a text message from Hayley.

The message read: I know what 2 do 4 U

CHAPTER 60

It was as if a light went on in her head, although the truth of what she'd discovered felt more like all the lights went off. Abigail had read the book Reverend Cooper gave her all morning, determined to finish it. It was Saturday and she was free to do what she wanted, no school, or homework, or therapy sessions to distract her. She sat cross-legged on her bed, the heavy book on her lap. Scratches was curled up against her back, being denied his usual spot in the warmth of her lap.

Most of the book provided little insight. Abigail already knew everything there was to know about angels. At least that's what she thought until she neared the end of the book. The shocking revelations she encountered in the final section were like a heavy curtain that had fallen on her, the weight forcing her down in a net of darkness. She continued to read, though each line frightened her more than the last with its truth. Abigail forced herself to plow through the material, each page shattering the reality of what she thought she knew.

When she finished, she slammed the cover closed, which caused a cry of protest from Scratches. Abigail rested her hand on the faded leather and stared at the worn cover. It all made sense now. She finally understood what the angel told her and had come to the horrifying realization of her daddy's true situation.

This had become about much more than just her daddy's soul. This was about his life and it was in danger. There was a demon chasing after him and Abigail understood now she could not trust the angel to save him. The book showed her there was a finer line between good and evil than she ever imagined. Her daddy needs to fight for his own soul, but he is in a battle for his life he doesn't know he's in.

Separation from God was death. A walking death. Spiritual death. For angels, eternal death. But for humans there was still hope. For her daddy there was still hope. God was forgiving and because of His grace, that death can be undone. Lost souls can be redeemed. Abigail got that, but the book said there are beings out there who look for the spiritually dead and feed off them by making them actually dead.

This is what the angel warned her about. Something was after her daddy and waited for the opportunity to make him dead. Really dead. Ready to gobble up his soul as soon as it was free of God's protection. There was also something out there trying to break his spirit, to destroy his faith, making him susceptible. Food for the destroyer of souls that hovered near him. Abigail wasn't sure if those things were one and the same, or if there was more than one dark force working in tandem to take her daddy away from her forever.

Why couldn't Daddy just believe? It's so obvious there is a God; how could anyone question it? There's no doubt. God is real and it's obvious. How does he not see that? If he believed, there would be no danger. Daddy would be OK. He has to believe—he just has to.

Abigail felt herself losing her grip, her body disconnecting itself from her mind. She felt hot. The room closed in around her and grew darker. She needed to break free of the thick air that grabbed at her. Abigail threw the book at the wall and screamed. It made a loud, satisfying thump and for a brief moment, the room expanded allowing her to breathe. Better. But it only lasted a second.

Her world quickly began to contract again and enfold her with its darkness. Abigail grabbed a stuffed bear and twisted the arms until they ripped and tore free, leaving cotton stuffing sticking out from the amputated torso. She threw the arms across the room, which landed silently on the floor, then proceeded to pull at the head, grunting with the strain until it too came free. This time she aimed for her dresser when she threw the remaining bear parts and succeeded in knocking off a few items. Picture frames shattered and left pools of broken glass poking up dangerously from the carpet. A small jewelry box flew off and sent its contents spilling on the ground with a clatter of plastic on metal. The sounds eased the pressure and lightened the space that threatened to crush her. Abigail noticed screaming helped too. So she let loose.

She was vaguely aware of her cat's dark form fleeing from

the room. She screamed as she got off her bed. She screamed as she swiped every book off every shelf of her bookcase. She screamed as she pulled open her drawers and slammed them shut again. Abigail screamed until her mama burst into the room.

"Abigail, what happened? What's going on?"

Abigail stopped screaming and stood still, her entire frame rose and fell with each heavy breath. She knew she was supposed to look people in the eyes when addressed, but she couldn't make eye contact right now. The best she could do was shift her gaze from side to side. As her eyes scanned back and forth, she noticed her mama's hands. She was holding them funny. Something wasn't right, but Abigail couldn't sort it out.

The graveness of her daddy's situation was like a coffin being nailed shut around her, leaving her helpless to do anything but lie in the darkness of the truth and breathe in the stale air of anxiety. Abigail needed to break free. She closed her eyes as tight as she could and let loose a scream that surged up from somewhere deep inside her. She screamed for her daddy.

She gave it everything she had and hoped it would be enough.

CHAPTER 61

She heard the scream first. Then a bang reverberated through the walls of the house. Alice's head jerked up at the sudden noise and she slipped with the knife she was using to cut carrots for the girls' lunches. The blade sliced into the tip of her finger and Alice breathed in sharply at the cold sting. She looked down to see blood quickly running from the wound and cursed. It was more than just a nick. Alice snatched a kitchen towel off the counter and wrapped her finger to prevent getting blood all over the place. Of course the towel was white.

There was a crash that sounded like breaking glass. She heard Abigail screaming then a thunder of objects hitting the floor above her like it was raining bricks. What in the world? Alice ran to see what was wrong, taking the stairs two at a time. As she reached the top she heard drawers being slammed. The twins were coming down the hall toward Abigail's room to check out the disturbance. More likely to see what kind of trouble Abigail was going to get in than out of any sort of concern for her well-being. Either way, Alice stopped them in their tracks with a quick thrust of her head, indicating they had better return to their room. Now.

Abigail's occasional tantrums had gotten worse as she got older, but Alice was unprepared for the war zone she laid her eyes on when she threw open Abigail's door. Books in haphazard piles, every shelf and vertical surface area relieved of its contents.

"Abigail, what happened?" She still held the towel around her finger and tried to keep it wrapped thick enough so no red stain seeped through. The sight of blood would do Abigail in for sure.

Alice's sudden appearance seemed to give Abigail pause. She had clearly been exerting herself, and looked exhausted. Maybe the tantrum was over. It would be a record if it was, but then again, by all appearances, Abigail did a couple hours' worth of damage in a few minutes. She didn't make eye contact, which wasn't unusual when Abigail had one of her fits, but what she did next was.

It started as a low rumble then Abigail screamed like she'd never heard her scream before. "Daaaaaaddy! DaddyDaddyDaddyDaddy…" Abigail was stuck in a loop. This was bad. Alice wasn't sure it was safe to let Abigail out of her sight so she stayed put.

"Sarah! Sydney! Bring me my phone, quickly!"

She could hear the sounds of the twins scrambling to find her cell phone in the background, but she dared not look away. What was taking them so long? Abigail's screaming seemed to be getting louder, if that was possible.

"It's not in your charging dock," Sarah hollered.

"It's not in your purse, Mom," Sydney shouted. "Where is it?"

Those girls couldn't find their own rear ends if they were sitting on them. Alice was about to give them a piece of her mind when it occurred to her. She reached back and felt her rear end. The phone was there. She had slipped it into her back pocket when she finished talking to her sister while starting lunch in the kitchen. Alice dug it out.

"Girls, I got it."

Abigail's behavior had her a bit unnerved, not to mention trying to hold a phone and dial with one hand wrapped in a towel was a bit tricky. Alice tried to pull up Lucas's contact, hit the wrong one, swore, backed out of it, then tried again. She tapped the call button and finally it rang.

"Come on, Lucas, pick up," she said through clenched teeth.

The phone continued to ring, then eventually sent her to his voice mail. Alice swore again and hung up. She hit redial, hoping he would see it was her calling and pick up. This time it went straight to voice mail. She pulled the phone from her ear and looked at it in disbelief, like it was some foreign technology, placed in her hand by an alien race. She trembled with frustration, unable to shake the one thought that ran through her mind as her daughter screamed herself hoarse.

Did he just turn his phone off?

CHAPTER 62

"Are you ready for your surprise?" Hayley was smiling, clearly pleased with herself.

"My what?" Lucas pretended not to know what she was talking about.

Hayley swatted him on the shoulder. "I told you I was going to make it up to you for taking such good care of me and my ice leg." She had slipped into her Dutch accent again.

"Oh, right. You know, you really don't have to…"

"Don't be silly. It's my pleasure to do something for you in return."

Lucas felt a flutter in his chest, his armpits instantly moist. He wasn't sure where she was going with this. Was she coming on to him? What was she going to do? His mind instantly came up with any number of fantasies of how she might repay the favor. No, this was ridiculous. His wild imagination ran in high gear, fueled by the idea she was possibly attracted to him, which he was certain she was not. He was too old for her.

"So anyway, I knew we would be in this area today and I live super close, so I thought I would make you a nice lunch at my place. What do you say?"

She looked at him with her sparkling eyes that smiled on their own. Lucas felt the tightness in his muscles flow out of him. He didn't realize he was so tense until it left him. Lunch. Lucas almost laughed out loud at the innocence of it. Food was not where his mind was headed, but they had been out all morning taking depositions for one of their cases and he was starved.

"That sounds perfect. Thank you. But seriously, you don't—"

"Will you stop already? It's just lunch."

Lucas followed her home. They parked in front of a quaint old craftsman style house, squeezed in among a whole block of homes that were identical except for their color. There was no garage, no yard, and barely two feet between neighbors. Hayley waited for him at the bottom of her walkway. As he approached her, his cell phone buzzed in his pocket. He pulled it out and squinted against the glare on the screen.

It was Alice. He really didn't want to talk to her right now. If he answered, she'd probably ask what he was doing and then he'd have to explain he was at Hayley's house having lunch and there was no way that was going to come out right. As innocent as it was, he would sound guilty of something, he was sure of it. So Lucas turned his phone off.

"Ready?"

"I am," Lucas said as he dropped his phone back into his pocket.

DARK ANGEL

He followed her up a short set of concrete steps to the front door. As Hayley stuck a key in the lock, Lucas noticed there was no deadbolt. He glanced back at the surroundings. In a neighborhood like this, she should probably have a deadbolt. He almost said something, but decided the last thing he wanted right now was to sound like her father.

They stepped inside and Lucas saw an office to the left and a living area to the right with a couch and a long coffee table littered with notebooks, journals, and pads of paper with scribbling all over them. The couch had cigarette burns on the arms and the cushions looked like they had invisible people sitting on them. The place smelled like lavender. Against the far wall was a synthesizer on a stand and an acoustic guitar propped against it. In the corner, Lucas saw a rack of stereo equipment, but no TV. He looked back at the papers on the table. They were filled with words, most of which had been crossed out, and a lot of doodles in the margins. They must be song lyrics Hayley was working on for her band.

Still walking, Lucas pointed at the coffee table. "Are those—" but as he turned toward her, he realized she had already stopped in front of him. She was turning back to face him which brought her closer and he couldn't stop his momentum in time. He practically walked right over her. They both reached out and grabbed each other for balance. Hayley giggled, but neither one let go.

Her smile slowly faded as she continued to stare into his eyes. Lucas felt the heat rise from his toes all the way up through his shoulders. It was hard to breathe. Why didn't either of them pull away? Coming here was a mistake. But Lucas hadn't felt like this in a long time. He just wanted to feel good. To feel loved. Wanted. Needed. Not as a father or husband, but as a man. He leaned closer to Hayley and she didn't back off. She gazed into his eyes, her mouth parted ever so slightly as she slowly drew her tongue across her lips.

Lucas couldn't think straight. The heat had spread to his head and blocked out everything. All sounds were muted. All thoughts were gone. He could only feel and what he felt was too hard to resist.

Lucas found his lips on hers. He wasn't sure who made the move, but it happened. Lucas knew he had just crossed a line there was no going back from. What had he done? He pulled back abruptly.

Hayley looked disappointed. "Is everything OK?"

No, everything was not OK. He was about to throw everything away—his family, his integrity, possibly even his job. He knew this was a mistake, but he couldn't resist the temptation. He wasn't strong enough. He'd already committed adultery in his heart; would doing the physical deed truly make things any worse? Lucas knew he should turn and leave right then, but he couldn't seem to move. Instead he let his eyes wander over every curve of Hayley's perfect body. When he made contact with her expectant eyes again, he said, "No. I mean, yes. Everything is fine. I just can't believe this is happening."

Hayley's smile returned and she pressed her lips hard against his and he pulled her into him.

As they tore at each other's clothes, Lucas was certain he heard someone laughing, but it didn't sound like Hayley. Then he realized it must be him. He felt giddy. Why shouldn't he? He was about to experience heaven.

* * *

It wasn't Lucas who was laughing. It was the demon floating invisibly in the corner.

I've almost got you now, Lucas. And it's not heaven you are headed for.

CHAPTER 63

He felt a powerful release. It felt like months of tension built up in every muscle and tendon were blown out in one vigorous burst of passion. They had managed to make it to the bedroom and now Lucas lay with his head on Hayley's bare chest and let his body melt into hers. The guilt set in immediately.

"Mmm...," Hayley purred. "I could go to sleep."

Lucas didn't say anything. There was no way he could sleep right now. He already felt the tension return to his body as the implications of what he had done settled in. Rather than think about Hayley and enjoy the moment, he found his mind drift to his wife and family. All of a sudden, the phone call from Alice he ignored earlier seemed somehow important. He had an unpleasant feeling he couldn't shake.

Unable to stand it any longer, Lucas sat up then reached down to the floor and dug through his crumpled pants for his phone.

"Hey, come back," Hayley said in mock frustration as she grabbed the sheets and rolled over, turning her back to Lucas.

When he switched his phone on, his fears were justified. Thirteen messages. Something was definitely wrong. Lucas called his voicemail and listened to a panicked Alice as his sense of trepidation grew. He didn't even bother to listen past message number four.

"Hayley, I have to go. Family emergency."

She turned her head and faced him with a big pout, but when she saw the look on his face, she got serious. "Is everything alright?"

"I don't know. I'm sorry, I really need to go."

"Yeah…" She paused, thinking, then closed her eyes and shook her head. "I mean of course. You should go." Another pause. "Lucas, are we good?"

Lucas couldn't deal with this right now. "Yeah, we're good." He leaned over and kissed her in an effort to mask the fact they weren't at all good, but the kiss only felt awkward and inappropriate. He quickly got dressed, thankful for an excuse to get out of there, even if he was just leaving one uncomfortable situation for another.

Lucas slunk out to his car, his shame a dark cloud over his head. They never did get around to lunch, which was fine since he'd completely lost his appetite. As he drove away, he didn't dare look back at the house to see if Hayley watched him leave. He couldn't look at her right now. Lucas wished desperately there was a way he could make this un-happen.

Now that he had slept with Hayley, her attractiveness seemed to all but disappear, as if some magical spell he had been under was broken by the act. She was just a girl. A beautiful girl, yes, but just a girl and not the goddess he had made her out to be. His infatuation with her was completely gone. What had he done?

Lucas felt sick to his stomach. He pulled over, opened his door and retched onto the pavement. The sudden wave of nausea satisfied, Lucas pulled his door closed, leaned back and closed his eyes. He sat there for 10 minutes and tried to will away what he had done. He had made the biggest mistake of his life and there was no taking it back, no matter how badly he wished he could.

Alice could not find out about this. Ever. It would crush her. Humiliate her. She didn't deserve that. How was he going to face her? He couldn't, not yet. He wasn't ready.

Then his phone buzzed again.

CHAPTER 64

The front door flung open right as he was about to reach for the handle. Alice stood there, her hair a nest of frizz and flyaways, her shirt torn at the shoulder. She had a large, padded bandage wrapped around her left index finger. "Where have you been?" she said in a hushed tone.

"I…" Lucas fumbled for the right words, but she didn't wait for them to come.

"I've been calling you for the last two hours. Why didn't you pick up? You knew it was me calling. What have you been doing?"

That last question dug in his gut like a hot poker. "You know what I was doing. I had depositions to take today. I turned my phone off so there wouldn't be any interruptions and forgot to turn it back on when we were done." A plausible lie. Lucas had to remind himself to make eye contact.

Alice stared him down. "What aren't you telling me?"

Lucas was already fumbling the infidelity ball. She was going to see right through him. He had to recover quickly. "Nothing, I just… I'm worried about Abigail and now I feel horrible about turning off my phone. I'm sorry." Time to turn it around. "How is she? Fill me in."

She stared at him for another beat then looked him up and down as if deciding whether he was worthy to be let in. She stepped back from the doorway and signaled Lucas to enter the house. "She's asleep now. Finally wore herself out." Alice still spoke in a near whisper.

Lucas poured himself a glass of water, if for no other reason than to have something to occupy his hands, and they sat at the kitchen table. She explained everything that happened and how she held on to Abigail for nearly an hour to prevent her from hurting herself or breaking anything else before she eventually collapsed from sheer exhaustion.

"Are you sure restraining her when she's like that is the best—" Lucas's sentence was cut short by the blades of daggers thrown by Alice's eyes. "No, I'm sure you did the right thing," he corrected himself. "Good job," he added lamely.

Talking about it seemed to calm her down. They sat in silence for a couple minutes, then Lucas asked, "Do you know what set her off this time?"

Alice closed her eyes and shook her head. "I haven't the slightest." She took Lucas's hands in her own. "I'm sorry I snapped at you earlier."

"Don't be sorry. I deserved it, believe me."

"I was just so scared. I don't know what's going on with

DARK ANGEL

Abigail lately. This was the worst I'd ever seen her."

Lucas noticed a spot of red soaking through the padding on her finger. "How did this happen?" he lifted her hand.

"Abigail's outburst startled me when I was cutting carrots."

"Let's take a look," Lucas said as he unwrapped the bandage. The cut looked long and deep and was still bleeding. "You need to go to urgent care for this; you're going to need stitches."

"I know, I just didn't have a chance to go. Once Abigail fell asleep, I wasn't sure what kind of state she'd be in when she woke up. I couldn't leave the twins to watch her, it might have been too much for them to handle if she woke up."

Lucas nodded. "How did the girls react to Abigail's episode today?"

"You know, they're in their own little pre-teen world. They hardly pay attention to what is going on around here. To them it probably seemed like just another tantrum. But it wasn't. This one was different. I don't know what it is, but whatever is going on, it all seems to be centered around you somehow."

"Well, I'm home now. Why don't you go get that finger taken care of? I've got things handled here." This would be a good time to score some extra points. "I'll get something started for dinner."

Alice looked at him for a second like he was a stranger, then smiled. "Thank you, Lucas."

As she grabbed her keys and purse and headed out the door, Lucas remained seated at the kitchen table and thought about what Alice said. *It all seems to be centered around you somehow.* It was as if Abigail knew Lucas was screwing up his life and was trying to warn him. How could she possibly know what he'd been up to though? Maybe there was something to all her talk about angels. He sure could use an angel to look out for him these days.

Too bad he didn't believe in them.

CHAPTER 65

Lucas sat in his office early the next morning and stared at his cup of coffee, wishing he had something stronger to add to it. He had skipped his usual early run with Hayley so he could have time alone with his thoughts. It was Sunday and he knew the office would be dead at this time. Dead. Something Lucas began to wish he was.

Yesterday, Abigail had woken up just before dinner and immediately came running down the stairs calling for him. When she saw him, she rambled on about angels, talking so fast he couldn't follow her. The whole time she kept glancing over his shoulder as if someone might be sneaking up on him. After a while, he could no longer resist the urge and turned around to see for himself there was no one there.

He tried to focus on what she was saying, but he was too wrapped up in his own thoughts about what he had done earlier that day. He couldn't put it out of his mind, even long enough to listen to his daughter who clearly was concerned about him. He tried to pacify her with nods and "uh-huhs", but he wasn't hearing her and hated himself for it. Though not as much as he hated himself for what he had done to his wife.

Today, Abigail seemed to be back in control of herself and looked forward to going to church. She apparently had some book she wanted to discuss with Reverend Cooper. So Lucas felt safe escaping to work where he could be away from everything. From everyone. At least for a while. It was only a matter of time before Hayley showed up and he'd have to face her. What was he going to say to her? Lucas really wished his coffee was something else, never mind it was only seven in the morning.

Two hours later there was a knock on his doorframe. Hayley. The site of her caused bile to rise and burn his throat to remind him he had played with fire.

"Hey, Lucas." Concern tugged at the corners of her eyes. "I missed you running today. You're not avoiding me, are you?"

"No, no. I just needed extra time with my family this morning." Was he even capable of uttering a word of truth anymore? "You know, after the issue that came up yesterday." That's all he offered on the subject and could tell she was considering asking him about it, but he changed the subject before she could. "Listen, I have a bunch of stuff I'm in the middle of, but why don't we go get coffee in an hour?"

Hayley perked up at this. She probably thought it was a date. She started to approach him, but Lucas held up his hand and stopped her short. "Let's keep it professional in the office."

She winked at him. "OK, Mr. Daniels. See you in an hour."

Hayley sashayed back out with a giant grin.
   If only she knew what she was in for.

CHAPTER 66

Finally her mother had the good sense to let her talk to him again. *Maybe she's finally seen the light and gets how important this is.* Abigail clutched the book in her hands and stood with her mother and sisters, waiting ever so patiently to be addressed while Reverend Cooper chatted with other grown-ups about today's sermon. *Was he ever going to come over and talk to her? Did he not see her standing there with his book to return to him?* She glanced at her sisters. Sarah and Sydney fussed with their dresses and hair, *like anyone cares what they look like. Why were they always so fixated on trying to impress people with their looks? Not people. Boys.* It seemed like all they talked about now was boys. Abigail couldn't understand what the big deal was. *How were boys any different than girls? Well maybe girls would at least notice when someone was waiting to talk to them.*

When Reverend Cooper turned to them, before he had a chance to say anything, Abigail thrust the book at him and said, "Here." Then, "Thank you for loaning me this."

Reverend Cooper chuckled. "Well hello to you too, Abigail. Hello, Alice. Hello, girls."

Abigail wondered if her sisters ever got tired of being addressed as "girls" because the people addressing them didn't know which one to call Sarah and which one to call Sydney.

"Abigail, you finished the book already? It took me four months to get through when I read it. You've had it for only a week. Didn't you find the reading a bit dry?"

"Dry? Of course it was dry. Books are supposed to be dry. If you get them wet, it can ruin them. I didn't get it wet." Abigail now shuffled her feet and cast her glance from side to side. "I did throw it against the wall once. Sorry." She forced herself to make eye contact again. "I kept it dry the whole time."

Reverend Cooper laughed, but in a kind way. "Never mind. What did you think?"

Her mother piped in. "Actually, I want to talk to you about this."

"Sure, sure. Where is Lucas this morning?" Silence. "I see. Why don't you all come with me to my office where we can talk about this in private."

"Ugh, how long is this going to take?" Sydney whined while Sarah let out a big sigh.

"Girls, please…" Mama said, and let out an even bigger sigh.

Reverend Cooper looked at the twins. "You two are welcome to go hang out in the youth room and play foosball or watch TV while I talk to your mother and sister." He glanced at their mother, his eyebrows raised. "If it's OK with you, Alice?"

She looked at Sarah and Sydney a moment, then said, "You two behave yourselves. We'll come get you when we're done."

"Yes!" they both said in unison, and pumped their fists in the air.

As they ran down the hall, Mama called after them, "You stay in that room and don't go anywhere else." But they were already out of sight.

Reverend Cooper smiled, a twinkle in his eye. "Shall we?" he said as he gave a slight bow, his right arm outstretched.

Once they settled into his office, Reverend Cooper leaned forward, resting his forearms on the arms of his chair, fingers steepled together, pointed at the floor. "Alice, why don't you go first?"

CHAPTER 67

Lucas and Hayley sat at a back corner table in Legal Grounds, as far from the other patrons as possible. He was certain she thought he was looking for privacy so they could talk sweet nothings, but in truth he didn't want anyone to overhear their conversation because he wasn't sure how she was going to react. A conversation he was sure would go quickly south.

Normally, Hayley would drink tea, but today she insisted on ordering, "Whatever he's having." Great. Was this some form of bonding for her? Hayley sat across the small table grinning at him from ear to ear.

They made small talk for a while, mostly about work, then Hayley leaned across the table and lowered her voice. "You know, my place is close. Why don't we head back there for a bit?" She gave him a wink.

A week ago that would have seemed sexy. Today, it seemed

ridiculous. Lucas could feel an ulcer quickly forming in his gut. "Listen, Hayley, uh…" Lucas saw the smile drop from her face like it was knocked off and he was the one who delivered the blow.

"What is it?"

Lucas had thought all morning about what he was going to say. About how he loved his wife and had his family to think about. He was going to explain how they needed him and though things were often crazy, he didn't want to give up what he had. He didn't know what he had been thinking and yesterday was a mistake. He shouldn't have let it happen, especially since he was her superior at work. Then he would reassure her she was smart, beautiful and talented and it's not that he didn't want to be with her, but he was a married man with a family. He wasn't ready to give that up. Not even for her and the guilt he felt for what he did was just about killing him.

He had so much to say, but didn't know how to start so he stared at the lid on his latte.

Hayley moved her head slowly side to side and said through lips that didn't move, "No, no, no, no." Tears emerged and ran down her cheeks like raindrops. "No!" She gave the table a small shove with both hands, causing it to scrape the floor with more volume than a table of its size should. A few heads turned in their direction.

"Hayley…" The look on her face made his heart crack like it was made of so much glass.

"You used me!"

"No, Hayley, it's not like that at all. I—"

"It's exactly like that. You charm me, make me think you're

interested in me, then as soon as you have me, you drop me like yesterday's news."

Lucas wasn't sure that even made sense, but he wasn't going to correct her. She was clearly very emotional. "It's not about you, Hayley."

"Oh, it's not you, it's me? That's the line you're going to give me? You can do better than that, Lucas. What are we, in high school? I gave myself to you, body and soul. I thought we had something special, but apparently I'm just some conquest to you."

"Hayley, please. Calm down, we can talk about this."

"Don't tell me to calm down!" She slammed her hand down on the table.

If they weren't looking before, every eye in the place was on them now. So much for a private corner. They may as well have been standing on the drink counter, front and center.

"Just tell me one thing," she said quietly. "Are we over?"

Lucas looked into her eyes, swollen with tears, and searched for the right thing to say. But he had no words. He couldn't bear to look at her anymore so he dropped his eyes to the cup in his hands and nodded.

Hayley stood, and wiped her eyes with each sleeve. "I will not be taken advantage of." Her voice wavered as she tried not to cry. She turned and walked two steps then spun back around jabbing an index finger at him. "You will pay for this, Lucas Davenport." This time her voice was steady and hard as steel.

Lucas felt a shiver run down his spine, like a drop from a melting ice cube, as she stormed out. He thought he'd hit an all-time low after what he did yesterday, but he was wrong.

Things just got so much worse.

CHAPTER 68

Abigail couldn't sit still. She practically bounced out of her seat in Reverend Cooper's office, she was so pent up with information. Couldn't he see that? Why was he asking her mama these questions? She doesn't know what's going on. She didn't read the book. But Abigail knew better than to interrupt. She would try her best to wait her turn. It was something her aids were working with her on this year.

"Lucas is... he's really struggling with his faith right now. He has grown distant and I think it's particularly affecting Abigail." She took a sudden interest in a spec of lint on her pants. "It's affecting all of us." After a pause she continued, "But Abigail especially. She's having more and more violent episodes. All this angel business is getting the best of her. I like to think I have a strong faith and an open mind, but some of the things Abigail says... I don't know. I can't help but think she's created monsters out of her fears because she doesn't know how to handle what she doesn't understand. She senses her father is going through stuff right now and I worry she's created demons and angels as a way to explain it all. I don't know what to think anymore. I'm in the dark and Lucas won't let me in. He's just… I can't…"

She broke down and buried her face in her hands to hide her tears. Why, Abigail had no idea because it was obvious she was crying by the sound of her sobs and heaving of her shoulders.

"I'm not making anything up!" Abigail was done waiting her turn. "I do understand what's going on now. It's all in the book."

Her mama stopped crying and looked up. "Yes, that book. Something she read has brought this all to a head and I'm hoping you can clear things up for us."

"There's nothing to clear up, Mama. The book explains it all."

"What does it explain, Abigail?" Reverend Cooper asked.

"About what's happening to my daddy. I understand now what the angel was saying about his life being in danger, not just his soul. The demon trying to get him must have been a malakh ha-mavet."

Reverend Cooper nodded. "Interesting, go on."

"Your book talked all about them on pages 437 through 512."

"Abigail, your photographic memory never ceases to amaze me." Reverend Cooper shook his head.

"Eidetic," Abigail said.

"I beg your pardon?"

"I have an eidetic memory, not photographic."

"She not only remembers everything she's seen and done, but

when and where she saw or did it," her mama interjected. "It's like she was given Google access to her own brain. She can recall with perfect precision every experience stored in her head."

"I see. Fascinating." He turned back to Abigail. "So what makes you think the demon was a malakh ha-mavet?"

"It's all in there. It explains the dead birds, and what the angel said about him losing his life once his soul is lost. That's what they do. Punish the sinners with death."

"You had dead birds?"

Her mama ignored the question. "What are these malakh hammer-vets?"

"Ha-mavet," Abigail corrected.

"However you say it, what are they?"

"They are mentioned many times in the Bible," Reverend Cooper explained. "They were used by God in extreme situations to carry out his righteous penalty of death. Most notably when He destroyed Sodom and Gomorrah, at the Passover when He killed every firstborn in Egypt, and in Jerusalem when He killed 185,000 men of King Sennacherib's Assyrian army. Each of these and many other similar acts were carried out by the malakh ha-mavet, which is Hebrew for angel of death. These very powerful angels were created as destroyers. It's in their blood, so to speak, to punish the godless by taking their lives."

Her mama's body stiffened, like someone dumped a bucket of ice water on her. "That's what demons are?"

"No, demons are the fallen angels. A malakh ha-mavet acts under the orders of God. But if they do anything against His will, they are cast out forever. Once any type of angel is separated from God, they can never be reconciled and then become servants of Satan." He turned his attention back to Abigail. "What makes you so sure there is a fallen angel of death after your father? Even as an angel, it's conceivable a malakh hamavet could be a danger to your father if he were to completely lose his belief in God."

"Because, the angel who talked to me told me there was a demon after him."

"When Satan fell, one-third of the angels followed him. I'm not sure it's likely any angels have fallen since. They've already picked their sides."

"But it's possible."

Reverend Cooper narrowed his eyes and puckered his lips, then relaxed his face. "It's possible," he admitted.

"If this is all true, what do we do?" her mama asked.

"Do you think you can get him to come in and talk with me?"

"That's highly doubtful at this point."

"Then you will need to help him find his faith. He is going to need you now, more than ever. My suggestion is you do everything you can to help him believe again. Even if he resists you, hold on to him and don't let go."

"But he hasn't been listening to us," Abigail said. "What if he still won't listen?"

Reverend Cooper stood, walked to the door and opened it for them. "Then we pray. Hard."

CHAPTER 69

It was a long afternoon of avoiding both work and family. Lucas couldn't bring himself to face either one. He didn't want to go for a run, the rain was coming down with the same sheer intensity his life seemed to be crumbling under. After three cups of coffee and hours of driving aimlessly around Old Town, Lucas could avoid home no longer. He reminded himself no one knows what he did. All he needed to do was act normal. Whatever that was. Lucas was no longer sure what normal looked like for him.

"Lucas, we need to talk," Alice said seriously when he stepped through the front door.

Her eyes bored into him and Lucas felt a fist of anxiety squeeze its fingers around his intestines. *She knows.* Did Hayley tell her? She couldn't have. Or could she…

"Luc? Hello?"

Lucas focused his attention back to Alice and saw something

different in her eyes this time. Concern? "About what?" he asked tentatively.

"I'm worried about you. Abigail and I had a talk with Reverend Cooper today. There are some things we should discuss."

The relief Lucas felt hit him like an ocean wave, only to have the riptide of realization pull him back into a state of frustration. "Is this more talk about angels? I don't want to hear it," he said a little too defensively.

"I know you don't, but you need to hear this. We think there are some very powerful spiritual beings following you. Threatening you. Tearing you away from God."

"I'm not sure there is a God to be torn away from. Tell me what one thing about my life points to evidence there is a God? We make our own decisions and reap the benefits or consequences of our own actions. I find it hard to believe there is a supreme being looking out for us." Alice's expression showed no indication of surprise at any of this. "Think about it. Does it really make sense each and every person on this planet could be part of some master plan? That one God is pulling magic strings that control everyone's lives?"

Abigail appeared out of nowhere. "The fool says in his heart there is no God, Daddy."

"Excuse me?" Lucas spun on her. He was not going to be called a fool by his 10-year-old.

"It's Psalms 14:1, Daddy."

She was quoting the Bible to him. This was not a battle he could win. He needed to nip this in the bud with a pre-emptive strike. "Abby, your mother and I are having a conversation. I need you go to your room, right now."

"Luc," Alice touched his arm. "Please, Abigail is worried about you. At least listen to what she has to say. She probably understands what's going on better than I do."

"It's obvious God is real, Daddy," Abigail continued. "What about the bombardier beetle?"

"The bombar... the what? What are you talking about?"

"I'm talking about the bombardier beetle. Do you think a creature like that could have been created by random chance?" She flailed her arms wildly, to accent her point.

"I'm sure they naturally evolved the way they did to adapt to their habitat." Lucas didn't know where she was going with this, but he was pretty sure he didn't like it any better than the Bible quoting.

"Naturally evolved? Daddy, do you know how they defend themselves? It's amazing, really. They have these separate compartments where they store two different chemicals. When they are threatened, they squeeze muscles that push the chemicals through tubes into a mixing chamber where they combine. The reaction causes a pressure buildup that forces the valves on the storage compartments to close. This protects the beetle's insides from the now poisonous chemical which partially becomes a gas, that explodes it from the rear of his abdomen with a loud pop. He can do this about 500 times per second."

Abigail bounced on her toes and looked at the space between him and Alice with a peculiar grin, like she was waiting for a specific response. "What?" was the best he could come up with.

"Daddy, don't you get it? He attacks his enemies with machine gun acid farts! Ha!"

Lucas hadn't seen her smiling like this in he couldn't remember how long. He almost didn't want to spoil the moment, but he was in no mood. "What does that have to do with God?"

"Do you think that happened by accident? If you got all the greatest minds on the planet together, they couldn't design something this brilliant in a million, billion years."

Lucas had no response to that. "OK, Abby, I'll think about the bombardier beetle. But right now I need you to go to your room."

As Abigail trudged off to her bedroom, she called out, "Insects totally prove the existence of God, Daddy!"

He watched her disappear up the stairs, then looked back at Alice with a weak smile. "Whose kid is that?"

"She's your daughter, Luc. Holds endless facts right up there." She tapped Lucas's forehead.

"But she's got your faith. I'm sorry, I wish I had it. I don't know what to believe these days. I don't even know who I am anymore." He dropped his head and sobbed. The pressure of work, home, life, his little secret, it overwhelmed him and he had to let it out. Alice pulled him into her arms. He buried his head in her shoulder and could smell the faint honey scent of her hair. "I'm just so lost."

She stroked his head and spoke quietly into his ear. "I know. But it's not your being lost that worries me."

Lucas pulled back and searched her face. "Then what is it you're worried about?"

"I'm worried about who's going to find you."

CHAPTER 70

Monday morning Lucas sat at his desk, filled with apprehension. He didn't want to see Hayley. How were they going to work together now? Things were more than awkward between the two of them. She should have been in by now and the anticipation of facing her made his heart rate climb. He wanted to get it over with and get on with the day. Lucas was so lost in his thoughts, he jumped when his desk phone rang.

It was Louise, the receptionist. "Mr. Wall wants to see you in his office right away."

Something in his gut told him this wasn't a good thing. He walked down the hall at a slower than usual pace, like a man on death row walking his last mile. Marcus Wall's office door was open and Lucas could see him furiously filling out paperwork. He did not look happy. Of course, Marcus Wall never looked happy.

"You wanted to see me, sir?"

"Have a seat." Wall gestured at a chair with his left hand without looking up. "And close the door."

Lucas turned and closed the door, then took a deep breath before he turned back around. Why did he feel like he was 15 and had just been called into the Principal's office? He had to settle down and quit reading too much into everything. He was going to give himself an ulcer. Lately he had been popping Tums like candy, but it did no good. He sat and waited silently as his stomach acid burned through another layer of lining.

After what seemed like hours, Wall set down his pen and looked up at Lucas. He paused to give a frustrated sigh then said, "Hayley came to see me this morning. She has filed a sexual harassment claim against you."

Lucas felt the room spin. He dropped his head into his hands and waited for his equilibrium to return.

Apparently unconcerned by the fact Lucas nearly passed out in his office, Wall continued. "I understand you two had sexual relations. Is this true?"

Lucas's self-preservation instinct told him to deny it, but he knew better. He forced himself to make eye contact, opened his mouth, then closed it again and dropped his gaze to the floor.

"That's not the answer I wanted to hear."

"It was consensual." Lucas met his eyes again. "What did she tell you?"

Marcus Wall folded his hands and rested them on his desk. "Lucas, you are her mentor, which means you are in a position of power over her. Whether it was truly consensual is a bit of a gray area. I'm afraid there will have to be an investigation. I'm very disappointed in you, Lucas. Do you fully understand the ramifications of your actions?"

Lucas had a good idea, but Wall didn't wait for his answer.

"Your potential partnership with us is in jeopardy, obviously. Worst case, you could be disbarred if your actions are deemed inappropriate enough. Effective immediately, you are suspended from work until we conclude our investigation."

Lucas felt like the building had collapsed on him. He was paralyzed. Couldn't move, couldn't speak.

"Immediately means now, Lucas."

Lucas forced himself out of the chair and pulled the door open to leave.

"Oh, and one more thing, make sure you are available the next couple of days. The investigators will need to take a statement from you."

Lucas didn't say a word, just kept walking. He could still hear Marcus Wall's voice behind him.

"Very disappointed, Lucas. Very disappointed."

CHAPTER 71

It had been nearly two weeks since Lucas was suspended from work. Every day he pretended to go to the office. He put on a suit and left early each morning as he usually did. Alice could not know what happened. It was his hope everything would resolve itself, he'd get back to work and no one would be the wiser. But if this ordeal didn't end soon, he wouldn't be able to keep covering it up. He told his side of the story to the investigators from the bar association as well as giving a formal statement at work for the internal investigation going on there.

So he waited, but he was running out of things to fill his day. He went for a long, solitary run each morning, had become intimately familiar with every exhibit at the Tacoma Art Museum, and spent the rest of his time at the downtown public library where he worked on his resume and researched his situation and options. He concluded he probably wouldn't be disbarred, but would almost certainly lose his job. He couldn't keep up this façade much longer and was about out of ways to kill time. If he spent any more hours at the art museum, they would probably offer him a job. Unfortunately, he might actually need it.

For lack of anything better to do, Lucas headed to Legal Grounds for coffee and hoped he didn't run into Hayley there. He paid for his grande non-fat latte and was looking for a table to sit at when he noticed someone waving an arm. Kevin. He wandered over to say hi.

Kevin said, "Hey, Lucas, join me. I could use the company."

The truth was, Lucas could use some company too so he pulled out a chair and had a seat.

"What's been going on, Lucas? I haven't seen you at the courthouse in a couple weeks."

Lucas wasn't sure if he should say anything about his situation. Not exactly the kind of thing you want to tell people about, but yet he needed someone to talk to about it. He obviously couldn't talk to Alice about what was going on. Lucas had come to the unfortunate realization over the last couple weeks he pretty much had nobody to confide in. He was alone in this and didn't know what to do. He had to talk to someone and Kevin seemed as safe a bet as anyone.

Lucas told him the whole story about what happened with Hayley and what was going on at work. Kevin listened intently, his blue eyes almost seemed to glow.

"So that's what I've been doing because I just can't face Alice. I don't know what to do, but I can't keep…" He raised his hands in resignation, unable to finish his sentence.

Kevin bobbed his head. "That's rough, man. You are definitely in a tough spot. I warned you Hayley was into you."

"Yeah, well why is she doing this to me?"

"She's hurt, no doubt. If she can't have you, she wants to make your life miserable. Hayley is only doing this out of revenge. The truth will come out. I'm sure everything will work out with your job." He took a sip of his coffee. "If anything, she will probably be the one who gets into trouble."

That was mildly comforting, but even if things went down that way, Lucas was still concerned by the fact his affair was bound to surface in the process. "How do I get through all this without Alice finding out? Because if she does, even if I save my job, I might lose everything else."

Kevin stared thoughtfully at the table for a while, then said, "I think you should come clean with her. Lay it all out on the table before she finds out some other way. She needs to hear it from you."

"You think I should admit what I did? Are you insane?"

"I'm serious, man. Listen, my parents have been married forever. They always told me the secret to their relationship was trust and honesty. They never kept anything from each other. It's better to be honest about your mistakes than to keep secrets." Kevin reached across the table and put his hand on Lucas's shoulder. "I think you know in your heart coming clean is the right thing to do."

Lucas felt a warm tingling where Kevin's hand was. His words seemed to make sense even though they were counter to Lucas's instincts. "I'll be honest, the idea of confessing to Alice scares me to death."

"I promise it won't kill you. Yeah, it will be a tough conversation, but think about it—does she love you?"

"Yes, of course."

"If she really loves you, would she stop loving you because of this one mistake?"

"I don't know, maybe."

"She will be angry initially, but she won't stop loving you. There is something there, a special bond you two have built over the years. That kind of love doesn't go away like a switch that gets turned off."

"You're probably right," Lucas admitted. The more he thought about it, the more sense it made. He felt a strange sense of peace as Kevin removed his hand from his shoulder. "Yes, I'm going to do it."

Lucas stood. "I'm glad I ran into you today. I needed this talk. Needed to be set straight."

"You got it, man." They shook hands. "Be strong, Lucas."

As Lucas walked away, he heard Kevin's voice, but it was in his head, not out loud. He heard it all the way home.

"Go, confess your sins."

CHAPTER 72

It was still early in the day and the girls would be in school. This was the perfect time to come clean with Alice. Lucas was parked in his driveway and sat in the car going over what he would say. He couldn't seem to find any words that would lessen the blow he was about to give and time was running out. The girls would be home soon and Lucas needed to have this conversation now, before he lost his nerve. He would have to wing it.

"Luc, you startled me!" Alice said when he entered the house. "I didn't expect to see you so early. What a nice surprise." Then she saw the expression on his face and asked, "Is everything all right?"

"We have to talk." Lucas ushered her into the family room and gestured at the couch. "Please."

She looked at him for a couple seconds then hugged her arms

to her chest. "I think I'll stand."

He decided to lay it all out. "Something's happened, something I'm not proud of. The thing is…"

"What, Lucas?"

"The thing is, I haven't been going to work these past couple weeks. I've been suspended, but I didn't want you to know." Lucas looked down at the floor. "So I pretended to go."

"What are you talking about? Why were you suspended?"

This was the hard part. Harder than he imagined it would be. Lucas tried to say the words, but he couldn't make any come out. He made himself look her in the eye, but that's all he could do. It seemed the silence would never be broken, then he saw her features soften. She relaxed and dropped her arms.

"Luc, whatever happened I'm sure it wasn't your fault. You can tell me."

"No, it was my fault. I brought this on myself."

"Well I'm sure it wasn't intentional. They will see that. You've done so much good work for them, they can overlook one little mistake right?" Alice reached for him.

She was trying to comfort him. Who was this amazing woman he married? A beautiful person inside and out that he didn't deserve, that's who. She was making this harder, so he stepped back from her open arms, which she let fall back to her sides.

"Whatever happened, we'll get through this, Luc. It's going to be OK. Just tell me—"

"I had an affair," he cut her off.

Alice recoiled as if she had been slapped in the face. "You… what?"

"I slept with someone from work."

He saw her eyes well up with tears and had to look away, which is why he never saw it coming. He actually did get slapped in the face. Harder than he thought she would have been capable of. The sting on his cheek almost felt good in a way. For once, he felt something real. He deserved it, though he knew he deserved much worse.

Alice buried her face in her hands and her body shook as she sobbed. She slowly looked up and said in a quivering voice, "Who was it?"

"Alice, I'm so sorry—" She slapped him again, even harder than the first time.

Then, as if releasing a little pressure made it too difficult to contain her rage, she gave up and let it all escape. Alice beat at his chest and face. Her arms swung wildly, without precision, but occasionally making solid contact. "How. Could. You. Do. This. To. Me," she cried between blows. Lucas threw up his hands to protect his face, but didn't try to stop her. He let her ride it out until she exhausted herself.

When she finally stopped he said, "You have every right to be mad, but we can work through this."

"Get out," she said almost in a whisper. Her arms were stiff at her sides as she clenched and unclenched her fists.

"Please, can we talk about this?"

"Get out. Right. Now." Something about the tone in her voice frightened him. It was too calm.

He looked at her tear streaked face and felt his glass heart, already cracked and damaged, shatter into a thousand pieces, cutting him up inside with the razor sharp shards of his deception. "I'll be gone before the girls get home," he said softly.

Lucas grabbed a duffel bag from his closet and threw some clothes in it. He went into the bathroom and put his razor, toothbrush, toothpaste, and a few other basic toiletries into his Dopp kit and put it in the bag. He unplugged his phone charger and grabbed the book he was reading off his nightstand and added them. Then Lucas took a quick look around the bedroom and spotted a picture of Alice and the girls on the dresser and stuck it in the bag too.

When he went downstairs, Alice was waiting at the front door, holding it open.

"Alice…"

"Just. Go."

Lucas nodded and walked through the door, his head hung low. He threw the bag in the backseat and climbed in the car. As he backed down the driveway, he noticed a vehicle in his rearview mirror, parked across the street. He noticed it because there weren't usually any cars there.

He also noticed as he pulled onto the street, the same car came up behind him and followed him as he drove away.

CHAPTER 73

He tried to tell himself it was his imagination. But he couldn't shake the feeling he was being followed. Lucas wasn't sure where he was going, he was just driving and yet every turn he made, the same beat-up Volkswagen Golf that had been parked outside his house stayed behind him making the same turns. Trying to rationalize it, he decided it must be an investigator checking up on him. But why would they tail him? If they had questions, they would call.

He was being paranoid, he decided. Making things up in his mind to avoid the true reality he faced, which was that he had nowhere to go. Lucas had no family close by and no friends he would be comfortable asking to crash with. He needed to find a hotel. Alice needed time to cool off, maybe just for the night, then he could return home and begin to work things out with her. But something in his gut told him this was going to take more time than that. How long was he going to need a place? One night? Two? A week?

Lucas thought about his girls. What would Alice tell them? How would she explain why Daddy wasn't home? He wondered when he would get to see them and where. Could he go home just to spend time with them? Somehow he didn't think Alice was going to allow him in the house for a while.

None of this was playing out the way he envisioned. Why did he ever listen to Kevin? He was starting to believe he made a mistake by coming clean. Everything was quickly falling apart and Lucas was afraid there may now be too many pieces to be able to pick up and put back together the way they belong.

There was a Silver Cloud Inn on Ruston Way, Lucas remembered. He had passed it countless times on his runs along the waterfront. It was close and would be as good a place as any, so Lucas headed there and ten minutes later pulled into the parking lot. He had forgotten about the VW that was following him until he saw it pull up and park a couple stalls away. Lucas was unsure he should get out of his car. He couldn't see who was driving the other vehicle, it was never close enough for him to make out the driver.

The way his day had gone, how could it get any worse? Lucas got out and decided to face whatever came his way. He watched as a long-haired, twenty-something male, dressed all in black, got out of the VW. Definitely not an investigator. Lucas felt his stomach knot up. This couldn't be good. But when the young man turned to walk toward him, Lucas recognized who it was. Hayley's brother, Christian. He relaxed a little, but when Christian reached him, he smashed his fist into Lucas's jaw without a word. Lucas went down.

Before he knew what was happening, Christian had dropped on top of him and threw more punches into his face and gut.

"Nobody hurts my sister," Christian said, spittle flying from his lips as he continued to take out his wrath with his fists.

Lucas didn't bother to fight back. He just laid there and took it, believing he deserved every punch. He had gone numb anyway. His body tingled and his face was wet with blood, but he didn't feel pain. Then Christian stood, gave him a swift kick to the ribs with a heavy black boot, then another and another. Lucas felt that. He thought he might pass out from the pain, or maybe he was dying. Lucas no longer cared. He had officially hit rock bottom and lost his faith in everything. In himself, in the world, and most certainly in God.

Through swollen eyes with vision tinged in red, Lucas saw Christian walk away. Then everything went dark.

When he came to, he wasn't sure how much time had passed. Something was pulling him back to life, completely against his wishes. He saw a face hover above him, but couldn't make it out. Someone was trying to help him.

"Leave me alone," he said. His tongue felt foreign in his mouth.

"You're going to be OK," the stranger said and lifted his head a little.

Lucas stared at the face, which started to come into focus. Something nagged at him, like he should know who it was. Then he recognized it. It was different somehow, but there was no forgetting that face.

"You!" he said.

The stranger abruptly released his head, letting it slam back onto the concrete. Everything went dark again.

CHAPTER 74

Margaret walked down Ruston Way, on her route home from her GED prep class at Tacoma Community College. The bus stopped closer to her house, but she liked to get off early and walk along the waterfront and reflect on how fortunate she was. She gained a whole new perspective on life after the ordeal with that robbery gone bad and the demon creature who killed her boyfriend then almost killed her. There was murder in its eyes one minute, then all of a sudden it was gone. She had been given a second chance and she wasn't going to screw this one up.

So she walked and counted her blessings every day. Turns out, her parents did love her and had missed her terribly. They took her back in and said she could live with them as long as she needed to, until she was on her feet again. She was back in school. Once she passed the GED, she would be able to enroll in the EMT program at TCC. Margaret was still counting these blessings when a car nearly took her out as it peeled out of a parking lot. The driver looked like a metalhead.

"Hey! Watch it!"

The driver responded with his middle finger stuck out his window as he drove away.

"Loser," she said to herself.

She happened to glance into the lot where he came from to make sure no one else was going to barrel out behind him and noticed a pair of legs sticking out from behind a car. The parking lot was obscured by bushes along the walkway, so she never would have seen it had she not looked in as she crossed the entrance.

"Oh, my gosh," she said as she ran to check on the person lying on the ground.

When she got to the body, she dropped to her knees and checked for a pulse. He was alive and breathing, but badly beaten. She'd seen JD leave many people in this condition, herself included. This man would be OK, but he couldn't be left here like this. She tried to revive him by shaking his shoulders.

"Sir? Sir! Can you hear me?" She gave him another shake and his eyes fluttered, then slowly opened.

He tried to say something, but all that came out was, "Lib eee anagnhh."

"You're going to be OK," she said and gently lifted his head.

The man looked at her, clearly struggling to focus, then recognition flashed in his eyes.

"You!" he exclaimed.

Instantly, she realized who it was she held in her hands. It was the man she almost shot in his own home when she and JD tried to steal that wedding ring. She had lost a little weight, removed her facial piercings and returned her hair to its natural chestnut color, but he definitely recognized her. Margaret was so shocked by this turn of events, she jerked her hands away without thinking and heard his head hit the pavement with a sickening thud.

He was out cold again and Margaret was starting to freak out. She couldn't leave him like this now. She looked up and saw they were at the Silver Cloud Inn. Margaret knew she should bring him inside and call for a medic or something. But then people would start to ask questions. Who was she? Did she know this man? Questions she didn't want to answer because he knew who she was and as soon as he came to, he'd have her thrown in jail. She couldn't let that happen. She was finally getting her life together and working hard to make something of herself. This could ruin everything. She should just run and leave him here. Something inside wouldn't let her do that, though.

Then Margaret noticed he held his car keys in his right hand. She bit her lower lip and quickly looked around. There was nobody else in sight. She tentatively took the keys from his hand, sure any second he would wake up and catch her. But he didn't. He didn't even stir when she awkwardly picked him up and shoved him into the back seat of his own car. Margaret climbed in behind the wheel, closed the door and put the key in the ignition.

She sat there and contemplated the absurdity of what she was thinking about doing. Margaret knew it would be a mistake, but didn't see what choice she had. He had seen her and recognized her and now she needed to deal with it. She took a calming breath in through her nose and let it out slowly through pursed lips. As long as she didn't draw any attention to herself, she could pull this off.

Margaret started the car and slowly pulled out of the parking lot. She was extra careful not to take out any pedestrians.

CHAPTER 75

When he opened his eyes, Lucas could only see out of one of them. The other remained swollen shut. His head felt as if it was being squeezed like the last milliliter in a toothpaste tube and his torso didn't feel any better. He tried to scan the room with what little vision he had, but didn't recognize his surroundings.

He was lying on a couch in an unfamiliar living room. The place was decorated not unlike his parents' house. There was an oak hutch with teapots lined across its top, a glass display case filled with collectible figurines, cheap framed prints of famous paintings hung on the walls, doilies on 50-year-old furniture, and a musty smell in the air. Or maybe that was the smell of dried blood in his nose? He couldn't tell. Where was he? Lucas tried to sit up, but as soon as he moved he felt sick to his stomach and the pressure of the invisible vice on his head increased twofold.

"Whoa there, don't try to get up," said a female voice from

his blind side.

Lucas turned his head so he could see who it was with his good eye. She was now at his side, and placed a cold cloth on his forehead which immediately relieved some of the pressure. He studied her for a moment then it all came back to him. The girl from the robbery. Lucas was instantly tight as a bowstring, ready to loose an arrow of anger guided by fletching made of confusion.

"What am I doing here? What do you want with me? Are you planning to finish me off?" It hurt to talk.

"Oh my gosh, no," she said. "I'm going to take care of you."

That didn't sound psycho at all. "Who are you?"

"My name is Margaret. You were beaten pretty bad. Do you remember what happened?"

Lucas was having a hard time reconciling the strange juxtaposition of this twentyish young woman and the décor of the house. Something wasn't right. "Where are we?"

"It's my parent's house. I live with them. Don't worry, they are on a trip."

That only made Lucas worry more. Why did she bring him here? Whatever it was she was up to, he was helpless to stop her.

"Do you want me to call your wife or someone for you?"

Lucas almost said yes as an automatic response, then he remembered how he got into his current situation, so he said, "No, no one."

There was an awkward silence then Margaret said, "It was an accident."

"What?"

"That I almost shot you. I didn't want to have a gun, but my boyfriend made me. I didn't know what I was doing. You startled me when you came down the stairs and the gun just… went off. I'm so sorry. The whole night was a mess. There weren't supposed to be guns or kids and nobody was supposed to get hurt. I was kinda messed up back then and got sucked into that whole thing by my boyfriend." She knelt next to him. "I'm different now, you'll see. Please, please let me take care of you to show how sorry I am about everything. And I hope you will forgive me and not call the cops or whatever. I brought you here to prove to you I was different. To make you see I've changed."

"What about your boyfriend?"

Margaret looked away. "He's gone."

Lucas wasn't sure what that meant, but clearly he was out of her life now. Part of him wanted to pull out his cell phone and call the police right then. But he didn't think he could manage to do even that much himself right now. He didn't suppose he could ask her to call the police for him. Truth was, he needed her right now. And besides, he'd given up caring about anything so why not let her help.

"OK," he said.

She smiled at him and reached over to pick something up from an end table. "Here's some ibuprofens, do you think you could manage to swallow these?" She offered him four small pills and a glass of water.

Lucas took the pills and popped them in his mouth. He sipped some water to wash them down, but it mostly ran down his chin.

"Easy, not too fast." She helped him tip the glass until he had enough in his mouth to swallow the pills. "I'll let you rest now. Try to get more sleep. We can talk later."

Lucas closed his eyes. Sure, talk later. Was that really ibuprofen she gave him? He wasn't actually sure. Maybe she was testing him out before she decided whether or not to let him live. He wasn't sure he passed the test. Lucas soon drifted back to sleep, not particularly caring if he woke again or not.

CHAPTER 76

The sunlight pouring through the windows and the scent of bacon and coffee roused him from his slumber. The rumble in his stomach told him he was still alive, but Lucas wasn't sure he was thrilled to come to this conclusion. He had slept through the night and had to admit the sleep had done him good. The pain had lessened some, more numb now than hurting. Until he sat up. Then it felt like a hot fire poker being pressed into his side and Lucas let out an involuntary yelp.

"I think you might have a fractured rib or two," Margaret said from the direction of the sounds and smells of breakfast. She came out of what Lucas presumed was the kitchen. "You're going to want to get that checked out. Are you hungry? I made eggs."

"No." He was starving. The look of disappointment on her face gave him some satisfaction though. Lucas looked at her for a few seconds. "Why are you doing all this?"

"When I saw you lying in that parking lot and recognized who you were, I freaked out. I feel so bad about what happened, you know… before. And I didn't want to leave you, but I also didn't want to risk helping you there and have you come to before I had a chance to explain myself." She lowered her voice and looked at her bare feet. "So I brought you here, hoping I could convince you not to turn me in." She looked up and made eye contact again. "And maybe to forgive me?"

Lucas said nothing.

"I want to do the right thing." Margaret didn't seem to know what to do with her hands, so she alternated playing with her hair and rubbing them on her thighs as she continued. "If you want to call the cops on me, go ahead. But I swear I've turned my life around. I'm going to do something positive, something that will make a difference. I've been working on my GED, then I'll go to EMT school and everything is going great and I've probably thrown that all away by bringing you here, but I…" she slumped her shoulders and looked down again, her voice barely a whisper. "I couldn't leave you like that, not again."

Lucas was actually a little touched, but he had a hard time getting past the fact she came into his house with a gun and nearly shot him to death. And yet, he was in so much pain right now, he didn't have the energy to deal with any of this. Margaret looked at him expectantly though, so he needed to say something. He said the only thing he could think to say. "How about that breakfast?"

Margaret helped him off the couch and they sat quietly at the kitchen table as they ate scrambled eggs and bacon with English muffins and strawberry jam. The uncomfortable silence was broken by Lucas's phone ringing.

Lucas looked at the screen on his phone. It was the office. Maybe they were ready for him to come back to work. "This is Lucas."

"Lucas, Marcus Wall here. I'm calling to let you know we've completed our investigation into the incident with Hayley Simons."

"Glad to hear it, sir. Can I come back to work now?"

"Lucas we've found your behavior in this matter to be irresponsible, inappropriate, unprofessional, and inexcusable. We have terminated your employment effective immediately. Please come by and get your things from the office by the end of the week."

"That's it? It was one instance of poor judgment, that's all. You're letting me go just like that?"

"Just like that. End of the week, Lucas." Then Wall hung up.

Margaret had been listening to Lucas's end of the conversation and when he put his phone down, she asked, "What is going on with you? First you get yourself beat up and now, clearly that was more bad news."

"I'm destroying my life, apparently." Lucas paused, not sure how much he should say or why he would want to say anything at all to this girl. But she was here and he had no one else to talk to. "I've ruined my marriage, lost my family as I know it, and now I've lost my job too. Life is so fragile, Margaret. You think you've got it all together, but if you pull the wrong thread, everything unravels."

Margaret nodded. "I was there, my life unraveling. Then I

remembered God is what holds us together. It's when we try to take control of our own destiny things start to fall apart."

Lucas looked at her incredulously. She, of all people, was the last one he expected to be trying to save his soul. He was done with this business about God and about saving his soul. His was not a soul worth saving anyway.

Lucas pushed his plate forward. "Look, I appreciate all your help. Don't worry, I won't call the cops. Let's just call it even, but I really need to go."

"Where will you go?"

"I don't know," Lucas admitted. "To hell, I suppose."

CHAPTER 77

Saturday morning Lucas woke up, went to the bathroom, looked at himself in the mirror, and thought about shaving. Then decided, what for? He shuffled over to the kitchen area in his room at the Extended Stay America. He'd ended up here because when he called Alice as he was leaving Margaret's place earlier in the week, she made it very clear he wouldn't be returning home anytime soon, if at all.

He told her about losing his job, hoping she would take pity on him.

"I'm sorry, Lucas. I really am because that is going to make things difficult financially right now. But you sort of deserve this and it doesn't change what you did to me. I can't take you back, I just can't right now. Maybe not ever," she'd said.

So much for pity. Then, on top of that, she told him to come get whatever stuff of his he was going to need. *Clear out your office, Lucas. Clear out your house. Clear out your life. It's over.* She suggested he do it during the day when the girls were at school and to let her know when he was coming so she could be gone while he was there. That suited him fine since he didn't want any of them to see his face right then. He didn't tell her about getting beat up. It clearly wasn't going to gain him any sympathy either. Why bring it up?

So Lucas found a more long-term housing solution that had weekly rates and picked up enough things to get by for a while. At least the place came with a fully stocked kitchen. All he had needed from the house were his laptop and more clothes. Nothing important. What he really needed was his family. But that wasn't possible right now.

He looked in the gaudy, gold-framed mirror that hung in the entry and decided his face looked almost human again. The swelling was gone and the bruising had lightened. He decided he was ready to face the girls again. He needed to see them, to make sure they knew this mess had nothing to do with them, that Daddy screwed up and he missed them terribly. It was time. He found his phone and called Alice.

"What is it, Lucas? Do you need to come by to get more stuff?"

"Well, hello to you too."

"I really don't want to talk to you yet. What do you want?"

No small talk then, right to the point. "I want to see the girls."

A pause. "They're not ready to see you yet. They feel betrayed. They're too angry right now."

They weren't ready? Or Alice wasn't ready? Was she projecting her feelings of betrayal onto them? "What did you tell them, exactly, about what happened?"

"I told them their father loved another woman in a way a man is only supposed to love his wife. The twins understood what I meant by that."

"What about Abigail?"

"She asked, what way is that? So I told her you kissed someone else. That seemed to satisfy her for now. She's bound to question why all this happened over a kiss sooner or later."

"Alice, I need to see my girls. And they need to see me. They need to know I still love them, even though I hurt you. Please, honey."

"Don't call me that."

"Sorry, habit."

"I think it's too soon. Let the girls cool off. When they are ready to see you again, I promise I'll call." A pause, then, "I gotta go now."

The line went dead. Lucas looked at his phone incredulously. He was half tempted to call her right back then thought better of it. She obviously needed to cool off herself. His stomach told him what he needed was food. Although the lobby provided complimentary grab-and-go breakfast, Lucas didn't feel much like venturing out. Not even down a mere two flights of stairs. He didn't have much food on hand, but he would make due.

When he reached into the cabinet for a frying pan, he winced at the sharp stab in his side. He lifted his shirt and checked the tape. It had come loose. Time to change it. Lucas had gone to see his doctor after leaving Margaret's and x-rays showed he did genuinely have two fractured ribs. The doctor had shown him how to stretch adhesive tape from his sternum, over the injured ribs, to his spine in order to restrict movement of the fractured area, which eased some of the pain.

Lucas padded back to the bathroom, popped a couple ibuprofens, and re-taped his rib cage. Feeling better, he returned to the kitchen, started the coffee maker and fixed himself a couple of poached eggs and buttered toast, then sat at the table to eat.

He picked at his breakfast and looked around the small space with the olive green furniture and cheap hotel artwork on the walls. He had nothing personal here except the picture of his family, which he kept by the bedside. His personal case files and what few miscellaneous documents and supplies he was able to grab before he was quickly ushered out of his office, make that his ex-office, were in boxes stacked in one corner. This was his existence now. All he had worked for his entire life amounted to zilch. There was nothing to show for the life he thought he was building out of love and faith. Now Lucas knew for sure there was no God, because God wouldn't be this much of a son of a—

Lucas's thoughts were interrupted by a knock at the door. The sound threw him off guard. Nobody knew he was here… except Alice. Did she bring the girls after all? But wouldn't she have called him back? Lucas glanced over at his phone on the counter and noticed the light was blinking. He had a message. That had to be her. Lucas's heart swelled. It was the first time he'd felt anything but pain and disappointment in as long as he could remember. The feeling was almost foreign to him, but it didn't stop an involuntary smile as he threw open the door.

He was convinced he would see Alice and the girls standing there, which is why he wasn't remotely prepared for what actually waited for him on the other side of the door.

CHAPTER 78

She was already agitated when she came down the stairs. Not having her daddy around was a deviation from her routine, and routine was critical. She needed it for comfort, for peace of mind. Something happened she didn't completely understand and everything changed. Daddy was gone and Mama cried all the time. Abigail was sure the wolves had gotten him. When she stepped into the kitchen, Abigail overheard her mamma talking on the phone.

"…it's too soon. Let the girls cool off. When they are ready to see you again, I promise I'll call."

"Mama? Is that Daddy, Mama?"

Her mama glanced at her then said into the phone, "I gotta go now."

"That was Daddy, wasn't it, Mama? I'm ready to see him. I want to see him now, Mama! He's in trouble, I know he is."

"Your father is in trouble, all right. He did a very bad thing."

"Why is everyone so mad at Daddy? Don't you see he needs us? Whatever is happening is not his fault, it's not!"

"It is his fault, Abigail, and now is not a good time."

Abigail balled and un-balled her fists and blinked her eyes. "Now is the only time, Mama. He needs help right nowwww!" Abigail let the last word slide into a full-on scream that didn't stop until she ran out of breath.

"Abigai—"

"Nowwwwwww," Abigail managed to scream the word longer this time.

"OK, OK. If I take you, do you think you can manage to get a hold of yourself?"

She nodded. Surprisingly, Abigail felt instantly in control again. The thought of seeing her daddy had a calming effect that allowed her to hold it together. Order would come back to her world if she could just see her daddy.

Mama grabbed her purse and rooted around inside until she pulled out a set of keys. Then she called upstairs, "Sarah! Sydney! Come down, please." When the twins appeared, she said, "I'm taking Abigail to see Daddy. Are you ready to see him too?"

Sarah and Sydney looked at each other, crossed their arms and said, "No," together.

"That's Fine. I'm going to let you stay here. Behave yourselves until I get back." She looked at Abigail. "Let's go."

As they walked to the front door, Abigail heard Sydney say, "I'll be in charge."

Sarah responded with, "Why should you be in charge?"

"Because I'm the responsible one."

"You? Responsible? Ha! You can't even get in the shower without forgetting to take your underwear off."

"That only happened one time!"

As they stepped outside, Mama hollered back, "Girls, you're both in charge." Then shut the door.

"How can they both be in charge, Mama?" Abigail asked as they walked to the car. "By definition, in charge means to have control or supervision over someone else. They can't both be in charge. One of them has to be in charge of the other or else no one is in charge."

Her mama sighed. "Then no one is in charge."

"But you didn't say no one is in charge. You said they were both in charge. How are they—"

"Abigail! Just… get in the car."

Abigail did as she was told, but felt compelled to make her point one last time. "They can't both be in charge, Mama."

Her mama climbed in and started the car, put it in gear, then put it back in park. "I guess we better let your father know we're coming." She fished around in her purse for her cell phone then dialed and put it to her ear. After a long pause she said, "Lucas, it's me. Abigail insisted on seeing you, so… we're on our way." She started to take the phone away from her ear, then put it back and said, "I hope you're home when we get there."

She put the phone back in her purse. "He didn't answer, Abigail. Maybe we shouldn't go."

Something gnawed at Abigail. Why didn't he answer? She had to make sure he was OK. "Mama, we have to go. We're already in the car and you said you'd take me. Let's go."

Her mama looked at her for a few seconds then said, "You're right, I did. He's probably in the shower or something." Then she put the car back in gear and pulled out of the driveway.

Twelve minutes later they pulled into a parking lot. There was a big sign that said Extended Stay America Efficiency Studios. "This is where Daddy lives?"

"For now, yes." She parked, then pulled her phone out again and looked something up. "Let's see, he's in room 213. Are you sure you're ready, Abigail?"

Abigail jumped out of the car and ran toward the building. She heard her mama yelling behind her.

"Parking lot, Abigail. Parking lot!"

By the time she caught up, Abigail was in the lobby and had already pushed the elevator button. When it didn't come fast enough, Abigail said, "Stairs," and headed up the staircase without waiting for a response.

On the second floor there were signs on the wall with ranges of room numbers and arrows pointed in various directions. "This way," Abigail said pointing to the left.

They walked slowly down the hall as Abigail scanned the room numbers on both sides. She quickly realized the odd numbered rooms were on the left side and the even numbered rooms on the right. She was then able to pick up her pace and focus only on the numbers on the left side of the hallway. When they got to room 213, they found the door slightly ajar.

"That's odd," her mama said.

Abigail was about to go in, but her mama said, "Wait." She checked her phone again then said, "Yes, this is the room he told me he was in. We should knock."

But instead of knocking, Abigail reached out her hand and slowly pushed the door all the way open.

CHAPTER 79

It took him a while to track the human down, but Dante finally zeroed in on him. Somehow, Lucas had dropped off his radar and had moved around to unexpected places. Admittedly, Dante hadn't been paying as much attention to him as he should have been. He didn't care enough. Until now.

Lucas had lost his last shred of faith, which according to God's own rules made him Dante's for the taking now. It was this fact that allowed Dante to hone in on where he was. He had found the place where Lucas was staying, and as he surveyed the building, there appeared a darkness that didn't exist a moment ago. He knew it was Lucas who was now like a black hole among hundreds of little beacons of light. The very space around him was being sucked into the dark abyss formed by the complete absence of his spiritual light.

He could have materialized in front of Lucas in his natural

form, but what was the fun in that? He decided to toy with him a bit first, so he maintained his human appearance and walked right in to the hotel, ignoring the nervous glances from the staff behind the counter. Dante easily found the room Lucas was in and knocked on the door so he could get in without making a scene. The ridiculous smile on the man's face made it clear he had been caught off guard, which made it easy for Dante to push his way in before Lucas could react.

He was aware the door hadn't shut all the way behind him as he marched to the middle of the room, but that was of no concern. Nobody could touch him and no one was going to save Lucas from his fate.

Lucas managed a weak, "Who are you? What do you want?"

No screaming, no cry for help. This human had completely given up. Dante wanted more of a reaction. He wanted to see the fear in the man's eyes. He was going to have to take this to the next level.

"It's time for you to die," he said, his voice like gravel.

His body shuddered as his wings took form and began to unfold. He could feel the heat behind his eyes as he grew larger, almost consuming the small space. Dante watched Lucas's reaction as his transformation completed. There it was. He saw fear and trepidation contort Lucas's face. That was more like it.

Dante felt the anticipation of the kill. His thirst about to be quenched by human suffering and death. He would have to be careful not to let his need overpower him or it would all be over before he barely got started. These opportunities didn't come often enough, so he tried to make them last. He felt himself reaching that point of no return though, where the need overtook all control and left him unable to hold back even if he wanted.

Without warning, there was a flash of light in the room. Lucas's look of terror quickly turned to confusion as the angelic figure appeared.

This was just the distraction Dante needed.

CHAPTER 80

What stood before him was more beast than man. Besides his imposing size, his skin color had a death-like pallor. The man stood there in a long, black leather coat and glowered at him with eyes that seemed to look right into his soul. Not that they would find anything there. There was something familiar about this stranger. Had he seen him before somewhere? Maybe this guy was sent by Hayley. He did look a bit like a metalhead. A really scary biker metalhead. And there Lucas stood with a stupid smile on his face, his body not having yet reacted to what his mind already realized.

Next thing he knew, the man had pushed his way into the room and Lucas just let him. He could have at least tried to close the door on him, but he reacted too late. As if it would have done any good. This guy had him overpowered five times over. As the man pushed past him, Lucas saw the inverted cross on the back of his coat and it dawned on him why he looked familiar. He had seen him in the coffee shop. The man was in the center of the room now and turned back to face Lucas.

Lucas struggled to speak, still in shock. "Who are you? What do you want?"

He expected to get pummeled again, but what happened next was inconceivable. The man said, "It's time for you to die," then proceeded to shape-shift into something both majestic and horrid.

He grew taller and his leather coat turned to black feathery wings, like he was becoming a gigantic raven. The creature's eyes glowed red. Lucas watched a lot of scary movies, but even on screen he had never seen a sight this frightening. This was some sort of demon. The thing towered over him and seemed to shake like it struggled to control its own body.

Just when he thought he'd seen everything, he was shocked again when a bright flash appeared in the middle of the room. Another being appeared. This one did not scare him, but was no less shocking. Before him was a white winged, human-looking apparition that glowed with a soft yellow light. An angel. It must be. It was the most beautiful thing he'd ever seen. Lucas was astounded. Could it be Abigail was right all along?

Lucas dared to look it in the face, though the brightness hurt his eyes. "Are you truly an angel?" Its light dimmed so it no longer hurt to look at, but Lucas still couldn't make out any facial features.

"I'm here to take you home," it said.

Lucas felt relief at first, then confusion. What did he mean by take him home? Home to his house on J Street where he belonged with his family? Home to heaven? Was there a heaven?

"So there is a God?" he asked.

"No," the white angel answered with a voice that calmed Lucas to his core. "God is dead."

The news should have unhinged him, but instead Lucas felt the cool satisfaction one feels when one is proved right, even if what is proved is bad news.

The angel continued, "It's just us spiritual beings left to roam the earth, amusing ourselves."

"Blasphemer!" the dark one shouted. "God is alive and at work in this world. You will show some respect."

Lucas was a little perplexed. What was going on? He must have slipped into madness.

"Don't believe this demon," the white one said. "He doesn't want you to believe in me, but he is the deceiver. I am the one who was sent to watch over you."

"What do you mean, watch over me?"

The white angel then grew smaller as its wings disappeared. The glow faded until it was completely extinguished, leaving a man standing there. A man he recognized. His jaw dropped.

Lucas couldn't believe who he saw before him.

CHAPTER 81

Positioned in front of Lucas was Seamus White, the street guitarist, in the flesh. Lucas was bewildered. It was all like some sort of bad dream. He struggled to make sense of everything as realizations swarmed around in his mind, making connections that seemed impossible, yet answered so many questions. Had God been in his life all along? It now seemed so true, yet how was it everything went so wrong?

"It's me, brother," Seamus said in his distinctive Irish accent. "I'm the one that got you a job when you needed one."

The demon creature grunted. "A job that introduced you to temptations you weren't prepared to handle. Money. Success. A woman."

This threw Lucas off. The thing actually had a point. That job did seem to be the start of his downfall. Would God have put him in that position? Or maybe the other being had told the truth.

Maybe God was dead and humans are nothing more than the playthings of angels.

"He's right," Lucas said to Seamus. "Though I did need a job, my life only got worse after I took that one."

Seamus smirked at him. "I've done so much more for you. You have no idea all the ways I've looked out for you. I've been with you every step of your journey, trying to keep you safe."

"I only saw you a couple times, what are you talking about?"

Seamus shook his head. "Not like this."

He generated a glow again, the bright light consuming his form until he was nothing but a blur. Then the light faded until he revealed himself in a new form.

"Perhaps you recognize me now?" It was Kevin. "I saved your life that day in the court house. You see? I have walked with you and protected you. Call me your guardian angel." He smiled a beautiful smile.

Lucas now understood why Kevin had those impossible good looks. He always thought Kevin was somehow too attractive for a man. Turns out he wasn't a man at all.

"He only watched over you because at that point you were still destined for heaven. He wasn't done corrupting your soul and didn't want to lose it to God. He wanted it for his master," the dark creature said.

"Who's his master?" Lucas was afraid to know the answer.

"There is no heaven, Lucas," Kevin said. "Don't listen to him. Think about it, have I ever spoken anything but truth to you? I have guided you to do the right thing every time. I convinced you to come clean on your affair and you know that was the right thing to do."

The black beast said, "The devil uses truth to manipulate humans to his own purposes. He loves the truth because he can twist it to trick you, for truth without wisdom can easily lead one astray. He knew coming clean about your affair, while the right thing to do, would temporarily provide a challenge you weren't in a condition to handle. You lacked enough faith."

"Lies!" Kevin looked furious. "That demon will say anything to trick you."

Kevin transformed back to his angel form, a gorgeous vision of white. Only this time, though his form shimmered with a mild glow again, Lucas could see his face and it was still Kevin's.

Lucas was lost and confused. This angelic creature had clearly been with him, watching over him, yet everything he did for Lucas seemed to turn his life upside down. He also said God was dead and that made sense to Lucas. It explained why nothing good ever came of his faith. Why nothing good seemed to happen for him, despite his best efforts.

Then there was the dark angel, the demon creature. He insisted the white angel had purposely lead him astray, that God was alive. Yet he had come here to kill him. He looked like something out of the deepest, blackest part of hell. How could Lucas believe anything he said? He decided the white angel was right, God was dead. And now his angel had appeared to save him once again.

"So you are here to protect me from him?" Lucas asked Kevin, or whatever his angel name was.

"In a manner of speaking," he replied still smiling his brilliant smile. "I am not here to stop him from taking your life. I am here to protect you from his lies so I can usher you home when he does."

Lucas felt agonizing fear slither back into his soul and fill him with its poison. "Wh-what kind of angel are you?"

He heard a gasp come from behind him. Lucas turned to find Abigail standing in the open doorway. Alice was behind her with trembling hands over her mouth, muffling a scream, her eyes wide with shock.

Abigail said, "Daddy, that's not an angel."

CHAPTER 82

The air seemed to leave the room, making it hard to breathe. Lucas stared at Abigail in disbelief. If the beautiful creature that stood next to him, looking like a picture book angel, wasn't an angel at all, Lucas didn't know what was going on. He now felt more lost than ever. Why didn't anything make sense anymore?

"He's not the angel, Daddy," Abigail said pointing at Kevin. She swung her pointing hand over to the frightening beast with the black wings and red eyes and said, "That's the angel."

"What? This is the so-called angel you've been talking to? No, Abby, you're wrong. He has deceived you. He just told me he was here to kill me. Look at him, he's a demon. He even came in here wearing the satanic upside down cross."

The dark beast roared at this. Abigail started to walk into the room. Alice thawed out of her frozen state and threw out an arm to stop her, but too late. Abigail was already out of reach and

Alice hesitated to come in after her.

"Not satanic, Daddy. That's a St. Peter's Cross. It's a religious symbol of unworthiness. The satanic meanings are just made up stories. This isn't a demon, it's a malakh ha-mavet."

"That doesn't sound any better."

"It means angel of death. It's not here to turn your soul away from God, Daddy. It's here because you've already turned away."

"So God has sent a punisher after me?"

The dark angel, beast, whatever he was, stood silent. Alice's eyes flitted between it and Abigail.

"No, Daddy. God loves you and wants you to come back to him. He forgives you, but angels have free will. That means they can do whatever they want and not get in trouble as long as they don't break God's rules. This angel was made to kill and destroy. It almost can't help itself; it needs to do it. And as long as you've truly and completely turned away from God, it can get you."

"Enough!" Kevin said. "Lucas, are you going to believe this… this child?"

"I don't know what to believe."

"Well, you can believe there is no God and the Bible is all a lie. Proverbs will tell you the righteous will prosper, but look at your life, Lucas. You've lived the way of the morally upright, tried to be the faithful servant. What did it get you?"

Lucas had to admit, he had a point there. "It got me nothing but pain and heartache."

"Exactly, because the Bible is a fabrication."

Abigail approached Kevin. Alice, still standing in the doorway, yelled, "Abigail, please come back here!"

Abigail ignored her and walked right up to Kevin and said, "Both Job and Ecclesiastes say the righteous will suffer and the wicked will prosper." She turned to Lucas. "Living a moral life doesn't mean you'll have an easy one, Daddy."

"Silence, child!" Kevin's face darkened.

For the first time Lucas saw something there that looked evil. Then it clicked. Kevin actually was using truths to sway him down the wrong path and he fell for it again. That meant…

"So, this is a demon? Named Kevin?" he said, gesturing at Kevin.

"I am called Vetis," he said.

Then he seemed to shake as if he had trouble controlling himself, containing an eruption that tried to blast its way free. It's because Lucas finally saw the truth. That had to be it. He has seen the devil for who he is and the demon was losing his composure. Then it occurred to Lucas that Abigail stood right here in the presence of demons and angels and seemed unafraid. "Abby, aren't you scared?"

"No, Daddy. I have faith, so the angel isn't going to hurt me. And the demon, it can't touch me."

But Abigail was wrong, so very wrong.

CHAPTER 83

Vetis could control himself no longer. He had Lucas convinced there was no God and Dante was about to take Lucas's life. Everything had gone according to plan. That is, until this girl child showed up. She was ruining everything. The master would be most displeased with him if he failed. He was too close to lose this one. Out of frustration and rage, he did what he had to do. He became like a cloud of black vapor, then flew into the body of the troublemaking little girl, and possessed her.

He could tell as soon as he entered her body and mind, something was off about this girl. He didn't know what it was, but quickly found he was in trouble. He had intended to control her, but found nothing worked the way he expected. Normally a child's mind was easy to inhabit and influence, but with this one, he had to compete with too much. Her mind took in every aspect of the room; the colors, the arrangement of furniture, the materials, textures, artwork, photographs, positions of light switches, number of outlets on the walls. When he looked at the couch, he didn't see just a couch, he saw a tan microfiber sofa with rounded arms, wooden feet, three attached cushions on the back, each one with a button sewn into the middle, and three removable seat cushions. The couch faced west and it appeared the left side was the most used, based on the subtle indentation in the cushions. The middle cushion wasn't pushed as far back as the other two and had some sort of crumbs on it. Where a normal person would see a room full of objects, through this girl's mind he saw these objects as tessellations of tiny details. Everything, all at once. And not only visually, but audibly too. The sounds of screaming and crying, the traffic outside, the air system inside, the electrical buzz of the lights, it was overpowering and he couldn't seem to grab a foothold on her consciousness. There was no window into her mind left open for him to move about. He was cramped and stifled. This was not good.

Perhaps he had been rash to possess the girl. What did he think he would accomplish? He only knew he needed to shut her up. Now he was here and couldn't do anything. Vetis wasn't even sure he could get out. Enough subtlety, he would have to go into full-on physical possession. The kind demons didn't like to use because it was typically less effective, but yet was the only kind humans like to tell stories about or depict in their movies. He would take over this little body and rip it apart if need be. One way or another, she would be stopped and he would be free of her.

Vetis pushed out his essence to every corner of the girl's physical and mental being, consuming her completely, transforming her into something less human. Something demonic. He melded with her until they were one. As soon as he felt some sense of control, he released his wings. They were invisible to the humans, but caused the girl's form to float up over the others, who now watched with horror drawn on their faces like bad art. Dante was saying something, but Vetis couldn't make it out. Everything was so jumbled, it all sounded like noise. One thing was for sure, Dante wanted to attack him, to fight him all the way back to hell, only he couldn't. The black winged angel couldn't risk the life of an innocent. He may walk a fine line, but in the end, he was still an angel.

Feeling confident, Vetis attempted to speak to his captive audience, to communicate his lies and deceptions. To do the devil's work in its most extreme form. But once again, he couldn't make the girl's brain do his will. Never mind her brain worked in twists and tangles, there was something else at work here that prevented him from speaking his misleading truths, his words of deceit.

It wasn't merely the faith this girl had. Faith was usually fairly easy to crumble, especially in trusting, impressionable children. They may be good at taking things on faith, but they also believe almost anything they're told. Childlike faith is as much a weakness as it is a strength. But this child was different. Her faith was so much more than just a belief. Her faith was absolute. It was rock solid and unwavering. He was powerless. Best to cut his losses and get out before he was too weakened.

Vetis tried to leave the girl's body, but found himself caught in a web of twisted mental processes and perceptions. Her mind had a place for everything else, but there was no place for him.

He was everywhere in her body and he was nowhere. The child's brain wouldn't acknowledge him. He couldn't manipulate it like a normal mind. It fought him and he had to fight it for processing time like an application thread waiting for its turn on a computer's CPU. When he did get a chance to tap into her mind, it was like trying to drive a car with airplane controls. It was overwhelming, and he didn't understand how anything worked.

Desperate, Vetis let out a scream in frustration then threw the girl's small body against the nearest wall. He would fight his way out physically. It was the only way. He would be free if he had to kill her to do it.

CHAPTER 84

When he saw the demon take possession of Abigail, Dante knew Vetis was in trouble. He watched Abigail stiffen as she was penetrated by the demon's essence. Then she moved her head side to side, up and down, as if disoriented and confused. Dante had spent enough time around the girl to know she was different. Vetis took a big risk in trying to possess her. Perhaps if he had known more about the girl, he would not have tried this last-resort tactic. But he had focused all his attention on Lucas. A critical mistake.

Alice had overcome whatever hesitation she faced before and was fully in the room now. "Abigail? Oh my dear Lord, Abigail!"

Afraid to touch her daughter, but standing as near as she dared, Alice began crying and screamed, "No, not Abigail," over and over again.

"Abby, are you OK?" Lucas shouted. He turned to Dante and said, "What is happening to her? If you're really an angel, why aren't you doing anything about this?"

Dante watched as Vetis struggled to control Abigail. Her hands were now on her head, as if trying to block out the world. The demon didn't have her, not yet. Dante would do whatever he could to protect this child. As much as he despised humans, the faith in this one was astounding and something Dante could appreciate and respect. Here was a soul worthy of God, so Dante would set aside his grievances with the human race for this one. However, they were in a complicated spot. She is only a human child. She is fragile. Dante would have to wait until the demon left her and hope she survived.

"Demon, release her!" Dante shouted. "She is a child of God and you have no claim on her."

Dante resisted the urge to beat the demon out, it would only end badly. Then again, this would probably end badly anyway. But he waited, watching for an opening to present itself. Hoping for the opportunity to put a stop to this servant of the devil.

At first, Dante was grateful for the work Vetis had done on Lucas. The demon had turned the man away from the creator, thus providing him with another victim to satisfy his need. It was no big loss, just another human who was not worthy of God's love. Vetis only accelerated the inevitable. Ever since their battle outside the hospital, Dante had debated if the two of them should partner up, each one's goals benefiting the other. Only now, Vetis had gone too far. Dante couldn't allow such pure faith to be destroyed. The girl was off limits.

Dante had not expected this. Had he been prepared for the

possibility, he would have stopped Vetis from ever reaching her. But now the demon was inside her and Dante was forced to watch helplessly as Vetis continued to take an increasingly powerful hold. Abigail's eyes rolled back until they showed only the whites and her face darkened, her skin taking on an ashen tone. Black veins slowly drew themselves down her face, onto her neck, then reached down her arms to her fingertips. Alice's screams redoubled in intensity.

Lucas looked at him and yelled, "Do something!"

They both fell silent as Abigail's body rose up off the floor. Suspended about three feet in the air, she opened her mouth as if to speak, but no sound came out. She closed her mouth, then went into convulsions. He's trying to get out, Dante realized, but he's locked inside.

Then Abigail stopped moving. She became perfectly still, hanging there like a puppet, her hair over her face. The room was eerily silent as everyone watched to see what would happen next. It was the kind of silence you get when there is a large crowd of people being quiet enough to hear a pin drop, almost thunderous in its absence of sound. Unexpectedly, her face jerked up, her eyes now black pools, like oil, and she let out an inhuman scream, both deep and high-pitched. The sound of a hundred tortured souls.

Dante knew what was coming next and was powerless to stop it. Abigail's body flew across the room like a rag doll being thrown at the wall. Her body slid to the floor after impact and lay still for a brief moment. Just as Lucas took a step toward her, she was up again and flew toward the opposite wall. Lucas jumped back and cried out in surprise.

Alice screamed again, her tears flowing now. "Please, God, make it stop," she prayed.

Again, Abigail's body hit the wall and slumped to the floor. A small streak of blood was left behind. There was another brief pause then her limp body slowly lifted into the air once more. Her head drooped and limbs hung lifeless as she floated six feet from the floor. She had lost her left shoe at some point. Vetis seemed to be growing tired. In one last surge of effort, Abigail was thrown to the ceiling, where her head cracked the drywall with the impact. Again and again she was smashed into the ceiling with a sickening thud until something snapped and her body dropped in a small heap on the floor. Vetis was finally free. Free, but weakened and off-balance.

Unfortunately for him, Dante was prepared for this moment.

CHAPTER 85

This was his big chance. The demon had exhausted himself breaking free of the girl and appeared dazed as he floated back to the floor next to Abigail's motionless form. Dante knew it was now or never. He had to send Vetis back to hell. Dante launched himself on Vetis with a roar, his wings smashing lamps and pictures as he moved in for the attack. Vetis turned to face him, but didn't seem to register what was happening until too late.

Dante pounced and wrapped his giant wings around him, folding them both into a feathery cocoon. Vetis struggled with little effect. His face rapidly changed, morphing from Kevin's, to Seamus's, to countless others, unable to hold on to one for more than a fraction of a second. The moment one face took form, another would appear. Like an endless carousel of people, Vetis became anyone. He became everyone.

Dante squeezed tighter and bellowed, "Demon, be gone!"

Then his wings flew open as he threw his arms wide. Each hand held a powerful grip on Vetis's form, ripping it in half.

With a screech that sounded like scraping metal and caused the humans to cover their ears, Vetis dispersed into a cloud of black smoke which dissipated with the puff of air caused by Dante settling his wings behind his body.

The demon was gone. Beaten. Vetis was an immortal, but what Dante had done to him would put him out of commission for a long time. He wouldn't bother any humans for years, perhaps decades. Dante destroyed his physical form, but the spirit lived on, imprisoned in hell until he could regenerate into something that could exist in this world again.

He understood now. This was the great battle he'd sensed all along. It should have made him feel good. Destroying a demon was like the days of old. He hadn't felt anything like it for centuries. It should have satisfied his need the way the destruction of an entire city would. But Dante looked at the lifeless body of the young girl on the floor and felt greatly distressed. Why did he feel such things about a human? Why should it matter to him?

Lucas and his wife now hovered over the girl, crying, checking for any sign of life, but Dante knew it wasn't there. He could see the life force had fled from her. He felt something like pity for a brief moment, but it was quickly replace by anger. This whole situation was Lucas's fault. Because of the events that played out, Dante was not able to feel the respite from the constant ache for destruction he should be. If anything, his need was now greater. The demon was just a warm-up and now he had some real tribulation to unleash.

Dante remembered why he came here in the first place and turned his attention on Lucas.

CHAPTER 86

As soon as the demon was gone, obliterated by the black-winged angel, Lucas rushed to Abigail and dropped next to her. Alice was right there with him. She cried and reached out, but hesitated to touch Abigail's body.

"Is she alive?" Alice asked through her tears.

Lucas felt for a pulse, but couldn't find one. He looked at Alice unable to speak. He shook his head and closed his eyes.

Alice wailed, "No! Noooooo...."

"You're next, Lucas," the angel said.

Lucas did not expect this. He just lost his precious daughter while this so-called angel stood by and let it happen. The angel destroyed the demon only to turn around and still want to take his life too? Why? Why bother getting rid of the demon? Lucas became so enraged, he lost all sense of fear. He stood and faced the black-winged creature and looked him right in his burning red eyes.

"If God does exist, why would He let this happen? My daughter was innocent, pure, a true believer in spite of my personal beliefs. And yet here you are, supposedly one of His angels, and you let her die. Why didn't you protect her? Why didn't you protect me? I was almost killed a couple times these last few months. Where were you then?"

The angel said, "I was there. Why do you think you survived?"

"Why did it even almost happen in the first place? Nobody faces death that much in such a short amount of time."

"Fool! People face death constantly. If it weren't for my kind to look out for you, I'm not sure your race would survive. We save you from yourselves every day and you are none the wiser."

"No, I think it's because there is no God and you, whatever you are, are just here doing whatever you want!"

"I admit, I didn't work very hard to protect you. I don't care about you. That doesn't mean God hasn't been looking out for you. He has spoken to you, but you haven't listened. You don't deserve His love anyway."

"God hasn't spoken to me." Lucas said it like it was a question. "At first I thought I was listening for Him, but everything I did led me down this path of bad decisions and ultimately to the conclusion, He's simply not there."

"He was there all right, you didn't listen carefully enough. He is the still small voice, remember? You stupid humans have let the devil so far into your lives you can no longer hear God. The devil is loud. He screams promises of an easy life, lots of money, success, glamor. But all the while he also whispers lies that make you believe he's really giving you those things. No, you weren't listening for God. You were listening for what you wanted to hear. God tried to tell you to be less focused on your career and more focused on your family. He was driving you to them. But you didn't trust Him. Instead you listened to the voice that said you should focus on making more money."

Lucas dropped his head and sagged his shoulders. He knew what the angel said was true. He buried his face in his hands and cried.

"I'm sorry. I'm so, so sorry." Lucas dropped to his knees.

The angel grunted. "Sorry. That's the trouble with you humans. You're always sorry. And God always forgives you. No matter what you do, you always have forgiveness and salvation. Do you think I get forgiveness if I screw up?

You humans have it so good and yet you have no idea. You are ungrateful, unworthy sinners and He loves you anyway. So don't look to me for protection. I'd just as soon wipe out the lot of you than try to save you from yourselves. There's no one out there to save me. What makes you so special? You only have a short time on this earth to follow His way. An insignificant flash of time, yet it's still too hard for humankind to commit themselves to Him. The temptations of the world are too much for you. You are a weak species. I have all eternity to resist temptation, forced to wander your planet and only allowed to punish the lost souls. Lost souls like you, Lucas Daniels. Today, you die."

Lucas dropped back to his knees next to Abigail and bowed his head. As he prayed, he felt Alice put her hands over his, praying with him. He said, "Oh God, I don't know how to do this anymore, but what I do know is I believe in you. I see now where I've gone astray and I'm so sorry, Lord. Please have pity and save this life. I know it's in your power. I know in my heart you are there and can do it if it's your will. Please, God, there is so much this life could do in your name if only given the chance—"

"Enough!" Dante cut him short. "You can't decide to find God as a last ditch effort to save yourself. It doesn't work like that. You can't ask to see a miracle to believe they really happen. That's not what believing is all about."

"I don't need to see a miracle to believe anymore. I truly believe God can do this." Lucas stood again, ignoring the wincing pain in his ribs, and took one bold step toward the angel. "And I wasn't praying for my own life."

He pointed at his daughter. "I was praying for hers."

CHAPTER 87

The angel seemed caught off guard. He probably didn't expect Lucas would gladly offer himself up in sacrifice if that's what it took to save Abigail. He wasn't sure he could live with himself anyway, knowing her death was a result of his own lack of faith. Lucas was resigned to die, but he truly believed God could save Abigail and he intended to spend his last moments on this earth fighting for her.

Abruptly, the look on the angel's face changed from curiosity to something else. Fear? Then Lucas noticed the room getting brighter. A blazing, white light filled the room and the angel quickly dropped to one knee and bowed down low, as if a great king was about to enter.

The angel stole a look up at Lucas and Alice and said, "Close your eyes."

"What?"

"I said close your eyes!" The angel's voice shook the place like a sonic boom. He then bowed his head again.

Lucas glanced over at Alice and saw she had followed the angel's lead, so he knelt and closed his eyes too. The angel had looked afraid for the first time. What would possibly frighten a creature like that?

As the light grew brighter and more intense, he covered his face with his arm. Even with his eyes closed tight and buried in the crook of his elbow, the light was blinding. It was such a powerful brightness, it became deafening. Lucas felt like he was on the sun, surrounded by roaring, nuclear flames, only without the heat. As a matter of fact, Lucas felt an extreme coldness throughout his body. There was a great weight upon him that rendered him unable to move. His ears rang and his equilibrium was out of whack. He could feel the air pressure in the room tighten around his body and felt the sensation of the world crumbling down around them.

The temptation to look was almost overpowering, but Lucas knew he would be blinded if he did. How could he possibly see anything in a brightness that could penetrate his covered face like this anyway? No, looking wouldn't enable him to view what was going on. Lucas sensed it might literally kill him. He had to wait it out.

It seemed to go on forever and Lucas wasn't sure how much more his body could tolerate before it was crushed by the brightness and turned to dust. He tried to call out to Alice to see if she was OK, but he couldn't even hear his own voice in his head. Lucas had been rendered blind, deaf, and mute. He was nothing but a shell and powerless to do anything in this miniature apocalypse.

The weight on his body grew heavier, pushing him closer to the floor. Lucas felt a slight metallic taste in his mouth. Blood?

So this is it. This is how it ends for me.

CHAPTER 88

The moment he thought his body couldn't take any more, the light instantly disappeared. The pressure, the coldness, everything was gone. Lucas felt completely normal again so he risked opening his eyes. The angel stared at him with an odd expression.

Lucas asked, "What just happened?"

"Do you realize you were both in the presence of God… and lived through it?"

There was a small cough. "Daddy? Mama?"

Lucas jerked his head in the direction of his daughter. "Abby?"

Abigail slowly pushed herself up into a seated position. Alice gasped then gingerly touched Abigail, first on the head, then her arms, torso, and legs. Alice's fingers barely touched her, as if she were a china doll that would crack if the slightest pressure were applied.

Lucas gently lifted her chin and checked her eyes. They seemed perfectly dilated and he saw no cuts or trace of blood on her face.

"Abby, are you OK?" he asked.

"Yes, Daddy, I think so."

"Can you stand?"

Abigail pushed up with her legs and Lucas gently placed a hand on each shoulder to brace her as he stood with her. He looked her over and checked for signs of bruising or injuries of any kind. He found nothing. Not the slightest sign of the trauma he witnessed mere moments before.

"Does anything hurt, Abby?"

"No, Daddy. What happened, Daddy?"

"A miracle," he said. "That's what happened."

"Oh, praise the lord," Alice said and clapped her hands together and interlaced her fingers as she closed her eyes and tilted her face upward.

Overjoyed, Lucas wrapped his arms around Abigail without thinking and pulled her close. She hesitated for just an instant, then wrapped her arms around him and squeezed back. The pain in his ribs was excruciating, but he didn't care. He was holding his baby girl and she was alive.

A sudden thought put a knot in his stomach. Was the angel still going to take his life? Could he? Lucas had an undeniable belief in God now. He found some small solace in the fact Abigail was alive. It's what he prayed for and was all he really dared ask for. It was in God's hands now and Lucas was good with that.

Alice's voice shook him from his thoughts. "Um, Luc... do you see what you're doing right now?"

Lucas looked down and realized he was hugging Abigail. He immediately released her and said, "I'm sorry, sweetheart, I forgot. We thought we lost you and I just needed to hold you."

"It's OK, Daddy. It doesn't bother me. You can hug me—it feels good. It feels safe." She gave a single, assertive nod. "It makes me feel safe, Daddy."

Alice wasted no time and threw her arms around Abigail, who hugged her back. "Oh my sweet girl, it feels so good to hold you. I love you so much."

"I love you too, Mama."

Dante spoke up. "A small gift from God." He paused. "Your faith has saved her, Lucas, and yourself as well. I see it radiate strongly in you now."

Lucas never felt more alive. He noticed all his senses were heightened. His sense of smell was stronger, his vision improved. Colors looked brighter, sharper, clearer. When he paused to concentrate, he could hear his own heartbeat and feel the blood move through his body. He looked at Alice and could tell she experienced the same sensation. She had her arms up and turned her hands back and forth, looking at them like she was seeing them for the first time.

"What you are experiencing right now is the aftereffects of being in the presence of God," Dante said. "You are feeling a connection with all creation. It will wear off in time, but you would do well to remember this perception. This is only a hint at what you will experience in heaven. Only those who enter the kingdom of God can experience His true glory, but you've been given a taste of it."

"This is incredible," Lucas said, now examining his own hands. "I feel like a newborn, experiencing the world for the first time."

He looked at Alice and they smiled at each other the way they did on their wedding day. They held their gaze for a few moments, then the smiles dropped from their faces as reality settled back in.

Alice stepped up to him to look him in the eyes. "Listen, Luc… I see now there have been very powerful forces working against you, so maybe you aren't completely to blame for what has happened. Maybe I should give you a little slack, but ultimately you are responsible for your own actions and I can't forget that."

Lucas dropped his head. "I understand."

Abigail grabbed Alice's hand and squeezed it. "Please, Mama. Please forgive Daddy. He didn't know what he was doing. Please Mama, please. I want Daddy home. He belongs Home, Mama."

Lucas knelt down to be at eye level with Abigail, even though she looked away. "Your mom is right, Abby. I made my own choices. God gave us free will for a reason, and I messed it up. I can't blame God or the devil or anyone but myself."

Abigail was having none of it. "Mama, please, Mama!" Tears pooled in eyes that this time, looked directly into Alice's.

Alice felt the air go out of her lungs. Abigail making eye contact meant she was serious. "Abigail, I don't know if I can forgive your father."

Abigail's tear pools overflowed, waterfalling down her

cheeks, but she maintained eye contact.

Alice squeezed her hand back. "But I will try. I just need time."

Abigail yanked her hand free, wrapped her arms around Alice and buried her face in her abdomen.

Lucas jerked his head back up and looked at her with hopefulness. "Really? Do you mean that?" He couldn't believe he was getting so many second chances. A second chance with God. A second chance at life. And maybe even a second chance with Alice.

"All I can promise is that I will start down this long road to recovering our marriage with you. We'll just have to take it slow."

"I'm OK with slow," Lucas said.

"There will be counseling."

"I'm OK with counseling too."

Alice smiled a sad smile, like she was having a fond memory of something she would never see again, and took his hand in hers. Then he felt Abigail wrap her arms around his and Alice's waists as she pulled them together. He and Alice both rested their free hands on Abigail's shoulders and Lucas felt a surge of energy. Probably a symptom of his heightened awareness.

Unsure what happens next, Lucas looked over at the angel, who watched them, observing silently. Nobody said anything for a while, then he saw a change in the angel's expression that said he was done with him. For good. No words need be spoken. Lucas simply watched as the angel opened its wings and floated upward.

Just before it would have crashed through the ceiling, the

heavenly creature vanished.

CHAPTER 89

Maybe it was time to rethink his opinion on humans. Dante was impressed with Lucas's plea for his daughter's life. The man truly didn't care if he lived or died, didn't care what it took, he only asked for his daughter to be saved. And he prayed with such conviction, like a believer who truly understood God's power and believed in it with the faith of a child. Unwavering and absolute.

Lucas saved his daughter because the motivation behind his prayer was entirely selfless. Dante didn't think humans were capable of truly selfless acts. They love to act like they are being selfless in their actions, but humans always have an ulterior motive behind what they do. They never do anything that doesn't somehow benefit them, even if it's nothing more than to make them feel good about themselves. But Lucas didn't look to benefit in any way. He didn't even pray for his own life. His only prayer was for his daughter, that she might have a second chance. Only for her. Dante was intrigued by this turn of events.

Now this family, who had been torn apart by Lucas's actions, was coming back together through forgiveness, grace and love. As Dante watched Lucas and his family interact, he noticed how strong of a glow each of them had. Then Lucas and his wife held hands and touched their daughter. The glow that spread from them was remarkable. It was something greater than the sum of their individual glows. Something worthy of God.

Dante pondered what Lucas and his family went through to get here. He thought about the complete turnaround in Lucas's heart and the powerful effect it had on an entire family. He finally understood what great pleasure God must take in humans coming to this point by their own free will. Maybe humans are worth redemption after all, he decided.

As he came to this conclusion, Dante became aware of Lucas watching him expectantly, waiting for what? A sign? Some instruction? Where Lucas goes from here was not Dante's concern. That would be between him and God. He spread his wings and raised himself into the air, then became invisible so he could observe without anyone looking to him for what to do next. As he watched Lucas and his family, he felt something he hadn't felt in a long time.

Then Dante did something he hadn't done in nearly three millennia.

CHAPTER 90

It was over. All the pain he had gone through, the brushes with death, the struggles with his faith. Lucas felt truly grounded for the first time in his life. The uncertainty of the future no longer bothered him, because he knew everything would be OK. So he said it.

"Everything's going to be OK."

Alice smiled at him. There was kindness in her eyes, but also pain. "What's going to happen with your job, Luc?"

Lucas wasn't sure what the results of the Bar Association's investigation would lead to. He may never be able to practice law again. Maybe he didn't want to.

"I don't know. But I thought I'd start playing guitar again. Maybe teach lessons. I could join the worship band at church, perhaps."

"That sounds wonderful," Alice said.

He could hear uncertainty in her voice. He wasn't out of the woods yet, that much was clear. But somehow he knew, no matter what happened with Alice, he was going to be just fine.

"Listen, right now, my only job is to be with my family, to win back their love and trust."

"In that case," she said, "would you like to come over to the house and see the twins?"

Exactly the words he wanted to hear. "There's nothing I'd like more."

As he turned to go, Lucas noticed Abigail staring up at the ceiling. He followed her gaze and saw nothing there.

"Abby, do you still see the angel?"

"Yes, Daddy."

"What is it doing?"

Abigail shrugged. "It's just… smiling."

AUTHOR'S NOTE

I've always found angels to be fascinating creatures. We imagine them to be beautiful, powerful, and mysterious, but what we really know about them is, in truth, very little. This makes them the perfect subject to explore and create my own mythology around. The Bible mentions an angel in 2 Chronicles 32:21 that God sends to annihilate the Assyrian army. Every last soldier, regardless of rank, was killed in the blink of an eye. Nearly 200,000 men were wiped out without pity or discrimination. The horror of this is almost too hard to comprehend. But here's the thing—angels are believed to be finite in number and eternal, which means this particular angel is still around today. Think about that for a moment. There is a spiritual being out there, an agent of God, used once upon a time to crush hundreds upon thousands of human lives, but gone are the days when God would smite entire armies or destroy whole cities. I wondered what place this angel would have in the modern world. And what might he be doing in the present day? I suspect he must be looking for a good fight. These thoughts were the genesis of my story.

My second inspiration came from C.S. Lewis' *The Screwtape Letters*, which explores the idea that Christians go through peaks and troughs in their relationship with God. It is during the trough periods, when God pulls away, that the devil seizes the opportunity to tempt and persuade. And he doesn't do it loudly or blatantly, but rather works in subtle ways that you never see coming. This gave me the idea for a storyline with an intersection of a human struggling with his faith, a demon out to win his soul, and a centuries-old angel thirsty for battle.

And of course things are not always what you expect. We think of demons as scary creatures from some fiery underworld, but they are just as likely to appear as charming, persuasive beings who claim they can make your every dream come true. And why should angels be sandal-wearing, harp-playing, goody two-shoes? Some were created as instruments of God to inflict the righteous penalty of sin. They are God's harbingers of death. Now *that* sounds like a scary creature to me!

Regardless of who might be scarier, angels or demons, I believe there is a great battle going on over each and every one of our souls constantly, and that we are oblivious to the fact it is even happening. That is the scariest thought of all, but one I hope you enjoyed exploring with me. Thank you for reading.

Keep the faith,
-SM

ACKNOWLEDGMENTS

The process of creating this book was an adventure like no other I've undertaken in my life. It has been an extremely rewarding experience, but nothing makes one question their abilities or tests their perseverance quite like writing a novel. It's not enough to have a good story idea or even a talent for writing to be able to author a book. No, there is also research to be done, mental challenges to overcome, and a resoluteness one must dig deep to find in order to see a project like this through to the end.

It took an entire decade for me to turn an idea in my mind into what you hold in your hands right now. I never could have made it without the help and encouragement of many people along the way.

First and foremost, I want to thank my long-time friend and writing mentor, James L. Rubart, who not only inspired me to write this story, but who also taught me so much about the craft of storytelling. Thank you for sticking with me through the entire process these last ten years, encouraging me, critiquing (gently) and guiding me every step of the way. This wouldn't have happened without you!

A huge thank you to my editor, Josh Feinstein, for all his work on this book and for making me look like I might have done this before.

Thanks to Darhla Roberts, Jackie Smith, Tom Dykstra, John Higley, and Corrie Meddaugh, who read my early drafts and provided amazing and honest feedback. Their willingness to speak the cold, hard truth only made the story stronger.

Writing characters who are believable and well-developed doesn't come without a lot of help. I enlisted some subject matter experts to help me finesse my characters and storyline and they are owed so many thanks for adding reality and depth to my writing.

To my dad, Rev. Phil Meddaugh, who let me bounce ideas of faith and spirituality off of him. He didn't always agree with (or particularly like) some of my perspectives, but granted me my creative license for the purpose of the story without letting me cross any lines.

To Kathy Brewer, for answering my endless questions about raising a child with Asperger's. The insights and stories were invaluable to me in creating the character of Abigail and making her into something real that I fell in love with.

To Erik Ladenburg for help with the legal elements and what the life of a lawyer trying to run his own practice might look like both in and out of the courtroom.

To Andrea Boatman for her insights on parenting three pre-teen girls and in particular what having daughters who are twin sisters is like. Her stories and suggestions helped me bring that special kind of family chaos to the page.

Lastly, I want to thank my wife, Judy, for her love and support as I finished this book. She came into my life after I had already started on this journey, but never let me stray from the path. Her feedback and attention to detail were of enormous benefit to the story but her encouragement to follow my dreams were of even more benefit to me. She is my proof angels are watching over me.